TIM

Stephen Baxter wa[s] ...
he has a mathema... ...
Cambridge and a Ph.D from Southampton. Ba... ...
his first short stories to *Interzone* in 1986 and his first
novel, *Raft*, was published in 1991, to great acclaim. He
is married and lives in Buckinghamshire.

Praise for *Timelike Infinity*

'This is good science by someone who knows what he
is talking about'   *Sunday Telegraph*

'There are neat aliens, good plot reversals, much hand-
waving with physics and a pretty damn cosmic ending.
I didn't think they were writing them like this any
more . . . Hold on for the ride'   *Interzone*

'Baxter fully integrates his concepts in a streamlined,
engrossing drama with a nerve-rattling pace. Galaxy-
spanning imagination, as outrageously cosmic in scope
as any epic by Arthur C. Clarke or Greg Bear, is
harnessed to a sleek, turbo-charged narrative pulsing
with the urgency of countdown. Baxter is destined to
be one of the genre leaders for the Nineties'   *Starburst*

Voyager

STEPHEN BAXTER

Timelike Infinity

HarperCollins*Publishers*

Voyager
An Imprint of HarperCollins*Publishers*
77–85 Fulham Palace Road,
Hammersmith, London W6 8JB

The *Voyager* World Wide Web site address is
http://www.harpercollins.co.uk/voyager

This paperback edition 1997
1 3 5 7 9 8 6 4 2

Previously published in paperback by
HarperCollins Science Fiction & Fantasy 1993

First published in Great Britain by
HarperCollins*Publishers* 1992

ISBN 0 00 647618 X

Set in Linotron Palatino

Printed and bound in Great Britain by
Caledonian International Book Manufacturing Ltd, Glasgow

To my niece, Jessica Bourg

1

The flitter rose from occupied Earth like a stone thrown from a blue bowl. The little cylindrical craft tumbled slowly as it climbed, sparkling.

Jasoft Parz had been summoned to a meeting, in orbit, with the Qax Governor of Earth. Parz scoured a mind worn into grooves of habit by his years in the diplomatic service for reasons for this summons. It must be connected with the arrival of the damned wormhole, of course – that had stirred up the Qax like a stick in a hornets' nest.

But why summon him now? What had changed?

As his distance from the planet increased, so grew Parz's apprehension.

Alone in the automated flitter Parz watched shafts of cerulean Earthlight thread through the small ports and, twisting with the craft's rotation, dissect the dusty air around him. As always, the glowing innocence of the planet took his breath away. Two centuries of Qax occupation had left few visible scars on Earth's surface – far fewer, in fact, than those wrought by humans during their slow, haphazard rise to technological civilization. But still it was disturbing to see how the Qax-run plankton farms bordered every continent in green; and on the land, scattered and gleaming plains of glass marked man's brief and inglorious struggle against the Qax.

Parz had studied these mirrored landscapes from space – how many times before? A hundred, a thousand times? And each time he had struggled to recall the reactions of his youth on first seeing the sites of the destroyed cities. That liberating, burning anger; the determination not to compromise as those around him had compromised. Yes, he would work within the system – even carve out a career in the hated diplomatic service, the collaborative go-between of human and Qax. But his purpose had been to find a way to restore the pride of man.

Well, Jasoft, he asked himself; and what has become of those fine intentions? Where did they get lost, over all these muddy years? Parz probed at his leathery old emotions. Sometimes he wondered if it were possible for him genuinely to feel anything any more; even the city-scars had been degraded in his perception, so that now they served only as convenient triggers of nostalgia for his youth.

Of course, if he wished, he could blame the Qax even for his very aging. Had the Qax not destroyed mankind's AntiSenescence technology base within months of the Occupation?

Sometimes Parz wondered how it would feel to be an AS-preserved person. What would nostalgia be, for the permanently young?

A soft chime sounded through the flitter, warning Parz that his rendezvous with the Spline fleet was less than five minutes away. Parz settled back in his seat and closed his eyes, sighing a little as semi-sentient cushions adjusted themselves to the curvature of his spine and prodded and poked at aching back muscles; he rested his bony, liver-spotted fingers on the briefcase which lay on the small table before him. He tried to focus on his coming meeting with the Governor. This was going

8

to be a difficult meeting – but had they ever been easy? Parz's challenge was going to be to find a way to calm the Governor, somehow: to persuade it not to take any drastic action as a result of the wormhole incident, not to stiffen the Occupation laws again.

As if on cue the mile-wide bulk of the Governor's Spline flagship slid into his view, dwarfing the flitter and eclipsing Earth. Parz could not help but quail before the Spline's bulk. The flagship was a rough sphere, free of the insignia and markings which would have adorned the human vessels of a few centuries earlier. The hull was composed not of metal or plastic but of a wrinkled, leathery hide, reminiscent of the epidermis of some battered old elephant. This skin-hull was punctured with pockmarks yards wide, vast navels within which sensors and weapons glittered suspiciously. In one pit an eye rolled, fixing Parz disconcertingly; the eye was a gleaming ball three yards across and startlingly human, a testament to the power of convergent evolution. Parz found himself turning away from its stare, almost guiltily. Like the rest of the Spline's organs the eye had been hardened to survive the bleak conditions of space-flight – including the jarring, shifting perspectives of hyperspace – and had been adapted to serve the needs of the craft's passengers. But the Spline itself remained sentient, Parz knew; and he wondered now how much of the weight of that huge gaze came from the aware-ness of the Spline itself, and how much from the sec-ondary attention of its passengers.

Parz pushed his face closer to the window. Beyond the Spline's fleshy horizon, a blue, haunting sliver of Earth arced across the darkness; and to the old man it felt as if a steel cable were tugging his heart to that inaccessible slice of his home planet. And above the blue arc he saw another Spline ship, reduced by per-spective to the size of his fist. This one was a warship,

he saw; its flesh-hull bristled with weapon emplacements – most of them pointing at Parz, menacingly, as
if daring him to try something. The vast threat of the
mile-wide battleship struck Parz as comical; he raised a
bony fist at the Spline and stuck out his tongue.

Beyond the warship, he saw now, sailed yet another
Spline craft, this one a mere pink-brown dot, too distant
for his vision – augmented as it was by corneal and
retinal image-enhancing technology – to make out
details. And beyond that still another Spline rolled
through space. Like fleshy moons the fleet encircled the
Earth, effortlessly dominant.

Parz was one of only a handful of humans who had
been allowed off the surface of the planet since the
imposition of the Qax occupation laws, one of still fewer
who had been brought close to any section of the main
Qax fleet.

Humans had first emerged from their home planet
two and a half millennia earlier, optimistic, expanding
and full of hope . . . or so it seemed to Jasoft now. Then
had come the first contact with an extra-solar species –
the group-mind entity known as the Squeem – and that
hope had died.

Humans were crushed; the first occupation of Earth
began.

But the Squeem were overthrown. Humans had travelled once more from Earth.

Then the Qax had found a human craft.

There had been a honeymoon period. Trading links
with the Qax had been established, cultural exchanges
discussed.

It hadn't lasted long.

As soon as the Qax had found out how weak and
naïve humanity really was, the Spline warships had
moved in.

Still, that brief period of first contact had provided

humanity with most of its understanding about the Qax and their dominion. For instance, it had been learned that the Spline vessels employed by the Qax were derived from immense, sea-going creatures with articulated limbs, which had once scoured the depths of some world-girdling ocean. The Spline had developed spaceflight, travelled the stars for millennia. Then, perhaps a million years earlier, they had made a strategic decision.

They rebuilt themselves.

They had plated over their flesh, hardened their internal organs – and had risen from the surface of their planet like mile-wide, studded balloons. They had become living ships, feeding on the thin substance between the stars.

The Spline had become carriers, earning their place in the universe by hiring themselves out to any one of a hundred species.

It wasn't a bad strategy for racial survival, Parz mused. The Spline must work far beyond the bubble of space explored by humankind before the Qax Occupation – beyond, even, the larger volume worked by the Qax, within which humanity's sad little zone was embedded.

Someday the Qax would be gone, Parz knew. Maybe it would be humanity which would do the overthrowing; maybe not. In any event there would be trade under the governance of a new race, new messages and material to carry between the stars. New wars to fight. And there would be the Spline, the greatest ships available – with the probable exception, Parz conceded to himself, of the unimaginable navies of the Xeelee themselves – still plying between the stars, unnoticed and immortal.

The small viewport glowed briefly crimson, its flawed plastic sparkling with laser speckle. Then a translator box built somewhere into the fabric of the flitter hissed into life, and Parz knew that the Spline had established a tight laser link. Something inside him quivered further now that the climax of his journey approached; and, when the Qax Governor of Earth finally spoke to him in its flat, disturbingly feminine voice, he flinched.

'Ambassador Parz. Your torso is arranged at an awkward angle in your chair. Are you ill?'

Parz grimaced. This was the nearest, he knew, that a Qax would ever come to a social nicety; it was a rare enough honour, accorded to him by his long relationship with the Governor. 'My back is hurting me, Governor,' he said. 'I apologize. I won't let it distract my attention from our business.'

'I trust not. Why don't you have it repaired?'

Parz tried to compose a civil answer, but the forefront of his consciousness was filled once more with a distracting awareness of his own aging. Parz was seventy years old. If he had lived in the years before the coming of the Qax, he would now be entering the flush of his maturity, he supposed, his body cleansed and renewed, his mind refreshed, reorganized, rationalized, his reactions rendered as fresh as a child's. But AntiSenescence technology was no longer available; evidently it suited the Qax to have humanity endlessly culled by time. Once, Parz recalled, he had silently raged at the Qax for this imposition above all: for the arbitrary curtailment of billions of immortal human lives, for the destruction of all that potential. Well, he didn't seem to feel anger at anything much any more . . .

But, he thought bitterly, of all the plagues which the Qax had restored to mankind, he would never forgive them his aching back.

'Thank you for your kindness, Governor,' he snapped. 'My back is not something which can be fixed.

12

It is a parameter within which I must work, for the rest of my life.'

The Qax considered that, briefly; then it said, 'I am concerned that your functionality is impaired.'

'Humans no longer live forever, Governor,' Parz whispered. And he dared to add: 'Thank God.' This was the only consolation of age, he reflected tiredly – wriggling in the chair to encourage it to probe harder at his sore points – that meetings like these must, surely, soon, come to an end.

'Well,' said the Qax, with a delicate touch of irony in its sophisticated artificial voice, 'let us proceed before your bodily components fail altogether. The wormhole. The object is now within the cometary halo of this system.'

'Within the Oort Cloud, yes. Barely a third of a light-year from the Sun.'

Parz waited for a few seconds for the Qax to indicate specifically why he'd been brought here. When the Qax said nothing he drew data slates from his briefcase and scrolled down lists of facts, diagrams, running over the general briefing he had prepared earlier.

'It is an ancient human artefact,' the Qax said.

'Yes.' Parz retrieved an image on his slate – glowing frameworks against a salmon-pink background – and pressed keys to dump it through the tabletop and down the link to the Governor. 'This is a video image of the launch of the wormhole from the orbit of Jupiter, some fifteen hundred years ago. It was known as the Interface project.' He touched a fingernail to the slate to indicate the details. 'In essence, two tetrahedral frameworks were constructed. Each framework was about three miles wide. The frameworks held open the termini of a spacetime wormhole.' He looked up, vaguely, in the direction of the ceiling. Not for the first time he wished he had some image of the Governor on which to fix his

13

attention, just a little something to reduce the disorienting nature of these meetings; otherwise he felt surrounded by the awareness of the Governor, as if it were some huge god. 'Governor, do you want details? A wormhole permits instantaneous travel between two spacetime points by –'

'Continue.'

Parz nodded. 'One tetrahedral framework was left in orbit around Jupiter, while the other was transported at sublight speeds away from the Earth, in the direction of the centre of the Galaxy.'

'Why that direction?'

Parz shrugged. 'The direction was unimportant. The objective was merely to take one end of the wormhole many light-years away from the Earth, and later to return it.'

Parz's table chimed softly. Images, now accessed directly by the Qax, scrolled across his slate: engineering drawings of the tetrahedra from all angles, pages of relativistic equations . . . The portal frameworks themselves looked like pieces of fine art, he thought; or, perhaps, jewellery, resting against the mottled cheek of Jupiter.

'How were the tetrahedra constructed?' the Qax asked.

'From exotic matter.'

'From what?'

'It's a human term,' Parz snapped. 'Look it up. A variant of matter with peculiar properties which enable it to hold open the termination of a wormhole. The technology was developed by a human called Michael Poole.'

'You know that when humankind was brought into its present close economic relationship with the Qax, the second terminal of this wormhole – the stationary one, still orbiting Jupiter – was destroyed,' the Governor said.

'Yes. You do tend to destroy anything you do not understand,' Parz said drily.

The Qax paused. Then it said, 'If the malfunctioning of your body is impairing you, we may continue later.'

'Let's get it over with.' Parz went on, 'After fifteen centuries, the other end of the wormhole is returning to the Solar System. It is being towed by the *Cauchy*, a freighter of ancient human design; we speculate that relativistic effects have preserved living humans aboard the freighter, from the era of its launch.'

'Why is it returning?'

'Because that was the mission profile. Look.' Parz downloaded more data into the table. 'They were due to return about now, and so they have.'

The Qax said, 'Perhaps, since the destruction of the second, stationary tetrahedron, the wormhole device will not function. We should therefore regard this – visit from the stars – as no threat. What is your assessment?'

'Maybe you're right.'

'How could we be wrong?'

'Because the original purpose of the Interface project was not to provide a means of travelling through space . . . *but through time*. I am not a physicist, but I doubt that your destruction of the second terminus will have destroyed its functionality.'

Parz's slate now filled with a simple image of a tetrahedral framework; the image had been enhanced to the limit of the telescopic data and the picture was sharp but bleached of detail.

The Governor said, 'You are implying that we may be witnessing here a functioning time machine? – a passage, a tunnel through time which connects us to the humanity of fifteen centuries ago?'

'Yes. Perhaps we are:' Parz stared at the image, trying to make out detail in the faces of the tetrahedron. Was it possible that just beyond those sheets of flawed space was a Solar System free of the domination of the Qax – a system peopled by free, bold, immortal humans, brave enough to conceive such an audacious project as the Interface? He willed himself to see through these grainy pixels into a better past. But there was insufficient data in this long-range image, and soon his old eyes felt rheumy and sore, despite their enhancements.

The Qax had fallen silent.

With the image still frozen on the screen, Parz settled back into his chair and closed his aching eyes. He was growing tired of the Governor's game. Let it get to the point in its own time.

It was depressing to reflect on how little more had been learned about the Qax during the Occupation: even human ambassadors like Parz were kept at more than arm's length. Still, Parz had used his fleeting contacts to sift out fragments of knowledge, wisdom, glimpses of the nature of the Qax, all built into the picture that had been handed down from a happier past.

Like everybody else, Parz had never actually seen a Qax. He suspected that they were physically extensive – otherwise, why use Spline freighters to travel? – but, in any event, it was not their physical form but their minds, their motivation, that was so fascinating. He'd become convinced that it was only by knowing the enemy – by seeing the universe through the consciousness of the Qax – that men could hope to throw off the heavy yoke of the Occupation.

He had come to suspect, for instance, that comparatively few individuals comprised the Qax race – perhaps no more than thousands. Certainly nothing like the billions which had once constituted humanity, in the years before the development of AS technology. And he was sure that there were only three or four Qax individuals assigned to the supervision of Earth, orbiting in the warm bellies of their Spline freighters.

This hypothesis had many corollaries, of course.

The Qax were immortal, probably – certainly there was evidence that the same Governor had ruled Earth from the beginning of the Occupation. And with such a small and static population, and with all the time in the world, each Qax would surely come to know the rest of its species intimately.

Perhaps too well.

Parz imagined rivalries building over centuries. There would be scheming, manoeuvring, endless politicking . . . and trading. With such a small and intimate population surely, no form of formal policing could operate. How to build consensus behind any laws? How to construct laws which would not be seen to discriminate against individuals?

. . . But there were natural laws which governed any society. Parz, drifting into a contemplative doze, nodded to himself. It was logical. The Qax must work like so many independent corporations, in pure competition; they would swim in a sea of perfect information about each other's activities and intentions, kept in some semblance of order only by the operation of the laws of economics. Yes; the theory felt right to Parz. The Qax were natural traders. They had to be. And trading relationships would be their natural mode of approaching other species, once they started spreading beyond their own planet.

Unless, as in the case of humanity, other opportunities, too soft and welcoming, beckoned . . .

Parz didn't believe – as many commentators maintained – that the Qax were an innately militaristic species. With such a small number of individuals they could never have evolved a philosophy of warfare; never could they have viewed soldiers (of their own race) as expendable cannon-fodder, as a renewable resource to be husbanded or expended to suit the needs of a conflict. The murder of a Qax must be a crime of unimaginable horror.

No, the Qax weren't warlike. They had defeated humanity and occupied the Earth merely because it had been so easy.

Of course, this wasn't a popular view, and Parz had learned to keep it to himself.

'Ambassador Jasoft Parz.'

The Governor's sharp, feminine voice jarred him to full alertness. Had he actually slept? He rubbed his eyes and sat up – then winced at fresh aches in his spine. 'Yes, Governor. I can hear you.'

'I have brought you here to discuss new developments.'

Parz screwed up his eyes and focused on the slate before him. At last, he thought. He saw the approaching Interface tetrahedron, in an image as devoid of detail as before; the pixels seemed as large as thumbprints. The star background twinkled slowly. 'Is this a recording? Why are you showing me this? This is worse than the data I brought you.'

'Watch.'

Parz, with a sigh, settled back as comfortably as he could; the sentient chair rubbed sympathetically at his back and legs.

Some minutes passed; on the screen the tetrahedron hung on the rim of interstellar space, unchanging.

Then there was an irruption from the righthand side of the screen, a sudden blur, a bolt of pixels which lanced into the heart of the tetrahedron and disappeared.

Parz, forgetting his back, sat up and had the slate replay the image, moment by moment. It was impossible to make out details of any kind, but the meaning of the sequence was clear. 'My God,' he breathed. 'That's a ship, isn't it?'

'Yes,' said the Governor. 'A human ship.'

The Qax produced more reports, shards of detail.

The ship, camouflaged somehow, had exploded from the surface of the Earth. It had reached hyperspace within seconds, before the orbiting Spline fleet could react.

'And it made it through the tetrahedron?'

'Apparently a group of humans have escaped into the past. Yes.'

Parz closed his eyes as exultation surged through him, rendering him young again. So this was why he had been called to orbit.

Rebellion . . .

The Qax said, 'Ambassador. Why did you not warn me of the approach of the Interface device? You say that its mission profile was documented and understood, that it was due to return.'

Parz shrugged. 'What do you want me to tell you? A mission profile like that, based on the technology of the time, has uncertainty margins measured in centuries. It's been fifteen hundred years, Governor!'

'Still,' said the Governor evenly, 'you would regard it as your duty to warn me of such events?'

Parz bowed his head ironically. 'Of course. *Mea culpa.*' It probably made the Qax feel better to rail at him, he reflected. Well, to absorb blame on behalf of humanity was part of his job.

'And what of the human evacuees? The ship which escaped? Who built it? How did they conceal their intentions? Where did they obtain their resources?'

Parz smiled, feeling his papery old cheeks crumple up. The tone of the translator box continued as sweetly, as sexily even as ever; but he imagined the Qax boiling with unexpressed rage within its womblike Spline container. 'Governor, I haven't the first idea. I've failed you, obviously. And do you know what? I don't give a damn.' Nor, he realized with relief, did he care about his own personal fate. Not any more.

He had heard that those close to death experienced a calm, an acceptance that was close to the divine – a state that had been taken from humanity by AS technology. Could that describe his mood now, this strange, exult-ant calmness?

'Ambassador,' the Qax snapped. 'Speculate.'

'You speculate,' Parz said. 'Or are you unable to? Governor, the Qax are traders – aren't you? – not con-querors. True emperors learn the minds of their sub-jects. You haven't the first idea what is going on in human hearts . . . and that is why you are so terrified now.' His eyes raked over the faceless interior of the flitter. 'Your own, awful ignorance in the face of this startling rebellion. That's why you're scared, isn't it?'

The translator box hissed, but was otherwise silent.

20

2

Michael Poole's father, Harry, twinkled into existence in the middle of the *Hermit Crab*'s lifedome. Glimmering pixels cast highlights onto the bare, domed ceiling before coalescing into a stocky, smiling, smooth-faced figure, dressed in a single-piece sky-blue suit. 'It's good to see you, son. You're looking well.'

Michael Poole sucked on a bulb of malt whisky and glowered at his father. The roof was opaque, but the transparent floor revealed a plane of comet ice over which Harry seemed to hover, suspended. 'Like hell I am,' Michael growled. His voice, rusty after decades of near-solitude out here in the Oort Cloud, sounded like gravel compared to his father's smooth tones. 'I'm older than you.'

Harry laughed and took a tentative step forward. 'I'm not going to argue with that. But your age is your choice. You shouldn't drink so early in the day, though.'

The Virtual's projection was slightly off, so there was a small, shadowless gap between Harry's smart shoes and the floor; Michael smiled inwardly, relishing the tiny reminder of the unreality of the scene. 'The hell with you. I'm two hundred and seven years old. I do what I please.'

A look of sad affection crossed Harry's brow. 'You always did, son. I'm joking.'

Michael took an involuntary step back from the Virtual; the adhesive soles of his shoes kept him locked to the floor in the weightless conditions of the lifedome. 'What do you want here?'

'I want to give you a hug.'

'Sure.' Michael splashed whisky over his fingertips and sprinkled droplets over the Virtual; golden spheres sailed through the image, scattering clouds of cubical pixels. 'If that was true you'd be speaking to me in person, not through a Virtual reconstruct.'

'Son, you're four light-months from home. What do you want, a dialogue spanning the rest of our lives? Anyway these modern Virtuals are so damned good.' Harry had that old look of defensiveness in his blue eyes now, a look that took Michael all the way back to a troubled boyhood. *Another justification*, he thought. Harry had been a distant father, always bound up with his own projects – an irregular, excuse-laden intrusion into Michael's life.

The final break had come when, thanks to AS, Michael had grown older than his father.

Harry was saying, 'Virtuals like this one have passed all the Turing tests anyone can devise for them. As far as you're concerned, Michael, this is me – Harry – standing here talking to you. And if you took the time and trouble you could send a Virtual back the other way.'

'What do you want, a refund?'

'Anyway, I had to send a Virtual. There wasn't time for anything else.'

These words, delivered in an easy, matter-of-fact tone, jarred in Michael's mind. 'Wasn't time? What are you talking about?'

Harry fixed him with an amused stare. 'Don't you

know?' he asked pointedly. 'Don't you follow the news?'

'Don't play games,' said Michael wearily. 'You've already invaded my privacy. Just tell me what you want.'

Instead of answering directly Harry gazed down through the clear floor beneath his feet. The core of a comet, a mile wide and bristling with ancient spires of ice, slid through the darkness; spotlight lasers from the *Hermit Crab* evoked hydrocarbon shades of purple and green. 'Quite a view,' Harry said. 'It's like a sightless fish, isn't it? – a strange, unseen creature, sailing through the Solar System's darkest oceans.'

In all the years he'd studied the comet, that image had never struck Michael; hearing the words now he saw how right it was. But he replied heavily, 'It's just a comet. And this is the Oort Cloud. The cometary halo, a third of a light-year from the Sun; where all the comets come to die –'

'Nice place,' Harry said, unperturbed. His eyes raked over the bare dome, and Michael abruptly felt as if he was seeing the place through his father's eyes. The ship's lifedome, his home for decades, was a half-sphere a hundred yards wide. Couches, control panels and basic data entry and retrieval ports were clustered around the geometric centre of the dome; the rest of the transparent floor area was divided up by shoulder-high partitions into lab areas, a galley, a gym, a sleeping area and shower.

Suddenly the layout, Michael's few pieces of furniture, the low single bed, looked obsessively plain and functional.

Harry walked across the clear floor to the rim of the lifedome; Michael, whisky warming in his hand, joined him reluctantly. From here the rest of the *Crab* could be seen. A spine bristling with antennae and sensors crossed a mile of space to a block of Europa ice, so that the complete ship had the look of an elegant parasol, with the lifedome as canopy and the Europa ice as handle. The ice block – hundreds of yards wide when mined from Jupiter's moon – was pitted and raddled, as if moulded by huge fingers. The ship's GUTdrive was buried inside that block, and the ice had provided the ship's reaction mass during Michael's journey out here.

Harry ducked his head, searching the stars. 'Can I see Earth?'

Michael shrugged. 'From here the inner Solar System is a muddy patch of light. Like a distant pond. You need instruments to make out Earth.'

'You've left yourself a long way from home.'

Harry's hair had been AS-restored to a thick blond mane; his eyes were clear blue stars, his face square, small-featured – almost pixie-like. Michael, staring curiously, was struck afresh at how young his father had had himself remade to look. Michael himself had kept the sixty-year-old body the years had already stranded him in when AS technology had emerged. Now he ran an unconscious hand over his high scalp, the tough, wrinkled skin of his cheeks. Damn it, Harry hadn't even kept the colouring – the black hair, brown eyes – which he'd passed on to Michael.

Harry glanced at Michael's drink. 'Quite a host,' he said, without criticism in his voice. 'Why don't you offer me something? I'm serious. You can buy Virtual hospitality chips now. Bars, kitchens. All the finest stuff for your Virtual guests.'

Michael laughed. 'What's the point? None of it's real.'

For a second his father's eyes narrowed. 'Real? Are you sure you know what I'm feeling, right now?'

'I don't give a damn one way or the other,' said Michael calmly.

'No,' Harry said. 'I believe you really don't. Fortunately I came prepared.' He snapped his fingers and a huge globe of brandy crystallized in his open palm; Michael could almost smell its fumes. 'Bit like carrying a hip flask. Well, Michael, I can't say this is a pleasure. How do you live in this godforsaken place?'

The sudden question made Michael flinch, physically. 'I'll tell you how, if you like. I process comet material for food and air; there is plenty of carbohydrate material, and nitrogen, locked in the ice; and I –'

'So you're a high-tech hermit. Like your ship. A hermit crab, prowling around the rim of the Solar System, too far from home even to talk to another human being. Right?'

'There are reasons,' Michael said, trying to keep self-justification out of his voice. 'Look, Harry, it's my job. I'm studying quark nuggets –'

Harry opened his mouth; then his eyes lost their focus for a moment, and it was as if he were scanning some lost, inner landscape. At length he said with a weak smile: 'Apparently I used to know what that meant.'

Michael snorted with disgust. 'Nuggets are like extended nucleons –'

Harry's smile grew strained. 'Keep going.'

Michael talked quickly, unwilling to give his father any help.

Nucleons, protons and neutrons were formed from combinations of quarks. Under extremes of pressure – at the heart of a neutron star, or during the Big Bang itself – more extended structures could form. A quark nugget, a monster among nucleons, could mass a ton and be a thousandth of an inch wide . . .

Most of the nuggets from the Big Bang had decayed. But some survived.

'And this is why you need to live out here?'

'The first the inner Solar System knows of the presence of a nugget is when it hits the top of an atmosphere, and its energy crystallizes into a shower of exotic particles. Yes, you can learn something from that – but it's like watching shadows on the wall. I want to study the raw stuff. And that's why I've come so far out. Damn it, there are only about a hundred humans further from the Sun, and most of them are light years away, in starships like the *Cauchy*, crawling at near-lightspeed to God knows where. Harry, a quark nugget sets up a bow wave in the interstellar medium. Like a sparkle of high-energy particles, scattered ahead of itself. It's faint, but my detectors can pick it up, and – maybe one time out of ten – I can send out a probe to pick up the nugget itself.'

Harry tugged at the corner of his mouth – a gesture which reminded Michael jarringly of the frail eighty-year-old who had gone for ever. 'Sounds terrific,' Harry said. 'So what?'

Michael bit back an angry response. 'It's called basic research,' he said. 'Something we humans have been doing for a couple of thousand years now –'

'Just tell me,' Harry said mildly.

'Because quark nuggets are bundles of matter pushed to the extreme. Some can be moving so close to lightspeed that, thanks to time dilation, they reach my sensors barely a million subjective years after leaving the singularity itself.'

'I guess I'm impressed.' Harry sucked on his brandy, turned and walked easily across the transparent floor, showing no signs of vertigo or distraction. He reached a metal chair, sat on it and crossed his legs comfortably, ignoring the zero-gravity harness. The illusion was good this time, with barely a thread of space between the Virtual's thighs and the surface of the chair. 'I always was impressed with what you achieved. You, with Miriam Berg, of course. I'm sure you knew that, even if I didn't say it all that often.'

'No, you didn't.'

'Even a century ago you were *the* authority on exotic matter. Weren't you? That was why they gave you such responsibility on the Interface project.'

'Thanks for the pat on the head.' Michael looked into the sky-blue emptiness of his father's eyes. 'Is that what you've come to talk about? What did you retain when you had your head cleaned out? Anything?'

Harry shrugged. 'What I needed. Mostly stuff about you, if you want to know. Like a scrapbook . . .'

He sipped his drink, which glowed in the light of the comet, and regarded his son.

Wormholes are flaws in space and time which connect points separated by light-years – or by centuries – with near-instantaneous passages of curved space. They are useful . . . but difficult to build.

On the scale of the invisibly small – on Planck lengthscales, in which the mysterious effects of quantum gravity operate – spacetime is foamlike, riddled with tiny wormholes. Michael Poole and his team, a century earlier, had pulled such a wormhole out of the foam and manipulated its mouths, distorting it to the size and shape they wanted.

Big enough to take a spacecraft.

That was the easy part. Now they had to make it stable.

A wormhole without matter in its throat – a 'Schwarzschild' solution to the equations of relativity – is unusable. Lethal tidal forces would bar the wormhole portals, the portals themselves would expand and collapse at light-speed, and small perturbations caused by any infalling matter would result in instability and collapse.

So Poole's team had had to thread their wormhole with 'exotic' matter.

Space contracted towards the centre of the throat and then had to be made to expand again. A repulsive effect in the throat had come from exoticity, the negative energy density of the exotic matter. The wormhole was still intrinsically unstable, even so; but with feedback loops it could be made self-regulating.

At one time negative energy had been thought impossible. Like negative mass, the concept seemed intuitively impossible. But there had been encouraging examples for Michael and his team. Hawking evaporation of a black hole was a kind of mild exoticity . . . But the negative energy levels Poole had needed were high, equivalent to the pressure at the heart of a neutron star.

It had been a challenging time.

Despite himself Michael found memories of those days filling his head, more vivid than the image of the washed-out lifedome, the imperfect one of his father. Why was it that old memories were so compelling? Michael and his team – including Miriam, his deputy – had spent more than forty years in a slow orbit around Jupiter; the exotic-matter process had depended on the manipulation of the energies of the magnetic flux tube which connected Jupiter to its moon, Io. Life had been hard, dangerous – but never dull. As the years had worn away they had watched again and again as the robot probes dipped into Jupiter's gravity well and returned with another holdful of shining exotic material, ready to be plated over the growing tetrahedra of the portals.

It had been like watching a child grow.

Miriam and he had grown to depend on each other, completely, without question. Sometimes they had debated if this dependence contained the germ of love. Mostly, though, they had been too busy.

*

28

'You were never happier than in those times, were you, Michael?' Harry asked, disconcertingly direct.

Michael bit back a sharp, defensive reply. 'It was my life's work.'

'I know it was. But it wasn't the *end* of your life.'

Michael gripped the whisky globe harder, feeling its warm smoothness glide under his fingers. 'It felt like it, when the *Cauchy* finally left Jupiter's orbit towing one of the Interface portals. I'd proved that exotic material was more than just a curiosity; that it could be made available for engineering purposes on the greatest of scales. But it was an experiment that was going to take a century to unfold −'

'Or fifteen centuries, depending on your point of view.'

The *Cauchy* was dispatched on a long, near-lightspeed jaunt in the direction of Sagittarius − towards the centre of the Galaxy. It was to return after a subjective century of flight − but, thanks to time dilation effects, to a Solar System fifteen centuries older.

And that was the purpose of the project.

Michael had sometimes studied Virtuals of the wormhole portal left abandoned in Jovian orbit; it was aging at the same rate as its twin aboard the *Cauchy*, just as he and Miriam were. But, while Miriam and Michael were separated by a growing 'distance' in Einsteinian spacetime − a distance soon measured in light-years and centuries − *the wormhole still joined the two portals*. After a century of subjective time, for both Michael and Miriam, the *Cauchy* would complete its circular tour and return to Jovian orbit, lost in Michael's future.

And then it would be possible, using the wormhole, to step in a few hours across fifteen centuries of time.

The departure of the ship, the waiting for the completion of the circuit, had left a hole in Michael's life, and in his heart.

29

'I found I'd become an engineer rather than a scientist
. . . I'd restricted my attention to the single type of
material we could fabricate in our Io fluxtube accelera-
tors; the rest of exotic physics remained untouched. So
I decided –'

'To run away?'

Again Michael was stabbed by anger.

His father leaned forward from the chair, hands
folded before him; the grey light from the comet below
played over his clear, handsome face. The brandy glass
was gone now, Michael noticed, a discarded prop.
'Damn it, Michael; you had become a powerful man. It
wasn't just science, or engineering. To establish and
complete the Interface project you had to learn how to
build with people. Politics. Budgets. Motivation. How
to run things; how to manage – how to achieve things
in a world of human beings. You could have done it
again, and again; you could have built whatever you
wanted to, having learned how.

'And yet you turned away from it all. You ran and
hid out here. Look, I know how much it must have
hurt, when Miriam Berg decided to fly out with the
Cauchy rather than stay with you. But –'

'I'm not hiding, damn you,' Michael said, striving to
mask a flare of anger. 'I've told you what I'm doing out
here. The quark nuggets could provide new insight into
the fundamental structure of matter –'

'You're a dilettante,' Harry said, and he sat back in
his chair dismissively. 'That's all. You have no control
over what comes wafting in to you from the depths of
time and space. Sure, it's intriguing. But it isn't science.
It's collecting butterflies. The big projects in the inner
system, like the Serenitatis accelerator, left you behind
years ago.' Harry's eyes were wide and unblinking. 'Tell
me I'm wrong.'

Michael, goaded, threw his whisky globe to the floor.

It smashed against the clear surface, and the yellow fluid, pierced by comet light, gathered stickily around rebounding bits of glass. 'What the hell do you want?'

'You let yourself grow old, Michael,' Harry said sadly. 'Didn't you? And – worse than that – you let yourself stay old.'

'I stayed human,' Michael growled. 'I wasn't going to have the contents of my head dumped out into a chip.'

Harry got out of his chair and approached his son. 'It isn't like that,' he said softly. 'It's more like editing your memories. Classifying, sorting, rationalizing.'

Michael snorted. 'What a disgusting word that is.'

'Nothing's lost, you know. It's all stored – and not just on chips, but in neural nets you can interrogate – or use to feed Virtuals, if you like.' Harry smiled. 'You can talk to your younger self. Sounds like your ideal occupation, actually.'

'Look.' Michael closed his eyes and pressed his fingers against the bridge of his nose. 'I've thought through all of this. I've even discussed it with you before. Or have you forgotten that too?'

'There isn't really a choice, you know.'

'Of course there is.'

'Not if you want to stay human, as you say you do. Part of being human is to be able to think fresh thoughts – to react to new people, new events, new situations. Michael, the fact is that human memory has a finite capacity. The more you cram in there the longer the retrieval times become. With AS technology –'

'You can't make yourself a virgin by transplanting a hymen, for God's sake.'

'You're right.' Harry reached out a hand to his son – then hesitated and dropped it again. 'Coarse, as usual, but correct. And I'm not telling you that tidying up your memories is going to restore your innocence. Your thrill

31

at first hearing Beethoven. The wonder of your first kiss. And I know you're frightened of losing what you have left of Miriam.'

'You presume a hell of a lot, damn you.'

'But, Michael – there isn't an option. Without it, there's only fossilization.' Harry smiled ruefully. 'I'm sorry, son. I didn't mean to tell you how to run your life.'

'No. You never did, did you? It was always just a kind of habit.' Michael crossed to a serving hatch and, with rapid taps at a keypad icon, called up another whisky. 'Tell me what was so urgent that you had to beam out a Virtual package.'

Harry paced slowly across the clear floor; his silent footsteps, weight-laden in the absence of gravity and suspended over the ocean of space, gave the scene an eerie quality. 'The Interface,' he said.

Michael frowned. 'The project? What about it?'

Harry considered his son with genuine sympathy. 'I guess you really have lost track of your life, out here. Michael, it's a century now since the launch of the *Cauchy*. Don't you recall the mission plan?'

Michael thought it over. A century –

'My God,' Michael said. 'It's time, isn't it?'

The *Cauchy* should have returned to Sol, in that remote future. Michael cast an involuntary glance up at the cabin wall, in the direction of Jupiter. The second wormhole portal still orbited Jupiter patiently; was it possible that – even now – a bridge lay open across a millennium and a half?

'They sent me to fetch you,' Harry was saying ruefully. 'I told them it was a waste of time, that we'd argued since you were old enough to talk. But they sent me anyway. Maybe I'd have a better chance than anybody else of persuading you.'

Michael felt confused. 'Persuading me to do what?'

'To come home.' The Virtual glanced around the cabin. 'This old tub can still fly, can't she?'

'Of course she can.'

'Then the quickest way for you to return is to come in voluntarily in this thing. It will take you about a year. It would take twice as long to send a ship out to fetch you –'

'Harry. Slow down, damn it. Who are "they"? And why am I so important, all of a sudden?'

'"They" are the Jovian government. And they have the backing of all the intergovernmental agencies. System-wide, as far as I know. And you're important because of the message.'

'What message?'

Harry studied his son, his too-young face steady, his voice level. 'Michael, the portal has returned. And something's emerged from the wormhole. A ship from the future. We've had one message from it, on microwave wavelengths; we suspect the message was smuggled out, against the will of whoever's operating the ship.'

Michael shook his head. Maybe he *had* let himself get too old; Harry's words seemed unreal – like descriptions of a dream, impossible to comprehend. 'Could the message be translated?'

'Fairly easily,' said Harry drily. 'It was in English. Voice, no visual.'

'And? Come on, Harry.'

'It asked for you. By name. It was from Miriam Berg.'

Michael felt the breath seep out of him, against his will.

His father's Virtual crouched before him, one hand extended, close enough to Michael's face for him to make out individual pixels. 'Michael? Are you all right?'

3

Again Jasoft Parz was suspended in space before a Spline ship.

The freighter was a landscape of grey flesh. Parz peered into an eyeball which, swivelling, gazed out at him from folds of hardened epidermis, and Parz felt a strange sense of kinship with the Spline, this fellow client creature of the Qax.

Parz was aware of a hundred weapons trained upon his fragile flitter – perhaps even including the fabled gravity-wave starbreaker beams, purloined by the Qax from the Xeelee.

He wanted to laugh. A wall of non-existence was, perhaps, hurtling towards them from out of the altered past, and yet still they brandished their toy weapons against an old man.

'Ambassador Jasoft Parz.' The Governor's translated voice was, as ever, soft, feminine and delicious, and quite impossible to read.

Parz kept his voice steady. 'I am here, Governor.'

There was a long silence. Then the Governor said: 'I must ask your help.'

Parz felt a kind of tension sag out of him, and it was as if the muscles of his stomach were folding over each other. How he had dreaded this call to meet with the

Governor – his first journey into orbit since that fateful moment a week earlier when he had been forced to witness the humiliation of the Qax at the hands of the rebellious rabble who had escaped through the Interface portal. Parz had returned to his normal duties – though that had been difficult enough; even the rarefied diplomatic circles which controlled the planet were alive with talk of that single, staggering, act of defiance. At times Parz had longed to walk away from the heavy cordon of security which surrounded his life and immerse himself in the world of the common man. He would be destroyed as soon as they discovered he was a collaborator, of course . . . but maybe it would be worth it, to hear the delicious note of hope on a thousand lips.

But he had not the courage, or the foolhardiness, to do any such thing. Instead he had waited for the Governor to decide what to do. It would be quite within the imagination of the Qax to find a way to punish the planet as a whole for the actions of a few individuals.

Deaths would not have surprised Parz.

Paradoxically he had always found it hard to blame the Qax for this sort of action. To establish control of Earth and its sister worlds the Qax had merely had to study history and adapt methods used by humans to oppress their fellows. There was no evidence that the Qax had ever evolved such tactics as means of dealing with each other. The Qax were acting as had oppressors throughout human history, Parz thought, but still humanity had only itself to blame; it was as if the Qax were an externalized embodiment of man's treatment of man, a judgement of history.

But, in the event, nothing of the sort had happened. And now Parz had been called to another secure orbital meeting.

'Tell me what you want, Governor.'

'We believe we have made the Interface portal secure,' the Qax began. 'It is ringed by Spline warships. Frankly, any human who ventures within a million miles of the artifact will be discontinued.'

Parz raised his eyebrows. 'I'm surprised you've not destroyed the portal.'

Again that uncharacteristic hesitation. 'Jasoft Parz, I find myself unable to determine the correct course of action. A human vessel, manned by rebels against the Qax administration, has escaped fifteen centuries into the past – into an era in which the Qax had no influence over human affairs. The intention of these rebels is surely to change the evolution of events in some way, presumably to prepare humanity to resist, or throw off, the Qax administration.

'Parz, I have to assume that the past has already been altered by these rebels.'

Parz nodded. 'And were you to destroy the portal you would lose the only access you have to the past.'

'I would lose any possible control over events. Yes.'

Parz shifted his position in his chair. 'And have you sent anything through?'

'Not yet.'

Parz laughed. 'Governor, it's been a week. Don't you think you're being a little indecisive? Either close the damn thing or use it; one way or the other you're going to have to act.'

And all the time you procrastinate, he added silently, *the wall of unreality approaches us all at an unknowable speed* . . .

Parz expected a harsh reply to his goad, but instead there was again that hesitancy. 'I find myself unable to formulate a plan of action. Ambassador, consider the implications. These human rebels control history, over one and a half thousand years. I have tried to evaluate the potential for damage indicated by this, but no algorithm has been able to deliver even an order-of-magnitude assessment. I believe the danger is – in practical terms – infinite . . . My race has never faced such a threat, and perhaps never will again.'

Jasoft pulled at his lip. 'I almost sympathize with you, Governor.'

There had been a flurry of speculation about the effects of the rebels' escape into the past among what was left of the human scientific community, too. Could the rebels truly alter history? Some argued that their actions would only cause a broadening of probability functions – that new alternative realities were being created by their actions. Others maintained that reality had only a single thread, opened to disruption by the creation of the rebels' 'closed timelike curve', their path through spacetime into the past.

In either event, no one knew whether consciousness could persist through such a disruption – would Jasoft know if the world, his own history, altered around him? Or would he go through a mini-death, to be replaced by a new, subtly adjusted Jasoft? Nor were there any estimates of the rate – in subjective terms – at which the disruption was approaching, emerging from the past as if from the depths of some dismal sea.

To Jasoft such speculation seemed unreal – and yet it also lent an air of unreality to the world he inhabited, as if his life were all no more than a brightly painted surface surrounding a vacuum. He wasn't afraid – at least he didn't think so – but he sensed that his grip on reality had been disturbed, fundamentally.

It was like, he suspected, becoming mildly insane.

'Ambassador, report on what you have determined about the rebels.'

Jasoft pulled his slate from his briefcase, set it up on the tabletop before him and ran his fingers over its surface, drawing data from its heart. 'We believe the rebels constitute a group calling themselves the Friends of Wigner. Before this single, astonishing action, the Friends were dismissed as a fringe sect of no known danger to the regime.'

'We have a conscious policy of ignoring such groups,' the Qax said grimly. 'Adapted from the policies of such human colonial powers as the Roman Empire, who allowed native religions to flourish . . . Why waste effort suppressing that which is harmless? Perhaps this policy will have to be reviewed.'

Parz found himself shuddering at the menace implicit in that last, lightly delivered sentence. 'I'd advise against it,' he said quickly. 'After all, as you say, the damage is already done.'

'What is known of the vessel?'

Jasoft reported that the craft had been assembled underground on the small offshore island still called Britain.

During the decades of the Occupation there had been a programme to remove human capacity for space travel, and, systematically, ships from all over the Solar System and from the nearby stars – the small bubble of space embraced by humans before the Occupation – had been recalled, impounded and broken up in shipyards converted to crude wrecking shops. Nobody knew, even now, how many lone craft there were still avoiding the law of the Qax somewhere between the stars, but with the Solar System and the major extra-solar colonies invested, they could do little damage . . .

Until now. The rebel craft had apparently been constructed around the purloined remains of a broken, impounded freighter.

'And why the name?' the Qax asked. 'Who was this Wigner?'

Parz tapped his slate. 'Eugene Wigner. A quantum

38

physicist of the twentieth century: a near-contemporary of the great pioneers of the field – Schrödinger, Heisenberg. Wigner's subject was quantum solipsism.'

There was a brief silence from the Qax. Then: 'That means little to me. We must determine the intentions of these Friends, Jasoft; we must find a way to see through their human eyes. I am not human. You must help me.'

Parz spread his hands on the tabletop and gathered his thoughts.

Wigner and his co-workers had tried to evolve a philosophy in response to the fact that quantum physics, while universally accepted, was saturated with dazzling paradoxes which suggested that the external world had no well-defined structure until minds observed it.

'We humans are a finite, practical species,' Jasoft said. 'I live in my head, somewhere behind my eyes. I have intimate control over my body – my hands, my feet – and some control over objects I can pick up and manipulate.' He held his slate in his hands. 'I can move the slate about; if I throw it against the wall it bounces off. The slate is discrete in itself and separate from me.'

But this common-sense view of the universe began to fall apart as one approached the smallest scales of creation.

'Uncertainty is at the heart of it. I can measure the position of my slate by, say, bouncing a photon off it and recording the event in a sensor. But how do I record the position of an electron? If I bounce off a photon, I knock the electron away from where I measured it . . . Suppose I measured the electron's position to within a billionth of an inch. Then my uncertainty about the electron's momentum would be so high that a second later I couldn't be sure where the damn thing was within a hundred miles.

'So I can never be simultaneously sure where an electron is *and* where it's going . . . Instead of thinking of an electron, or any other object, as a discrete, hard little entity, I have to think in terms of probability wave functions.'

Schrödinger had developed equations which described how probability waves shifted and evolved, in the presence of other particles and forces. Parz closed his eyes. 'I imagine space filled with probability, like blue ripples. If I had vision good enough, maybe I could see the waves in all their richness. But I can't. It's like looking through half-closed eyes; and all I can make out is the shadowy places where the peaks and troughs occur. And I say to myself – there; that's where the electron is. But it isn't; it's just a crest of the wave . . . Where the wave function has its peaks is where I'm most likely to find my electron – but it's not the only possibility.'

'But the wave functions collapse on observation, of course,' the Qax prompted.

'Yes.' The link between quantum reality and the world of the senses – human senses – came when measurements were made. 'I run my experiment and determine that the electron is in fact, at this instant' – He stabbed the tabletop with a fingertip – 'right there. Then the position wave function has collapsed – the probabilities have all gone to zero, except in the little region of space within which I've pinned down the electron. Of course as soon as the measurement is over, the wave functions start evolving again, spreading out around the electron's recorded position.' Parz frowned. 'So, by observing, I've actually changed the fundamental properties of the electron. It's not possible to separate the observer from the observed . . . and you could argue that by observing I've actually evoked the existence of the electron itself.

'And there lies the mystery. The paradox. Schröd-inger imagined a cat locked in a box with a single unstable nucleus. In a given period there is a fifty-fifty chance that the nucleus will decay. If it does, the cat will be killed by a robot mechanism. If it doesn't, the cat is allowed to live.

'Now. Leave the box aside for its specified period, without looking inside. Tell me: is the cat alive or dead?'

The Qax said without hesitating, 'There is no para-dox. One can only give an answer in terms of prob-abilities, until the box is opened.'

'Correct. Until the box is opened, the wave function of the box-cat system is not collapsed. The cat is neither alive nor dead; there is equal probability of either state.'

But Wigner took Schrödinger's paradox further. Sup-pose the box were opened by a friend of Wigner's, who saw whether the cat were alive or dead. The box, cat and friend would now form a larger quantum system with a more complex wave function in which the state of the cat – and the friend – remained indefinite until observed by Wigner or someone else.

'Physicists of the time called this the paradox of Wig-ner's Friend,' Jasoft said. 'It leads to an infinite regress, sometimes called a von Neumann catastrophe. The box–cat–friend system remains indefinite until observed, say by me. But then a new system is set up – box–cat–friend–me – which itself remains indefinite until observed by a third person, and so on.'

The Qax pondered for a while. 'So we have, in human eyes, the central paradox of existence, of quantum physics, as set out by this Wigner and his chatter of cats and friends.'

'Yes.' Jasoft consulted his slate. 'Perhaps external reality is actually created by the act of observation. With-out consciousness, Schrödinger wondered, "Would the world have remained a play before empty benches, not existing for anybody, thus quite properly not existing?"'

'Well, Jasoft. And what does this tell us about the mindset of those who style themselves the Friends of Wigner?'

Parz shrugged. 'I'm sorry, Governor. I've no hypothesis.'

There was a lengthy silence then; Parz peered through the port of the flitter at the unblinking eye of the Spline.

Suddenly there was motion at the edge of Parz's vision. He shifted in his seat to see better.

The Spline freighter was changing. A slit perhaps a hundred yards long had opened up in that toughened epidermis, an orifice that widened to reveal a red-black tunnel, inviting in an oddly obscene fashion.

'I need your advice and assistance, Ambassador,' the Governor said. 'You will be brought into the freighter.'

Anticipation, eagerness surged through Parz.

The flitter nudged forward. Parz strained against his seat restraints, willing the little vessel forward into the welcoming orifice of the Spline.

The flitter passed through miles, it seemed, of unlit, fleshy passages; vessels bulging with some blood-analogue pulsed, red, along the walls. Tiny, fleshy robots – antibody drones, the Governor called them – swirled around the flitter as it travelled. Parz felt claustrophobic, as if those blood-red walls might constrict around him; somehow he had expected this aspect of the Spline to be sanitized by tiling and bright lights. Surely if this vessel were operated by humans such modifications would be made; no human could stand for long this absurd sensation of being swallowed, of passing along a huge digestive tract.

At last the flitter emerged from a wrinkled interface

into a larger chamber – the belly of the Spline, Parz instantly labelled it. Light globes hovered throughout the interior, revealing the chamber to be perhaps a quarter-mile wide; distant, pinkish walls were laced with veins.

Emerging from the bloody tunnel into this strawberry-pink space was, Parz thought, like being born.

At the centre of the chamber was a globe of some brownish fluid, itself a hundred yards wide. Inside the globe, rendered indistinct by the fluid, Parz could make out a cluster of machines; struts of metal emerged from the machine cluster and were fixed to the Spline's stomach wall, so anchoring the globe. A meniscus of brownish scum surrounded the globe. The fluid seemed to be slowly boiling, so that the meniscus was divided into thousands, or millions, of hexagonal convection cells perhaps a hand's-breadth across; Parz, entranced, was reminded of a pan of simmering soup.

At length he called: 'Governor?'

'I am here.'

The voice from the flitter's translator box, of course, gave no clue to the location of the Governor; Parz found himself scanning the stomach chamber dimly. 'Where are you? Are you somewhere in that sphere of fluid?'

The Qax laughed. 'Where am I indeed? Which of us can ask that question with confidence? Yes, Ambassador; but I am not *in* the fluid, nor am I *of* the fluid itself.'

'I don't understand.'

'Turbulence, Parz. Can you see the convection cells? There am I, if "I" am anywhere. Do you understand now?'

Jasoft, stunned, stared upwards.

*

The home planet of the Qax was a swamp.

A sea, much like the primaeval ocean of Earth, covered the world from pole to pole. Submerged volcano mouths glowed like coals. The sea boiled: everywhere there was turbulence, convection cells like the ones Parz saw in the globe at the heart of the Spline.

'Parz, turbulence is an example of the universal self-organization of matter and energy,' the Qax said. 'In the ocean of my world the energy generated by the temperature difference between the vulcanism and the atmosphere is siphoned off, organized by the actions of turbulence into billions of convection cells.

'All known life is cellular in nature,' the Governor went on. 'We have no direct evidence, but we speculate that this must apply even to the Xeelee themselves. But there seems to be no rule about the form such cells can take.'

Parz scratched his head and found himself laughing, but it was a laughter of wonder, like a child's. 'You're telling me that those convection cells are the basis of your being?'

'To travel into space I have been forced to bring a section of the mother ocean with me, in this Spline craft; a small black hole at the centre of the Spline sets up a gravity field to maintain the integrity of the globe, and heaters embedded at the core of the fluid simulate the vulcanism of the home sea.'

'Not too convenient,' Parz said dryly. 'No wonder you need a Spline freighter to travel about in.'

'We are fragile creatures, physically,' the Governor said. 'We are easily disrupted. There are severe constraints on the manoeuvrability of this freighter, if my consciousness is to be preserved. And there are comparatively few of us compared to, say, the humans.'

'Yes. There isn't much room, even in a planet-wide sea . . .'

'The greatest of us span miles, Parz. And we are

practically immortal; the convection cells can readily be renewed and replaced, without degradation of consciousness . . . You will understand that this information is not to be made available. Our fragility is a fact which could be exploited.'

This warning sent a chill through Parz's old bones. But his curiosity, drinking in knowledge after years of exclusion, impelled him to ask still more questions. 'Governor, how could the Qax ever have got off the surface of their planet and into space? You're surely not capable of handling large engineering projects.'

'But we are nevertheless a technological race. Parz, my awareness is very different from yours. The scales are different: I have sentience right down to the molecular level; if I wish, my cells can operate as independent factories, assembling high technology of a miniaturized, biochemical nature. We traded such items among ourselves for millions of years, unaware of the existence of the rest of the universe.

'Then we were "discovered"; an alien craft landed in our ocean, and tentative contact was established –'

'Who was it?'

The Governor ignored the question. 'Our biochemical products had enormous market value, and we were able to build a trading empire – by proxy – spanning lightyears. But we must still rely on clients for larger projects –'

'Clients like humans. Or like the Spline, who cart you around in their bellies.'

'Few of us leave the home world. The risks are too great.'

Parz settled back in his chair. 'Governor, you've known me for a long time. You must know how I've been driven crazy, for all these years, by knowing so little about the Qax. But I'm damn sure you haven't shown me all this as a long-service reward.'

45

'You're correct, Ambassador.'

'Then tell me what you want of me.'

The Governor replied smoothly, 'Parz, I need your trust. I want access to the future. I want humans to build me a new time Interface. And I want you to direct the project.'

It took Parz a few minutes to settle his churning thoughts. 'Governor, I don't understand.'

'The revival of the ancient exotic matter technologies should not be difficult, given the progress of human science in the intervening millennium and a half. But the parameters will differ from the first project . . .'

Parz shook his head. He felt slow, stupid and old. 'How?'

Through the flitter's tabletop the Qax transmitted an image to Parz's slate: an appealing geometrical framework, icosahedral, its twenty sides rendered in blue and turning slowly. 'The new Interface must be large enough to permit the passage of a Spline freighter,' the Governor said. 'Or some other craft sufficiently large to carry Qax.'

A traveller through a wormhole interface suffered gravitational tidal stresses on entering the exotic-matter portal framework, and on passing through the wormhole itself. Parz had been shown, now, that a Qax was far more vulnerable to such stress than a human. 'So the throat of the wormhole must be wider than the first,' he mused. 'And the portals must be built on a larger scale, so that the exotic-matter struts can be skirted –'

Parz touched the slate thoughtfully; the geometrical designs cleared.

The Qax hesitated. 'Parz, I need your co-operation on this project.' There seemed to be a note of honesty, of real supplication, in the Governor's synthesized voice. 'I have to know if this will cause you difficulty.'

Parz frowned. 'Why should it?'

'You are a collaborator,' the Qax said harshly, and Parz flinched. 'I know the ugliness that word carries, for humans. And now I am asking you to *collaborate* with me on a project whose success may cause great symbolic damage to humans. I am aware of how much the small success of the time-journeying rebels has meant to humans, who see us as oppressive conquerors —'

Parz smiled. 'You *are* oppressive conquerors.'

'Now, though, I am asking you to subvert this emblem of human defiance to the needs of the Qax. I regard this as an expression of great trust. Yet, perhaps to you this is the vilest of insults.'

Parz shook his head, and tried to answer honestly — as if the Qax were an externalization of his own conscience, and not a brooding conqueror who might crush him in an instant. 'I have my views about the Qax Occupation, my own judgements on actions you have taken since,' he said slowly. 'But my views won't make the Qax navies go away, or restore the technologies, capabilities and sheer damn dignity which you have taken from us.'

The Qax said nothing.

'I am a practical man. I was born with a talent for diplomacy. For mediation. By doing the job I do, I try to modify the bleak fact of Qax rule into a livable arrangement for as many humans as possible.'

'Your fellows might say that by working with us you are serving only to perpetuate that rule.'

Parz spread his age-marked hands, finding time to wonder that he was speaking so frankly with a Qax. 'Governor, I've wrestled with questions like this for long hours. But, at the end of it, there's always another problem to address. Something urgent, and practical, which

47

I can actually do something about.' He looked up at the ball of slowly seething liquid. 'Does that make any sense?'

'Jasoft, I think we are of like mind, you and I. That is why I chose you to assist me in this enterprise. I fear that the precipitate actions of these rebels, these Friends of Wigner, represent the gravest peril – not just to the Qax, but perhaps to humanity as well.'

Parz nodded. 'That thought's occurred to me too. Meddling with history isn't exactly a proven science . . . and which of us would wish to trust the judgement of these desperate refugees?'

'Then you will help me?'

'Governor, why do you want to travel *forward* in time? How will that help you with your problem from the past?'

'Don't you see what an opportunity this technology represents? By constructing a portal to the future I can consult with an era in which the problem *has already been addressed and resolved*. I need not make a decision on this momentous matter with any uncertainty about the outcome; I can consult the wisdom of those future Qax and refer to their guidance . . .'

Parz wondered vaguely if some sort of time paradox would be invoked by this unlikely scheme. But aloud he said, 'I understand your intention, Governor. But – are you sure you want to do this? Would it not be better to make your own decisions, here and now?'

The Governor's interpreted voice was smooth and untroubled, but Parz fancied he detected a note of desperation. 'I cannot take that risk, Parz. Why, it's entirely possible I will be able to consult myself . . . a self who knows what to do. Will you help me?'

The Qax is out of its depth, Parz realized. *It genuinely doesn't know how to cope with this issue; the whole of this elaborate new Interface project, which will absorb endless energy and resources, is all a smokescreen for the Governor's basic lack of competence.* He felt a stab of unexpected pride, of chauvinistic relish at this small human victory.

But then, fear returned through the triumph. He had been honest with the Governor . . . Could he really bring himself to trust the judgement of these Friends of Wigner, to whom accident had provided such power?

And, surely, this victory of procrastination would increase the likelihood that they'd all be left helpless in the face of the wave of unreality from the past.

But, Parz reflected, he had no choices to make.

'I'll help you, Governor,' he said. 'Tell me what we have to do first.'

4

With her message to Michael Poole dispatched and still crawling over the Solar System at mere lightspeed, Miriam Berg sat on coarse English grass, waiting for the Wigner girl, Shira.

Berg had built a time machine and carried it to the stars. But the few days of her return through the wormhole to her own time had been the most dramatic of her life.

Before her the lifeboat from the *Cauchy* lay in a shallow, rust-brown crater of scorched soil. The boat was splayed open like some disembowelled animal, wisps of steam escaping its still-glowing interior; the neat parallel slices through its hull looked almost surgical in their precision, and she knew that the Friends had taken particular pleasure, in their own odd, undemonstrative way, in using their scalpel-like cutting beams to turn drive units into puddles of slag.

The – murder – of her boat by the Friends had been a price worth paying, of course, for getting her single, brief message off to Poole. He would do something; he would be coming . . . Somehow, in formulating her desperate scheme, she had never doubted that he would still be alive, after all these years. But still, she felt a twinge of conscience and remorse as she surveyed the wreckage of the boat; after all this was the destruction of her last link with the *Cauchy*, with the fifty men, women and Friends with whom she had spent a century crossing light-years and millennia – and who were now stranded on the far side of the wormhole in the future they had sought so desperately to attain, that dark, dehumanized future of the Qax Occupation.

How paradoxical, she thought, to have returned through the wormhole to her own time, and yet to feel such nostalgia for the future.

She lay on her back in the grass and peered up at the salmon-pink clouds that marbled the monstrous face of Jupiter. Tilting her head a little she could still make out the Interface portal – the wormhole end which had been left in Jovian orbit when the *Cauchy* departed for the stars, and through which this absurd earth-craft of the Friends of Wigner had come plummeting through time. The portal, sliding slowly away from the earth-craft on its neighbouring orbit, was a thumbnail sketch rendered in cerulean blue against the cheek of Jupiter. It looked peaceful – pretty, ornamental. The faces of the tetrahedron, the junctions of the wormhole itself, were misty, puzzled-looking washes of blue-gold light, a little like windows.

It was hard to envisage the horrors which lay only subjective hours away on the other side of that space-time flaw.

She shivered and wrapped her arms around her body. After she'd landed on the earth-craft the Friends had given her one of their flimsy, one-piece jumpsuits; she was sure it was quite adequate for this fake climate, but, damn it, she just didn't feel warm in it. But she suspected she'd feel just as shivery in the warmest clothing; it wasn't the cold that was her problem, she suspected, but a craving to return to the safe metal womb that the *Cauchy* had become. During her century of flight, whenever she had envisaged the end of her journey, she had anticipated a pleasurable tremor on stepping out of a boat for the first time and drinking in the fresh, blue air of Earth . . . even an Earth of the distant future. Well, she hadn't got anywhere near Earth; and surely to God anybody would be spooked by a situation like this. To be stranded on a clod of soil a quarter-mile wide – with no enclosing bubble or force shell as far as she could tell – a clod which had been wrenched from the Earth and hurled back through time and into orbit around Jupiter –

She decided that a healthy dose of fear at such a moment was quite the rational response.

She heard footsteps, rustling softly through the grass.

'Miriam Berg.'

Berg raised herself on her elbows. 'Shira. I've been waiting for you.'

The girl from the future sounded disappointed. 'I trusted you, Miriam. I gave you the freedom of our craft. Why did you send this message?'

Berg squinted up at Shira. The Friend was tall – about Berg's height, a little under six feet – but there the similarity ended. Berg had chosen to be AS-frozen at physical age around forty-five – a time when she had felt most at home in herself. Her body was wiry, tough and comfortable; and she liked to think that the wrinkles scattered around her mouth and brown eyes made her look experienced, humorous, fully human. And her cropped hair, grizzled with grey, was nothing to be ashamed of. Shira, by contrast, was aged about twenty-five. Real age, soon to be overwhelmed by time, thanks to the Qax's confiscation of the AS technology. The girl's features were delicate, her build thin to the point of scrawny. Berg couldn't get used to Shira's clean-shaven scalp and found it hard not to stare at the clean lines of her skull. The girl's skin was sallow, her dark-rimmed eyes blue, huge and apparently lashless; her face, the prominent teeth and cheekbones, was oddly skeletal – but not unpretty. Shira was much as Berg imagined Earthbound city-dwellers of a few centuries before Berg's own time must have looked: basically unhealthy, surviving in a world too harsh for humans.

Berg would have sworn that she had even spotted fillings and yellowed teeth embedded in Shira's jaw. Was it possible that dental caries had returned to plague mankind again, after all these centuries?

What a brutal testament to the achievements of the Qax Occupation forces, Berg reflected bitterly. Shira was like a creature from Berg's past, not her future. And, now that Berg was deprived of the medical facilities of the *Cauchy* – not to mention AS technology – no doubt soon she, too, would become afflicted by the ills that had once been banished. My God, she thought; I will start to age again.

She sighed. She was close to her own time, after all; maybe – unlikely as it seemed – she could get back home. If Poole made it through . . .

'Shira,' she said heavily, 'I didn't want to make you unhappy. I hate myself for making you unhappy. All right? But when I learned that you had no intention of communicating with the humans of this era – of my era – of telling them about the Qax . . . then of course I had to oppose you.'

Shira was unperturbed; she swivelled her small, pretty face to the wreck of the boat. 'You understand we had to destroy your craft.'

'No, I don't understand that you had to do that. But it's what I expected you to do. I don't care. I achieved my purpose; I got my message off despite all of you.' Berg smiled. 'I'm kind of pleased with myself for improvising a radio. I was never a hands-on technician, you know –'

'You were a physicist,' Shira broke in. 'It's in the history books.'

Berg shivered, feeling out of time. 'I *am* a physicist,' she said. She got stiffly to her feet and wiped blades of grass from her backside. 'Can we walk?' she asked. 'This place is depressing me.'

Berg, casting about for a direction, decided to set off for the lip of the earth-craft; Shira calmly fell into step beside her, bare feet sinking softly into the grass.

Soon they were leaving behind whatever gave this disc of soil its gravity; the ground seemed to tilt up before them, so that it was as if they were climbing out of a shallow bowl, and the air started to feel thin. About thirty feet short of the edge they were forced to stop; the air was almost painfully shallow in Berg's lungs, and even felt a little colder.

At the edge of the world tufts of grass dangled over emptiness, stained purple by the light of Jupiter.

'I think we have a basic problem of perception here, Shira,' Berg said, panting lightly. 'You ask why I betrayed your trust. I don't understand how the hell a question like that has got any sort of relevance. Given the situation, what did you expect me to do?'

The girl was silent.

'Look at it from my point of view,' Berg went on. 'Fifteen hundred years after my departure in the *Cauchy* I was approaching the Solar System again . . .'

As the years of the journey had worn away, the fifty aboard *Cauchy* had grown sombrely aware that the worlds they had left behind were aging far more rapidly than they were; the crew were separated from their homes by growing intervals of space and time.

They were becoming stranded in the future.

. . . But they carried the wormhole portal. And, they knew, through the wormhole only a few hours' flight separated them from the era of their birth. It was a comfort to imagine the worlds they had left behind on the far side of the spacetime bridge, still attached to the *Cauchy* as if by some umbilical of stretched spacetime, and living their lives through at the same rate as the *Cauchy* crew, patiently waiting for the starship to complete its circuit to the future.

At last, after a subjective century, the *Cauchy* would return to Jovian orbit. Fifteen centuries would have worn away on Earth. But still their wormhole portal would connect them to the past, to friends and worlds grown no older than they had.

'I don't know what I was expecting exactly as we neared Sol,' Berg said. 'We'd run hundreds of scenarios, both before and during the journey, but we knew it was all guesswork; I guess inside I was anticipating anything from radioactive wastelands, to stone axes, to gods in faster-than-light chariots.

'But what I'd never anticipated was what we found. Earth under the thumb of super-aliens nobody has even seen . . . and look what came hurtling out to meet us, even before we'd got through the orbit of Pluto.' She shook her head at the memory. 'A patch of Earth, untimely ripp'd from England and hurled into space; a few dozen skinny humans clinging to it desperately.'

She remembered venturing from the steel security of the *Cauchy* into Jovian space, an envoy in her solo lifeboat, and tentatively approaching the earth-craft; she had scarcely been able to believe her eyes as the ship had neared a patch of countryside that looked as if it had been cut out of a tourist catalogue of Earth and stuck crudely onto the velvet backdrop of space. Then she had cracked the port of the boat on landing, and had stepped out onto grass that rustled beneath the tough soles of her boots . . .

For a brief, glorious few minutes the Friends had clustered around her in wonder.

Then Shira had come to her – related fifteen centuries of disastrous human history in as many minutes – and explained the Friends' intentions.

Within a couple of hours of landing Berg had been forced to crouch to the grass with the rest as the earth-craft plummeted into the gravity tube that was the wormhole. Berg shuddered now as she remembered the howling radiation which had stormed around the fragile craft, the ghastly, mysterious dislocation as she had travelled through time.

She hadn't been allowed to get a message off to the crew of the *Cauchy*. Perhaps her *Cauchy* shipmates were already dead at the hands of the Qax – if that word 'already' had any meaning, with spacetime bent over on itself by the wormhole.

'It has been an eventful few days,' she said wryly. 'As a welcome home this has been fairly outrageous.'

Shira was smiling, and Berg tried to focus. 'I'm glad you say that: *outrageous*,' Shira said. 'It was the very outrageousness of the idea which permitted us to succeed under the eyes of the Qax, as we planned. Come, let us talk; we have time now.'

They turned and began to stroll slowly back 'down' the rim-hill and towards the interior of the craft. As they walked, Berg had the uncomfortable feeling that she was descending into and climbing out of invisible dimples in the landscape, each a few feet wide and perhaps inches shallow. But the land itself was as flat as a tabletop to the eye. She was experiencing unevenness in the field which held her to this quarter-mile disc of soil and rock; whatever they used to generate their gravity around here clearly wasn't without its glitches.

Shira said, 'You must understand the situation. We knew, from surviving records of your time, that your return to the Earth with the Interface portal was imminent. If you had succeeded, a gateway to the free past might have become available to us. We conceived the Project –'

Berg looked at her sharply. 'What Project?'

Shira ignored the question. 'The Qax authorities were evidently unaware of your approach, but clearly, once they detected your vessel and its unique cargo, you would be destroyed. We had to find a way to meet you before that happened.

'So, Miriam. We had to build a space vessel, and in the full and knowing gaze of the Qax.'

'Yeah. You know, Shira, we're going to have to sort out which tense to use here. Maybe we need to invent a whole new grammar – future past, uncertain present . . .'

Shira laughed unselfconsciously, and Berg felt a little more human warmth for her.

They walked through a grove of light-globes. The globes, hovering in the air perhaps ten feet from the soil, gave out sun-like heat and warmth, and Berg paused for a few moments, feeling on her face and in her newly aging bones the warmth of a star she had abandoned a subjective century before. In the yellow-white light of the globe the flesh-pink glow of Jupiter was banished, and the grass looked normal, wiry and green; Berg ran a slippered toe through it. 'So you camouflaged your ship.'

'The Qax do not interfere with areas they perceive as human cultural shrines.'

'Hurrah for the Qax,' said Berg sourly. 'Perhaps they're not such bad fellows after all.'

Shira raised the ridges from which her eyebrows had been shaved. 'We believe that this is not altruism but calculation on the part of the Qax. In any event the policy is there – and it is a policy which may be manipulated to our gain.'

Berg smiled, her mind full of a sudden, absurd image

of rebels in grimy jumpsuits burrowing like moles under cathedrals, pyramids, the concrete tombs of ancient fission reactors. 'So you built your ship under the stones.'

'Yes. More precisely, we readied an area of land for the flight.'

'Where did you get the resources for this?'

'The Friends of Wigner have adherents System-wide,' Shira said. 'Remember that by the time of the first encounter with the Qax, humans had become a starfaring species, able to command the resources of multiple systems. The Qax control us – almost completely. But in the small gap left by that "almost" there is room for great undertakings . . . projects to match, perhaps, the greatest works of your own time.'

'I wouldn't bet on that,' Berg said with grim confidence.

They walked on, towards the heart of the craft. 'So,' said Berg, 'you got your ship ready. How did you get it off the planet and into space?'

'A stolen Squeem hyperdrive device,' said Shira. 'It cast a lenticular field around the craft, initially isolating it – and a surrounding layer of air – from the planet. Then the drive was used to hurl the craft into space, to bring it to the vicinity of your *Cauchy*. Then – after the rendezvous with your ship – the drive was used to carry the craft through the Interface.'

'The Squeem. That's the race humans came up against earlier, right? Before the Qax.'

'And who, in their defeat, afforded us much of the basic technology we needed to get out of the Solar System.'

'How will we defeat them?'

Shira grinned. 'Read your history books.'

'So,' Berg said, 'is the Squeem drive operating now?'

'Minimally. It serves as a radiation screen.'

'And to keep the air stuck to the ship, right?'

'No, the craft's gravity does that.'

Berg nodded; maybe here was a chance to get a little more meaningful information. 'Artificial gravity? Things have come a long way since my day.'

But Shira only frowned.

They approached the dwellings and workplaces of the Friends. The buildings, simple cubes and cones built on a human scale, were scattered around the heart of this landscape ship like toys, surrounding the old stones at the centre of the disc. The building material was uniformly dove-grey and – when Berg ran her fingertips over the wall of a tepee as she passed – smooth to the limit of sensation. But it was human-warm, without the cold of metal. This was 'Xeelee construction material', one of the many technological miracles which had apparently seeped down to mankind – and their foes, like the Squeem and the Qax – from the mysterious Xeelee, lords of creation.

Friends moved among the buildings, patiently going about their business. One small group had collected around one of the data capture devices they called 'slates', and were arguing over what looked like a schematic of the earth-craft.

They nodded to Shira, and to Berg with glances of curiosity.

Berg had counted about thirty Friends of Wigner aboard the craft, roughly split between male and female. They appeared to be aged between twenty-five and thirty, and all seemed fit and intelligent. Obviously this crew had been selected by the wider Friends organization for their fitness for the mission. All followed the shaved-skull fashion of Shira – some, Berg had noticed with bemusement, had indeed removed their eyelashes. But they were surprisingly easy to distinguish from each other; the shape of the human skull was, she was learning, as varied – and could be as appealing to the eye – as the features of the face.

'You've done well to get so far,' Berg said.

'More than well,' said Shira coolly. 'Our craft has successfully traversed the portal, without significant damage or injury. Our supplies – and our recycling gear – should suffice to sustain us in this orbit around Jupiter for many years. Long enough for our purposes.' She smiled. 'Yes, we have done well.'

'Yeah.' Berg sourly studied the busy knots of Friends. 'You know, it might help me a lot to understand you if you told me what the hell your Project is all about.'

Shira studied her sadly. 'That would not be appropriate.'

Berg took a stance before her, hands on hips, and set her face into what she knew would be a commanding scowl. 'Don't hide behind platitudes, Shira. Damn it all to hell, it was my ship – my Interface – which you used to get as far as you have. And it's the lives of my crew, lost on the wrong side of the wormhole, which have paid for the success you so complacently report. So you owe me a bit more than that patronizing crap.'

Shira's pretty, paper-fine face creased with what looked like real concern. 'I'm sorry, Miriam. I'm not meaning to patronize you. But I – we – genuinely believe that it wouldn't be right to tell you.'

'Why? At least tell me that much.'

'I can't. If you understood the Project then you would also see why you can't be told any more.'

Berg laughed in her face. 'Are you kidding me? Is that supposed to satisfy me?'

'No,' Shira said, grinning almost cheekily, and again, for a moment, Berg felt a tug of genuine empathy with this strange, secret person from the other side of time. 'But it really is all I can give you.'

Berg scraped her fingers across her wiry stubble of

hair. 'What is it you're afraid of? Do you think that it's possible I'll oppose you – try to obstruct the Project?'

Shira nodded seriously. 'If you gained only partial understanding, then that is possible. Yes.'

Berg frowned. 'I don't think you're talking about understanding – but about faith. Even if I knew what you were up to, I might oppose it if I didn't share the same irrational faith in its success. Is that it?'

Shira did not reply to that; her gaze was clear and untroubled.

'Shira, maybe you genuinely need my help,' Berg said. 'I'd rather not rely on the faith that my ship is going to fly, if I've got a chance of getting into the drive and making sure it does.'

'It's not as simple as that, Miriam,' Shira said. She smiled disarmingly. 'And I wish you'd stop pumping me.'

Berg touched the girl's elbow. 'Shira, *we're on the same side,*' she said urgently. 'Don't you see that?' She gestured vaguely in the direction of the inner Solar System. 'You've got the resources of five planets – of Earth itself – to call on. Once people understood what you're trying to avert – the nightmare of the Qax Occupation – you would be given all the help the worlds could muster. You'd have the strength of billions.'

'It wouldn't work, Miriam,' Shira said. 'Remember, we have developed fifteen centuries beyond you. There is little your people could do to help.'

Berg stiffened, drawing away from the girl. 'We could pack a hell of a punch, Shira. What if the Qax follow us back in time, through the portal? Won't you need help to stave them off?'

'We can defend ourselves,' Shira said calmly.

That sent a shiver through Berg, but she pressed on: 'Then imagine a hundred violently armed GUTships crashing through that portal, and into the future. They could do a hell of a lot of damage –'

Shira shook her head. 'A single Spline warship could scythe them down in a moment.'

'Then let's use the advantage of the centuries we've gained.' Berg slammed her fist into her palm. 'There's not a Qax alive at this moment who even knows humans exist. We could go and roast them in their nest. If you gave us the secret of the Squeem hyperdrive, we could build a faster-than-light armada and –'

Shira laughed delicately. 'You're so melodramatic, Miriam. So violent!' She made a wide cage of her hands. 'At this moment, the Qax already operate an interstellar trading empire spanning hundreds of star systems. The thought of an ill-equipped rabble of humans from fifteen centuries before my time having any hope of overcoming that might is risible, frankly. And, besides – we are not hyperdrive engineers. We could not "pass on the secrets" of the Squeem drive, as you put it.'

'Then let our engineers take it apart.'

'Any such attempt would result in the devastation of half a planet.'

Berg found herself bridling again. 'You're still being patronizing,' she protested. 'Even insulting. We're not complete dummies, you know; we are your ancestors, after all. Maybe you ought to have more respect.'

'My friend, your thinking is simplistic. We did not come here to attempt a simple military assault on the Qax. Even were it to succeed – which it could not – it would not be sufficient. Our purpose is at once more subtle – and yet capable of achieving much, much more.'

'But you won't tell me what it is? You won't trust me. Me, your own great-to-the-nth grandmother –'

Shira smiled. 'I would be proud to share some fraction of your genetic heritage, Miriam.'

Side by side they walked on, still heading towards the centre of the earth-craft. Soon they had cleared the belt of construction-material huts with their knots of busy people, and the hum of the Friends' conversation faded behind them; when they reached the centre of the craft it was as if they were entering a little island of silence.

And as the two women walked into the broken circle of stones, that seemed entirely appropriate to Berg.

There were no globe-lights here; the stones, hulking and ancient, stood defiant in the smoky light of Jupiter. Berg stood beneath one of the still-intact Sarsen arches and touched the cold blue-grey surface of a standing stone; it wasn't intimidating or cold, she thought, but friendly – more like stroking an elephant. 'You know,' she said, 'you could cause a hell of a stir just by landing this thing on Earth. Maybe on Salisbury Plain, a few miles from the original – which, of course, is standing there in the wind and the rain, in this time zone. If it were up to me, I couldn't resist it, Project or no Project.'

Shira grinned. 'The thought does have an appeal.'

'Yeah.' Berg walked towards the centre of the circle, stepping over crumbled fragments of rock. She turned slowly around, surveying the truncated landscape, trying to see this place through the eyes of the people who built it four thousand years earlier. How would this place have looked at the solstice, standing on the bare shoulders of Salisbury Plain, with no sign of civilization anywhere in the universe save a few scattered fires on the plain, soon dying in the dawn light?

. . . But now her horizon was hemmed in by the anonymous grey shoulders of the Friends' construction-material huts; and she knew that even if she had the power to blow those huts away she would reveal only a few hundred yards of scratched turf, a ragged edge dangling over immensities. And when she tilted her head back she could see the arc of Jupiter's limb, hanging like an immense wall across the universe.

The old stones were dwarfed by such grandeur. They seemed pathetic.

Absurdly she felt a lump rising to her throat. 'Damn it,' she said gruffly.

Shira stepped closer and laid her hand on Berg's arm. 'What is it, my friend?'

'You had no right to do it.'

'What?'

'To hijack these stones! This isn't their place; this isn't where they are meant to be. How could you murder all that history? Even the Qax never touched the stones; you said so yourself.'

'The Qax are an occupying power,' Shira murmured. 'If they thought it in their interest, they would grind these stones into dust.'

'But they did not,' Berg said, her jaw tight. 'And one day, with or without you, the Qax would be gone. And the stones would still stand! – but for you.'

Shira turned her face up to Jupiter, her bare skull limned in salmon-pink light. 'Believe me, we – the Friends – are not without conscience when it comes to such matters. But in the end, the decision was right.' She turned to Berg, and Berg was aware of a disturbingly religious, almost irrational, aspect to the girl's pale, empty blue eyes.

'How do you know?' Berg asked heavily.

'Because,' Shira said slowly, as if speaking to a child, 'in the end, *no harm will have come to the stones.*'

Berg stared at her, wondering whether to laugh. 'Are you crazy? Shira – you've burrowed under the stones, wrapped a hyperdrive field around them, ripped them off the planet, run them through the gauntlet of the Qax fleet, and thrown them fifteen hundred years back in time! What more can you do to them?'

Shira smiled, concern returning to her face. 'You know I will not reveal our intentions to you. I can't. But I can see you are concerned, and I want you to believe this, with all your heart. When our Project has succeeded, Stonehenge will not have been harmed.'

Berg pulled her arm away from the girl's hand, suddenly afraid. 'How is that possible? My God, Shira, what are you people intending to do?'

But the Friend of Wigner would not reply.

5

The flitter nestled against the Spline's stomach lining; small, clawlike clamps extended from the flitter's lower hull and embedded themselves in hardened flesh.

Jasoft Parz, watching the anchoring manoeuvre from within the flitter, felt his own stomach turn in sympathy.

He ran rapid tests of the integrity of his environment suit – green-glowing digits scrolled briefly across his wide faceplate – and then, with a nod of his head, instructed the flitter's port to sigh open. There was a hiss of equalizing pressure, a breeze which for a few moments whispered into the cabin, pushing weakly at Parz's chest. Then Parz, with a sigh, unbuckled his restraints and clambered easily out of his chair. Since the last time he'd visited the Governor inside his Spline flagship, back in Earth orbit a full year ago, the AS treatments had done wonders for some of his more obvious ailments, and it was a blessed relief to climb out of a chair without the accompaniment of stabbing agonies in his back.

Antibody drones had fixed a small, flat platform over the Spline's stomach lining close to the lip of the flitter's port; a compact translator box was fixed to it. Briskly Parz pulled himself out of the flitter and activated electromagnets in the soles of his boots to pin his feet to the platform. Soon he was done, and was able to stand in a reasonably dignified fashion.

He looked around. The hull of the flitter, resting beside him, was like some undigested morsel in the gut of the Spline. He turned his face up to the ball of boiling fluid suspended above him; alongside it, shimmering in the murky gloom of the Spline gut, was a Virtual of the scene outside – the icosahedral wormhole portal, a sliver of Jupiter itself. 'Governor,' he said. 'It's been a long time.'

The Governor's voice sounded from the translator box, slightly muffled in Parz's ears by the thick air. 'Indeed. A full year since those damned Friends of Wigner absconded. A wasted year, as we've struggled to put right the situation. And now we reach the climax, here in the shadow of Jupiter, eh, Parz?'

'I wouldn't say wasted,' Parz said smoothly. 'The building and launch of the new Interface portals was a great success; I was astonished at the rapid progress made.'

'Thank you for the part you played in that enterprise, Jasoft Parz.'

'My actions weren't for your benefit, in particular.'

'Perhaps not,' said the Qax. 'But what does your motive avail me, if the result is as I required? I understand that your motive was your personal reward, the AntiSenescence treatment which –'

'Not just that,' Parz said coldly. 'I happened to think that the revival of the old exotic-matter industries was a good thing for humans.' It had not been without cost, of course. With the single-mindedness available only in a command society, most of the human worlds – Earth, Mars, Luna, Titan – had been transformed into little more than exotic-matter factories, all their resources dedicated to the single goal. But the completion of such a massive project based on purely human technology – even a project instigated by the Qax – had done a great deal for the self-esteem of the race. 'After all, the damned thing was built and launched within six months, Governor.'

'I understand your pride,' the Governor said in its smoothly neutral feminine voice. 'And I'm glad to see that time has not withered your outspoken tongue, Ambassador.'

Parz said sourly, 'What is it you understand? Governor, you've underestimated us before, remember. The escape of the Friends –'

'Must I bolster your pride, Jasoft?' the Governor cut in. 'I have invited you here to witness the triumph of our work together.'

And indeed, Parz conceded, the Qax had summoned him here to Jovian space as soon as the showers of high-energy particles had begun to erupt from the mouth of the waiting portal . . . the first portents of an arrival from the future.

'After all,' the Qax went on, 'if it were not for the granting of AS treatment to you and a handful of your colleagues – treatment you were not reluctant to accept – you would not be standing here now lecturing me about the awesome potency of the human race. Would you? For you were close to the termination of the usual human lifespan, were you not?'

The relaxed contempt brought the blood to Parz's cheeks. 'Governor –'

But the Qax went on impatiently, 'Let us abandon this, Ambassador; on this day of days, let us dwell on our achievements together and not our differences.'

Parz took a deep breath of cool, blue human air. 'All right, Governor.'

'Your heart must have surged with pride when the new Interface was completed.'

Indeed it had, Parz remembered. At last the mouths of the Solar System's second spacetime wormhole had been threaded with icosahedra of blue-glowing exotic matter. For a few brief, magnificent weeks, the twin portals had sailed together around Jupiter's gravity well, the milky sheets of broken space stretched across the exotic-matter frames and glimmering like the facets of mysterious jewels.

Then had come the time for the removal of one of the portals. A massive GUTdrive vessel had been constructed: hovering over the portals the vessel had looked, Parz remembered, like a human arm, a clenched fist poised over a pair of fragile, blue-grey flowers.

The ship's huge GUTdrive engines had flared into life, and one of the portals had been hauled away, first on a widening spiral path out of the gravity well of Jupiter, and then away on a shallow arc into interstellar space.

Parz – like the rest of the human race, and like the Governor and the rest of the Qax occupation force – had settled down to wait out the six months of the portal's sublight crawl to its destination.

The first Interface ship, the *Cauchy*, had taken a century to bridge fifteen hundred years. The new ship took only half a year of subjective time to loop away from Sol and return; but, accelerating at multiples of Earth's gravity, it had crossed five centuries into the future.

Parz was not a scientist, and – despite his close connection to the project – found much of the physics of wormholes philosophically baffling. But, as he had travelled to the Jovian system and had gazed on the slowly turning jewel that was the Qax's returned icosahedral portal, the essence of the project had seemed very real to him.

On the other side of those misty, grey-blue planes was the future. If the Friends of Wigner had gained the advantage by escaping into a past in which no Qax had even heard of humankind, what greater advantage could those future Qax wield? Parz reflected ruefully. They had five centuries of hindsight, five centuries in which the outcome of the struggle between Qax and human had surely been decided one way or the other.

Only a year had passed since the escape of the Friends. Yet already those future Qax had the opportunity to twist events any way they pleased.

'You are pensive,' the Governor said, breaking into his thoughts.

'I'm sorry.'

'Come,' the Qax said, its translator-box voice softly beguiling. 'I don't think either of us would describe the other as a friend, Ambassador. But we have worked closely, and – once – grew to be honest with each other. Tell me what concerns you, while we wait on events.'

Parz shrugged. 'What an awesome weapon we have delivered into the hands of your successors, five centuries away. Imagine one of the great generals of human history – Bonaparte, for example – able to study, from history texts, the outcome of his greatest battle *before even taking the field.*'

'There is more than one possibility, Jasoft. Such a general might feel rendered helpless by the weight of historical evidence. Many wars are not decided by strokes of military genius – or by the heroism of a few individuals – but by the forces of history. Or, perhaps, the general might even be stricken with remorse, at the suffering and death his ambition had caused; perhaps he would even work to avert his battle.'

Parz snorted. 'Maybe. Although I can't imagine any Qax "general" feeling much remorse for human victims of a tyranny or a war, regardless of the outcome. When we learned of the escape of the Friends of Wigner, remember that we both felt mistrust at such awesome

70

power being delivered into the hands of any group, regardless of species. Should we not feel such mistrust of these Qax from the future?'

The Qax laughed softly. 'Now perhaps it is you who underestimate us. I am not without admiration for human achievements, baffled though I am sometimes by your motives.'

Jasoft peered through his faceplate at the soft, soapy bubbling of the sea-fragment hosting the Governor. 'For example?'

'The craft which bore away our Interface terminal was manned by humans. The vessel was essentially automatic, of course – and certainly immune to any possibility of mutiny by the human crew – but your experience of centuries of spaceflight persuaded me that there is no better guarantee of the success of a human-built ship than the presence aboard her of human engineers, with their ingenuity and adaptability – both physical and mental. And so we needed a human crew.'

'And you found no trouble getting volunteers. Despite the prospects of multiple-g travel.' Parz smiled. 'That isn't so surprising, Governor.'

'How so?'

'Not all humans are the same. We are not all as comfortable with our client-race status as –'

'As you, for example, Jasoft?'

'Right.' Parz stuck his chin out, feeling his stubbly jowls stretch; he didn't expect the Qax to read the gesture, but the hell with it. 'Correct. Not all humans are like me. Some want to get out of the box the Solar System has become, regardless of the cost. When will humans again be allowed to journey beyond the Solar System? And what's life for, but to see, to explore, to wonder? Maybe taking away our AS technology was a mistake for you; maybe the renewed cheapness of our lives – a few, paltry decades and then the endless darkness – has made humans more reckless. Harder to control, eh, Governor?'

The Governor laughed. 'Perhaps. Well, Parz; we should turn to our business. And how do you feel, now that the Interface is about to come into operation?'

Parz thought back over the long months of waiting after the construction and launch of the Interface. He had maintained a Virtual image of the stationary portal in his quarters throughout that time, listening to endless, baffling commentaries about relativistic time dilation, closed timelike curves and Cauchy horizons.

The future Qax must have been expecting the visitation from the past, of course. Perhaps some of the Qax alive in Parz's time would still be conscious and able to remember the launch.

At last the day of the ship's scheduled return to future Earth – the day on which the portal would begin to function as a time tunnel to the future – had come; and Parz had been joined in his silent vigil beneath Virtuals of the stationary Jovian icosahedron by an unseen congregation of millions. All over the Earth, and through the rest of the Occupied System, humans had watched the twinkling icosahedron with a mixture of fascination and dread.

Then, at last, the bursts of exotic particles from the wormhole terminus . . .

'I guess,' Parz said slowly, 'I feel something of what Michael Poole, the builder of the first Interface, must have gone through as he waited for his project to come to fruition.' But that first Interface project had, as Parz understood it, been initiated in the hope of filching some knowledge from future generations of mankind – and to test out the science of spacetime and exotic physics – and, Parz guessed, for the sheer, exuberant hell of it. A working time machine, in orbit around Jupiter? If you can build it, why the hell not?

Poole must have anticipated the opening of his wormhole with joy. Not feared it, as Parz had done.

'Yes,' the Qax said reflectively. 'And now –'

And now the Virtual image of the icosahedron exploded; darkness flecked with gold rained over Parz and he cried out, curled in on himself, cringing.

The Governor was silent; in Parz's ears there was only the ragged rasp of his own breath.

After long seconds Parz found the will to raise his head. The Virtual of the portal was still there, with the crack of Jovian light visible alongside it . . .

But now, before the portal, hovered a single ship. A bolt of night-darkness had erupted through the blue-grey face of the portal. The surface of the spacetime discontinuity still quivered seconds after the passage, sending distorted echoes of Jupiter's pink glow over the Governor's bubbling globe of Qax ocean.

The ship from the future spread wings like a bird's, a hundred miles wide. Night-dark canopies loomed over Parz.

'I am awed, Qax,' Parz said, his voice a whisper.

'No less I. Parz, the grace of this ship, the use of the sheet-discontinuity drive – all characteristics of Xeelee nightfighter technology.'

Xeelee . . . Parz felt his fear transmute into an almost superstitious horror that suddenly Xeelee might be made aware of the existence of humanity.

'But this is a Qax ship, nevertheless,' the Governor said. 'I have received call signatures . . . My successors must fare well in the centuries to come, to gain such an access to Xeelee technology.'

'You must be proud,' Parz said sourly. His heart still pounded, but already his fear was lapsing into irritation at the Qax's complacency.

'The wings are actual sheet-discontinuities in spacetime,' the Governor babbled on. 'Motive power for the

73

ship is provided by a nonlinear shear of spacetime – much as acoustical shock waves will propagate themselves through an atmosphere, once formed. And –'

'Enough.'

Parz's breath caught in his throat. The new voice, which had come booming from the translator box which rested on the platform beside him, was feminine; but where the Governor's synthetic voice was breathless, shallow and fast-speaking, the new voice was deep and heavy, almost harsh.

The Governor said, almost girlishly, 'I hear your voice. Who are you?'

'I am Qax.'

The Governor said, 'I do not recognize you.'

'That should not surprise you. I travelled through the wormhole Interface from your future. I am not yet sentient in this local frame.'

'Sir,' Parz said, determined not to show any awe or fear, 'I've got used to a Qax being laid out on the scale of miles, like the Governor and his fragment of mother-sea up there. But the body of your ship is much smaller. How can the awareness of a Qax be contained in such a constricted space?'

'Many things will change in the coming centuries,' the newcomer said. 'Many Qax will die, and many more will be formed; very few of the Qax now sentient will survive. And the forms which support our sentience will become greatly more varied. No longer will the Qax be able to afford the luxury of the ancient aquatic form; the Qax, scattered across the stars, must find new ways to survive.'

Parz could scarcely believe the implications of these words. 'Qax, what are you saying? What happens to the Qax? What is it that humans do to you?'

'First answer *my* question,' the Governor cut in, and Parz thought he could detect a note of aggrieved pride in the synthesized voice. 'Why did you not inform me of your approach? And why do we converse through this human translator box? We are Qax. We are brothers. Our forms may differ, but surely we can still communicate as the Qax have always done?'

'I want Jasoft Parz to hear and understand all that occurs here,' the new Qax said. 'Later, I will require his co-operation.'

Parz took an uneasy step back, feeling the edge of the metal platform under his feet. 'You know me?'

Again, a primitive awe rose in him, threatening to overwhelm him, as if he were some savage confronted by a shaman. But how could a Qax from five centuries into the future know of his existence? *But of course it does*, he thought, a touch of insanity bubbling in his thoughts. *The Qax is from the future; it knows everything about this sequence of events. It's probably watched this scene play itself out a dozen times . . .*

'Jasoft Parz, bear witness.'

Parz looked up.

Light, cherry-red, lanced through the hull of the Spline, a geometrically perfect line which pierced the heart of the Governor's ocean-globe. The flesh of the Spline peeled back from the wound, bubbling into immense blisters, and Parz was afforded a brief glimpse of space. The Virtual image of the nightfighter ship broke up into a cloud of pixels and vanished.

Jasoft closed his eyes, ran the last second of the Virtual scene through his mind.

The Qax ship, he realized. The weapon – the beam, whatever it was – had been fired by the Qax ship from the future.

'Xeelee technology, Jasoft Parz,' the new Qax said. 'The starbreaker . . .'

Where the cherry-red beam had struck, the surface of the ocean-globe seethed and steamed; huge bubbles erupted from the heart of the liquid, disrupting the delicate pattern of hexagonal turbulence cells. Mist wrapped around the churning globe.

'My God,' Parz breathed. 'You're killing it.'

'The beam consists of coherent gravity radiation,' the new Qax said, almost conversationally. 'The form of the ocean fragment is maintained by a small black hole at its centre. The action of the weapon has caused the equilibrium of the globe to be broken; it is now imploding towards the central singularity.'

The ball of liquid above Parz's head was completely obscured by mist now; it was like standing under a fat, spherical cloud. Droplets of fluid, round and heavy as mercury, splashed obscenely against Parz's faceplate. He wiped at the plate with a gloved hand. 'Qax,' he said angrily, 'I didn't know your species murdered each other.'

'The failure of the one you called the Governor, in permitting the escape of these rebel humans through time, is so catastrophic as to be criminal. If it troubles you, Parz, think of this as a culling, not a murder. A strengthening of my species through the elimination of the weak. The Governor of Earth was – hesitant. I am not.'

'A catastrophic failure?' Parz knelt again and pressed his face close to the translator box, shouting to hear his own voice over a rising wind. 'My God, Qax, I don't know what I expected from the future, but nothing like this . . . We humans terrify you. Don't we, Qax?'

'Yes,' the Qax said simply. 'But the fact of my apprehension should, perhaps, terrify *you*. For it is I, in this local frame, who wield the power –'

Parz shivered at that.

'And I do not fear *you*, Jasoft Parz,' the Qax went on.

Parz frowned. 'How flattering.'

'I have studied your earlier conversation with the

Governor. This new policy, of permitting selected humans access to the ancient AS technology is indeed a wise one. Because it divides you. And you, Jasoft Parz, you have accepted the payment of the Qax. You live, while your fellows die like insects.' The Qax laughed, and its synthesized laughter was dark, sinister in comparison with the Governor's. 'Your analysis of the value of potential immortality was valid. A human would far sooner throw away a life of a mere few decades than abandon the chance of immortality. Wouldn't you, Parz?'

'If you want my co-operation, why do you insult me?'

'Oh, I will have your co-operation.'

Parz lifted his head, letting the ghastly rain slide over his faceplate. 'You listen to me. The Governor, whom you seem to hold in such contempt, was *civilized*. Do you understand me? The framework within which we worked together – the Occupation – was not established by either of us. But the Governor strove for efficiency, not terror or brutality. And that was why I spent my life working with him; I felt it was the best way I could serve my species. But you. I've already seen you murder one of your own, since your irruption from the future only moments ago –'

The Qax laughed. 'You are honest, Jasoft Parz; perhaps that is why the Governor valued your presence so much. Listen. My purpose here is not to maintain the Occupation.'

Parz asked uneasily: 'Then what is it?'

'I will not stay in this local spacetime frame. My intention is to pass through the original human portal – to move still further back into time.'

'You're chasing the Friends of Wigner, the human rebels, back through time?'

'I intend to destroy those rebels, yes. And to achieve much more besides.'

Parz tried to imagine this Qax – an unprincipled killer with an admitted fear and loathing of humans – emerging into the unprepared Solar System of fifteen centuries earlier.

'And me?' Jasoft asked fearfully. 'What will I do, while you launch this assault on the past?'

'Why, you will accompany me, of course.'

'Dear God –' Primaeval ocean murk sleeted again over Jasoft's faceplate; he wiped at it ineffectually with the back of one gloved hand.

The Qax said, 'The Governor will remain conscious for some hours, although its sentience is diminishing already.'

'Is there pain?'

'Our business is concluded here. Return to your craft.'

Barely able to see through a sheen of ocean-stuff, Parz reached for the shelter of the flitter.

6

The GUTship *Hermit Crab* swept backside-first through a powered orbit around the swollen cheek of Jupiter.

Michael Poole sat in the *Crab*'s clear-walled lifedome with the Virtual of his father, Harry. The ship was rounding the dark side of the planet now, and the GUT-drive, blazing a mile beneath the transparent floor of the cabin, illuminated vast areas of an ocean of swirling cloud. Violet light was cast upwards through the cabin, and Poole noticed how his father's young, blond head had been given suitably demonic shadows by the processors in response.

'We're making quite an entrance,' Harry said.

'I guess so. If you like fireworks.'

Harry turned to his son, his blue eyes boyishly wide with wonder. 'No, it's more than that. You're the physicist, son, and I'm just a government functionary; and you understand it all better than I ever could. But maybe the wonder of it doesn't hit you with the same impact as it does a layman like me. We're harnessing forces lost to the universe since the first few seconds after the Big Bang —'

'Essentially. Except that you're talking about the first few *fractions* of a second . . .'

'GUT' stood for 'Grand Unified Theory', the

philosophical system which described the fundamental forces of nature as aspects of a single superforce. The heart of the *Crab*'s GUTdrive was a fist-sized chunk of hydrogen locked into a superconducting bottle and bombarded to creation physics temperatures. At such temperatures only the unified superforce could act. When hydrogen was bled from the bottle the superforce went through 'phase transitions', decomposing into the four familiar forces of nature – strong and weak nuclear, gravitational and electromagnetic.

And, just as steam releases heat when it goes through a phase transition by condensing to water, so at each transition of the superforce a pulse of energy was emitted.

Poole said to his father, 'The *Crab* uses GUT phase energy to flash comet ice to plasma; the superheated plasma is expelled through a superconducting nozzle . . .'

Harry nodded, peering down the mile of superstructure to the residual lump of comet which had brought them in from the Oort Cloud. 'Sure. But it was that same phase transition energy, liberated during the cooling period after the Big Bang, which drove the expansion of the universe itself.

'That's what seems so awesome, when you stop and think about it, Michael. We've spent a year scooting around the Solar System – and now we're making Jupiter himself cast a shadow – and we're doing it by harnessing the energies of creation itself. Doesn't it make you wonder?'

Poole rubbed the side of his nose. 'Yes, Harry. Of course it does. But I don't actually think that sort of attitude is going to help us all that much, in the next few days. I'd rather not feel awed by the workings of our own drive, right now. Remember we're going to be dealing with humans from fifteen centuries into the future . . . or for all I know, with artificial life forms, or with aliens, even.'

Harry leaned closer to Poole and grinned. 'Not all of us AIs are such terrible things, Michael.'

Poole narrowed his eyes. 'Push your luck and I'll pull your plug.'

Harry grumbled, 'Maybe these superpeople from the future will be advanced enough to recognize the rights of AIs. Such as the right to continuous consciousness, for instance. Anyway, I know it's all talk.'

'If you don't get your fingers out of my head then I'll shut you down, talk or not, you old fart.'

An alarm chimed through the lifedome. The *Crab*, sailing barely a thousand miles over a sea of purple clouds, was near its closest approach to the planet; and now the battered old ship swept around the limb of Jupiter and emerged into the light of the distant sun. Sol, shrunken by distance, lifted its rays through layers of cloud at Jupiter's flat-infinite horizon; there was a dazzling impression of the depth of the Jovian atmosphere as clouds cast thousand-mile-long shadows over each other. The cabin was flooded with brilliance. For a second Harry's Virtual image retained the purplish shadows cast from the cabin floor by the drive. Then the processor caught up and when Harry turned his face to the sun his profile was highlighted in yellow.

Then, like the rise of a second, angular sun, the Interface portal hurtled over the horizon towards them. Michael could see the firefly sparks of ships circling the portal, waiting for any new intrusion from the future. The *Crab*'s trajectory took her to within a few dozen miles of the portal; Michael stared out at the dazzling sky-blue of the portal's exotic tetrahedral frame, let his eyes linger over those cool lines and be drawn effort-lessly to the geometrically perfect vertices. The faces were like semitransparent panes of silvered glass; he could make out the watercolour oceans of Jupiter through the faces, but the cloud images were overlaid with a patina of silver-gold and were distorted, they swirled around in a fashion the eye could not quite track, like visions in a dream. And every few seconds a face would abruptly clear, just for a dazzling moment, and afford Michael a glimpse of another space, unfamiliar stars, like a hole cut into Jupiter.

The *Crab* swept on and away from the artifact; it dwindled rapidly behind them like an abandoned toy.

'My God,' Harry breathed. 'I didn't know how beautiful it was. I thought I could see stars in those faces.'

'You could, Harry,' Poole said softly. 'It really is a gateway to another time, another place.'

Harry leaned towards Michael. 'I'm very proud of you.'

Poole stiffened and pulled away.

Harry said, 'Listen, what do you really think we're going to find out here?'

'Aboard the craft from the future?' Poole shrugged. 'Since they haven't communicated with us apart from that single message from Miriam when they came through the Interface a year ago, it's difficult even to extrapolate.'

'Will humans still be recognizably human, do you think?'

Poole swivelled a glare at Harry. 'And are we "recognizably human"? Look at us, Harry; I'm an AS-immortal, and you're a semi-sentient AI.'

'*Semi*-sentient?'

'Superficially we look human enough, and we'd probably claim to be human, but I don't know if a man of, say, a thousand years ago would recognize us as members of the same species as himself. And now we're talking another fifteen centuries down the road . . .'

Harry wiggled his fingers in the air, pulling a face. 'A third arm growing out of the centre of the face. Disembodied heads, bouncing around on the deck like footballs. What do you think?'

Poole shrugged. 'If gross modifications like that are efficient, or serve a purpose, then maybe so. But I don't think any of that matters a damn, compared to what's going on *inside* their heads. And what they've built.'

'What about technology?'

'I guess I'd put singularity physics a long way up the list,' Poole said. 'The manipulation of spacetime curvature . . . We've already got a mastery of high-density, high-energy physics – that's the heart of the GUTdrive, and of the exotic matter which the Interface portals were built of.'

'And in fifteen more centuries –' Harry prompted.

'How far could we take this? I'd anticipate the manufacture of singularities themselves, on the scale of a few tons up to, maybe, asteroid masses.'

'What for?'

Poole spread his hands wide. 'Compact power sources. If you had a black hole in your kitchen you could just throw in the waste and see it compressed to invisibility in a fraction of a second, releasing floods of usable short-wavelength radiation. And how about artificial gravity? Bury a black hole at the centre of, say, Luna, and you could raise the surface gravity as high as you like.'

Harry nodded. 'Of course you'd have to find some way of keeping the singularity from eating the Moon.'

'Yeah. Then there are gravity waves, to be generated by colliding black holes. You could build tractor beams, for instance.' Poole settled back into his couch and closed his eyes. 'Of course, if they've taken this far enough, maybe they will have found some use for naked singularities.'

'And what's a naked singularity?'

'. . . Maybe we're going to find out.'

Now they were entering a region of space filled with ships; hundreds of drive sparks flitted over the patient ocean of Jupiter. The ships were too distant to afford any detail, but Poole knew that there must be Navy ships from the inhabited Jovian moons, science craft from the inner Solar System, and God-damned tourists and rubbernecks from just about everywhere. A subdued chatter in the background of the lifedome told him that signals were starting to come in from that motley armada – since the receipt of Berg's message a year earlier, Poole knew, Jovian space had been the centre of attention for most of the human race, and his own arrival here had been the most eagerly anticipated event since the emergence of the future ship itself.

He ignored the messages, letting Virtual copies of himself handle them; if there was anything devastating they'd let him know.

Peering into the crowded space ahead, and after his decades of isolation in the bleak outer lands of the Solar System, Poole felt a pang of absurd claustrophobia. He was driven on by curiosity as well as by a residual concern for Miriam Berg and her crew; but now that his year-long journey in from the Oort Cloud was complete he found he really, really didn't want to be here, back among the fetid worlds of humankind.

Harry was studying him, his youthful brow creased. 'Relax, son,' he said. 'It was never going to be easy.'

'Oh, for Christ's sake, shut up,' Poole snapped. Even as he spoke he was aware of an odd feeling of relief at having someone, or something, reasonably tangible outside his own head to react to. 'I should put you in an electronic bottle labelled "Dad", and take you out when I feel the need of another patronizing fatherly homily.'

Harry Poole grinned, unmoved. 'Just doing my job,' he murmured.

Now the *Crab*, drive still blazing ahead of her, was approaching the most dense knot of ships in the sky. The cloud of vessels, as if sensing the approach of the *Crab*, began to part.

Inside that firefly mist Michael could make out the lines of something huge, a splash of green against the murky pink of Jupiter.

'That's it,' Poole said, finding his voice hoarse. 'The ship from the future. Time to go to work . . .' He snapped a command into the air.

The crowded universe outside the lifedome was clouded by a sudden hail of pixels which danced like dust motes around the *Crab*, slowly congealing into planes, orbs and strands around the lifedome. Harry squirmed in his seat, mouth open, as he watched the huge Virtual take shape around the ship. At last they were looking out through eyes which were each at least a hundred yards wide, with eyelids which swept like rainstorms over the glistening lenses. A nose like a vast engineering project, with nostrils like rocket nozzles, obscured the *Crab*'s GUTdrive module; and huge sculpted ears sailed alongside the lifedome.

A mouth, whale-sized, opened moistly.

'My God,' Harry breathed. 'It's you, isn't it? We're looking out through your face.'

'I couldn't think of any other way to be sure we were identified properly. Don't worry: the Virtual is all show; it's not even as sentient as you are. It repeats a five-second phrase of greeting, over and over again.'

'So how will they hear what it has to say?'

'Harry, the Virtual is two miles high,' Poole said, irritated. 'Let them lip-read!'

Harry swivelled his head, surveying the nostrils, the cable-like hairs above the cabin, skin pores the size of small asteroids. 'What a disgusting experience,' he said at last.

'Shut up and watch the show.'

Now there were ships all around the camouflaged *Crab*. Poole recognized Navy ships which bristled with weapon ports, science platforms open and vulnerable, even one or two inter-moon skitters which should surely never have been allowed so close. Many of the larger craft followed the same basic design as the *Crab*, with drive unit and living quarters separated by a stem; from this distance the ships looked like lighted matchsticks, scattered through space.

'How do you think the men from the future will react to us?' Harry asked with sudden nervousness.

Poole, glancing across, saw Harry chewing a nail, a habit he remembered from a distant childhood. 'Maybe they'll shoot us out of the sky,' he said maliciously. 'What do you care? You're tucked up in bed on Earth, well away from any danger.'

Harry looked at him reproachfully. 'Michael, let's not go over that again. I'm a Virtual, but I have my identity, my sense of being.'

'You think you do.'

'Isn't that the same thing?'

'Anyway, I doubt if we're in any danger,' Poole said. 'The future people haven't made any attempt to use weapons so far; why should they now?'

Harry nodded grudgingly. 'True.' After the future ship had settled into its orbit around Jupiter there had been several attempts by Navy ships to approach the craft. The future humans hadn't responded, or fired on the Navy ships; they'd simply run away, faster than they could be tracked.

'Maybe they haven't any weapons,' Harry said.

Poole pursed his lips. 'That's possible, I guess. They do have their super-drive, though.'

'I know there's speculation that could be some kind of hyperspace drive,' Harry said.

'Maybe. But if that's true we've no idea how it works. It's not possible to extrapolate from existing technologies, the way I speculated about singularity technologies; a hyperdrive would represent a quantum leap.'

'Maybe it's not a human invention. Maybe it's alien.'

'Anyway, I don't think we're in any danger of being fired on; and if they want us to come in they'll not run away.'

'How reassuring,' the Virtual murmured.

Now the last few layers of craft peeled away before them, the GUTdrive fire-sparks scrabbling aside like scared insects.

The future craft was revealed, like a fragment of landscape emerging through a layer of cloud. The *Crab*'s drive died at last, and Poole's Virtual, mouthing its idiot words of greeting, loomed over a disc of green Earth a quarter-mile wide. Poole could clearly make out the ring of ancient stones at its centre, like grey-brown scars against the greenery. A belt of anonymous-looking dwellings encircled the stones, and beyond the belt grass grew as in some surrealist's vision, all the way to the edge of the world; the green of it clashed in his eyes with the purple-pink of Jupiter, so that it was as if the craft were encircled by a scar of indeterminate colour.

Close to the rim Poole made out a splash of metal, a scarred crater in the grass. Could that be a boat from the *Cauchy*?

Sparks of light, like entrapped stars, were sprinkled over this floating fragment of Earth. And here and there Poole could see tiny, insect-like forms crawling across the landscape. People? He imagined faces upturned in wonder to his own vast, smiling mouth.

He scanned the lifedome's instrument displays briskly, watching data chatter in on the lifeboat's mass

– about that of an asteroid – and its gravitational configuration and radiation characteristics.

'I've seen pictures and I've read about it,' Harry said, 'but I don't think I really believed it until now.'

'It looks more fragile than I expected,' Poole murmured.

'Fragile?'

'Look at it. Why build a timeship under a clod of earth like that, with so little protection . . . unless, perhaps, you wanted to hide what you were doing.'

'They can run, but they can't fight,' Harry said.

'Yeah. Maybe these aren't the heroic, superpowered gods from the future we anticipated after all. Maybe these people are refugees.'

Harry seemed to shiver. 'Refugees from what?'

'Well, at least they haven't fled from us yet. Come on; let's get to the boat and see if they will let us land.'

7

Michael Poole brought the *Crab*'s boat down near the grassy lip of the craft from the future, close to the wreckage of a lifeboat.

Followed by the Virtual of his father, he walked out onto a green plain. For a moment he felt disoriented. Beneath his feet there was grass, the blades coarse enough for him to feel them through the soft soles of his boots; globes the size of his fist hovered eight feet above him, giving off a Sol-like yellow warmth, and towards the centre of the disc-craft a concentration of the globes produced a cosy, Earthlike island of light. There was even a hint of blueness about the layer of atmosphere over the disc of land.

But above him – like some immense roof over creation – hung the banded clouds of Jupiter. It took a conscious effort not to cringe from that lowering sky.

'You know,' he said to Harry, 'I found it quite hard to step out of the boat. I feel naked, standing here.'

'I know what you mean.' Harry took a deep, theatrical sniff. 'But the air smells as good as the tests showed it to be. Why, you can even smell the grass growing.' He bounced on his toes. 'And near Earth-normal gravity, as we estimated from orbit.'

'Quit showing off,' Poole grumbled. 'It's hard to

understand how anyone could have the guts to ride through time clinging to this damn thing.' He thought of Berg huddled against this ground as the broken exotic-matter walls of the wormhole hurtled past her, and he felt an unfamiliar stab of protectiveness. Damn it, Berg could look after herself as well as anyone he'd known – certainly a lot better than he could himself – but nobody deserved to be put through such an experience.

His protectiveness began to fade to an uncertain guilt, as he wondered if he ought to hold himself responsible, if indirectly, for the chain of events which had resulted in this.

He watched Harry walk out of sight around the *Crab*'s boat; the craft, a cylindrical lump of metal still frosted from the chill of space, sat on this plain of grass as incongruous as a bullet on an altar-cloth.

'My God,' Harry called.

Poole followed his father. Harry stood, hands on hips, surveying the wrecked lifeboat they'd seen from the *Crab*.

The boat had been sliced open like a ripe melon. The laser-strokes through the hull were razor-sharp – almost pleasing in their clarity and neatness. Poole could see how the interior of the craft had been scorched and melted, and how partitions had softened and flowed towards the soil.

'Well, it's no ordinary wreck,' Harry said. 'And look.' He pointed to an intact hull panel. 'See the registration?'

'It's from the *Cauchy*. Harry, this is Miriam's boat, it has to be.' A kind of helpless panic surged through him. 'What the hell's been done to her?'

'Nothing, Michael. I'm all right. See?'

Poole whirled at the sound of the deep, slightly hoarse, and desperately familiar voice. He saw all of her as if in a blur – the tough, lively face, the thatch of cropped hair, eyes that looked soft with tears. Without willing it he found himself in her arms. Miriam was a few inches taller than Michael, and her slim body, encased in a coarse, pink jumpsuit, was tense for a moment, though her arms encircled his back; and then she relaxed, and the length of her body pressed against his. He buried his face in the soft warmth of her neck.

When he was able he released her, grasped her shoulders and peered into her face. 'My God, Miriam, I thought you were dead. When I saw the lifeboat —'

She smiled, her lips thin. 'Not very friendly of them, was it? But they haven't done me any harm, Mike; they just' — now the stiffness returned — 'they just stop me from doing things. Maybe I'm getting used to it. I've had a year of it now . . .'

'And the journey through time? How was that?'

Her face seemed to crumple, before she regained control. 'I survived it,' she said.

Poole stepped away from her with a sense of embarrassment. He was aware of Harry standing close beside him, but kept his eyes averted from Harry's face; he was two centuries old, and he was damned if he was going to put up with any more fatherly affection. Not right now.

There was a woman with Miriam, he saw now: as tall as Miriam, slightly scrawny, her thin, bony face young-looking and pretty — except for a dome of a shaven head, which Poole found it hard to keep his eyes away from. The woman regarded him steadily. Her pale-eyed gaze was somehow disturbing: Poole saw in it the naïvety of youth overlaid with a kind of blank impassivity.

Harry stepped forward to the girl and held out his arms. 'Well, Michael got his welcome; how about me?'

Michael groaned inwardly. 'Harry —'

The girl swivelled her head to Harry and took a neat

step back. 'That would be pleasant if it were possible, sir,' she said, her face solemn.

Harry grinned and shrugged theatrically. 'Are my pixels showing again? Damn it, Michael, why didn't you tell me?'

Berg leaned close to Poole. 'Who's the asshole?'

'Would you believe, my father?'

Berg screwed up her face. 'What an embarrassment. Why don't you pull the plug? He's only a Virtual.'

'Not according to him.'

'Michael Poole.' Now the girl, having extricated herself from Harry's attention, was facing Poole; her complexion was quite poor, the skin around her eyes bruised-looking and tired. Poole felt himself drawn to the weakness of this girl from the future – such a contrast to the high-technology superbeings he'd imagined in his wilder moments. Even the single-piece coverall she wore was, like Miriam's, of some coarse, cheap-looking artificial fabric.

'I'm Poole,' he said. 'You've already met my father.'

'My name is Shira. I'm honoured to meet you.' Her accent was modern-sounding but neutral. 'Your achievements are still famous, in my day,' the girl said. 'Of course we would not be here to meet you without your Interface project –'

Berg cut in sharply, 'Is that why you let them land, instead of blowing them out of the sky?'

'We would not have done that, Miriam Berg,' Shira said. She sounded vaguely hurt.

'Okay, but you could have cut and run with your hyperdrive, like you did from the other ships –'

The word hit Poole like a slap to the face. 'They *do* have a hyperdrive?'

Berg said sourly, 'Sure. Now ask if she'll let you inspect it.'

Harry pressed forward and pushed his young face

close to the girl's. 'Why have you come here, to our time? Why has there been only one message from this craft to the rest of the Solar System?'

'You have many questions,' Shira said, holding her hands up before her as if to ward Harry off. 'There will be time to answer you at leisure. But, please, you are our guests here; you must allow us to receive you into our hospitality.'

Harry pointed at the sliced-open wreckage of the *Cauchy* lifeboat. 'Some hospitality you've shown so far.'

'Don't be crass, Harry,' Poole said, irritated. 'Let's hear what they have to say.' He turned to the girl and tried to sound gracious. 'Thank you, Shira.'

'I'll take you to my home,' Shira said. 'Please follow me.' And she turned and led the way towards the centre of the earth-craft.

Poole, Harry and Berg trailed a few paces behind Shira. Harry's Virtual eyes flicked everywhere as they entered the loose maze of single-storey, grey-walled buildings which covered the central section of the craft.

Poole tried to keep from touching Berg, from grabbing her again as if he were a boy.

As they walked, Poole had the odd sensation that he was stepping into, and then climbing out of, shallow dimples in the grass-coated earth; but the area looked level, as far as he could see. The dimples seemed to be about a yard in width. He watched Shira covertly as she led them through the little village; she was walking gracefully, but he noticed how she, too, rocked backwards and forwards from the vertical by a few degrees, as if negotiating invisible potholes.

Harry, of course, sailed a fraction of an inch over the grassy surface.

Harry leaned close to Berg and whispered, 'She looks about twenty-five. How old is she really?'

'About twenty-five.'

'Don't kid me.'

'I'm serious.' Berg ran a hand through her wire-stiff crop of hair. 'They've lost AS technology . . . or, rather, had it taken away from them. By the Qax.'

Harry looked as if he couldn't believe it. 'What? How can that have happened? I imagined these people would be far in advance of us . . . That was part of the thrill of Michael's time-interface experiment in the first place.'

'Yes,' Poole said grimly, 'but it looks as if history isn't a monotonic process. Anyway, who are the Qax?'

'She'll tell you,' Berg said grimly. 'She won't tell you much else, but she'll tell you about the Qax. These people call themselves the Friends of Wigner.'

'Wigner?' Poole asked. 'Eugene Wigner, the quantum physicist?'

'As far as I know.'

'Why?'

Berg shrugged sadly, her bony shoulders scratching against the rough material of her jumpsuit. 'I think if I knew the answer to that, I'd know most of it.'

Poole whispered, 'Miriam, what have you found out about the gravity generator?'

Berg looked at him. 'Do you want the detail, or just a précis?'

'A précis will do –'

'Diddley squat. They won't tell me anything. I don't think they want to tell *anybody* anything. Frankly, I think they'd prefer I wasn't here. And they certainly weren't enamoured of me when I smuggled out my signal to you.'

'Why me?' Poole asked.

'Partly because I thought that if anyone could figure out what's going on here it would be you. And partly because I thought that you had a better chance than anyone else of being allowed to land here; yours is about the only name from our era these people know. And partly –'

'Yes?'

Berg shrugged, on the edge of embarrassment. 'Because I needed a friend.'

Walking beside her, Poole touched her arm.

He turned to the Virtual. 'Harry, these invisible dips in the landscape –'

Harry, surprised, said, 'What dips?'

'They're about a yard apart,' Poole said. 'I think they're caused by an unevenness of a few per cent in whatever's generating the gravity in this place.'

Berg nodded. 'I figured out that much. We must be climbing in and out of little gravity wells, right?'

'Harry, tell me if the dips are consistent with a distribution of point masses, somewhere under the surface in the body of the craft.'

Harry nodded and looked unusually thoughtful.

'What does he know?' Berg asked.

'I'm not asking him,' Poole said patiently. 'I'm really asking the boat. Miriam, Harry's like a camouflaged terminal to the boat's central processor; one of the main reasons – no, *the* main reason – for bringing him along is that the future folk might find him easier to accept than a packful of lab equipment.'

Harry looked pained, but he kept 'thinking'.

They reached what was evidently Shira's 'home', a conical ten-feet-tall tepee. There was an open triangular entrance. Smiling, Shira beckoned them in. Poole ran a fingertip over the edge of the doorway; the dove-grey material of the tepee was rigid, vaguely warm to the touch – so not metallic – and felt more than sharp enough to cut flesh.

Two of the fist-sized light-globes hovered near the

roof of the tepee, casting softened double shadows; they bobbed like paper lanterns in response to random currents in the air. The inner walls were blank of decoration – they bore the same dull dove-grey sheen as the exterior – and the floor area, fifteen feet across near the base, contained a single piece of furniture, a low, hard-looking bed, and what looked like thick rugs, or perhaps scatter-cushions.

They stood around awkwardly. Interestingly, now they were inside the tepee Harry seemed to be having trouble with his resolution; his face and limbs crumbled into sugar-cube-sized pixels, and then reassembled.

Shira bade them sit, and left them.

Stiffly, Berg and Poole pulled a couple of the cushions to the centre of the floor and sat, a few inches apart; Harry made a show of sitting on the bed, but the resolution was so poor that from time to time he broke up into such a cloud of disparate pixels that Poole could see right through him, to the grey wall. Poole laughed. 'You look terrible,' he said.

'Thanks,' Harry said, his voice indistinct. 'It's the material of the walls; it's blocking the signal from the boat. What you're getting is scattered through the doorway.'

'What about the gravity wells?'

Harry nodded, his face furred with pixels. 'You were right. The dips are consistent with point masses, ten million tons each, set out in a hexagonal array a yard under the surface we stand on . . . Here comes Shira.'

Shira floated through the doorway, smiling, bearing three plates on a tray. 'From our kitchens. I'm sorry there's nothing for you,' she said to Harry. The Virtual's reply was lost in a defocused blur – mercifully, thought Poole.

The light-globes, clearly semi-sentient, dipped closer to their heads, casting an incongruously cozy light over the meal. The globes didn't seem to be aware of Harry, though, and drifted through his head and upper chest; Harry, stoical, ignored them. Poole wasn't hungry but he used the plain metal cutlery Shira handed him to cut into his meal curiously. The food was hot. There was something which had the fibre of a white meat, and a thick vegetable like cabbage, soft as if overboiled. Shira poured a clear, sparkling drink from a bottle into small blue beakers; sipping it, Poole found it had a sweet, mildly alcoholic tang, like a poor wine.

'It's good,' he said, evoking a polite smile from Shira. 'What is it?'

'Sea food,' said Berg around a mouthful. 'The meat stuff is based on an edible fungus. And the green sludge is processed seaweed.'

Shira nodded slightly, in assent.

'Sounds efficient,' Poole said.

'It is,' said Berg sourly. 'Although that's all it is. Mike, they've shown me some pictures of their Earth. Cities flattened. The continents bordered by thick, chlorophyll green: offshore farms. The produce from what's left of the planet's arable dry land is exported off-planet. The complex molecules are highly prized, apparently, and raise a good price. For the Qax. Michael, they've turned the planet into a damn factory.'

Dark speculations filled Poole's head. Shira's poor physical state, the confiscation of AS technology, the occupation of Earth by an alien power . . . When he'd envisaged the future to which he had built a bridge he'd foreseen strangeness, yes, but *progress* . . . dignity.

Instead, here was this shabby girl with her flavourless food . . .

He asked Berg, 'Who do the Qax get a good price from?'

She turned to him with a thin, strained smile. 'You've a lot to catch up on, Michael. It's a big galaxy out there.

A jungle. Dozens, hundreds of races competing for resources.'

Poole put his plate down beside him on the rug, and faced Shira calmly. 'I'm full of questions,' he said. 'And the fragments Miriam has learned have only added to them. I know you're reluctant to share what you know, but –'

'I won't deny that,' Shira said, graciously enough. Her eyes were warm. 'But you are a scientist, Michael Poole; and the skill of a scientist is in asking the right question.' She gestured, indicating the tepee, her fragment of world. 'From all you have seen today, what is the right question, do you think? Ask it and I shall try to answer you.'

Harry, a blur of pixels, murmured: 'The right question? But how –'

Poole shut out Harry's voice and tried to focus, to find the key to all this teeming strangeness, a way into the girl's bizarre world. 'All right,' he said. 'Shira – what are the walls of the tepee made of?'

Shira nodded, a faint smile on her thin lips. 'Xeelee construction material,' she said.

'And who,' asked Poole carefully, 'are the Xeelee?'

Shira sipped her wine and, thoughtfully, answered him.

The Xeelee owned the universe.

When humans emerged from the Solar System, limping along in the first sublight GUTdrive ships, they entered a complex universe peopled by many intelligent races. Each race followed its own imperatives, its own goals.

When humans dealt with humans, in the days before interstellar flight, there had always been a residual bond: they all belonged to the same species, after all.

There had always been a prospect of one day communicating, sharing, settling down to a mutually acceptable system of government.

Among the races men encountered, as they peered in awe about their suburb of the Galaxy, there was no bond; there was no law, save the savage laws of economics.

Not two centuries after Poole's time, Earth had been captured and put to work by the group-mind aquatic creatures called the Squeem.

Harry whistled. 'It's a tough place out there.'

'Yes,' Shira said seriously. 'But we must regard junior races like the Squeem – even the Qax – as our peers. The key advantage held over us by the Squeem, in those first years, was hyperdrive technology.' But the hyperdrive, like many other of the key technological components of the local multispecial civilization – if it could be called that – was essentially Xeelee in origin.

Wherever men, or any of the races men dealt with, had looked, the Xeelee were there, Shira said. Like gods, aloof from the rest: all-powerful, uncaring, intent on their own vast works, their own mysterious projects.

'What are those projects?' Poole asked.

Nobody knew, Shira said. It was hard to be sure, but it seemed that the other junior races were just as ignorant.

Berg leaned forward. 'Are we sure the Xeelee exist, then?'

'Oh, yes,' said Shira with certainty.

The Xeelee were aloof . . . but a little careless. They left fragments of their technology around for the junior races to pick up.

'We think this stuff is trivial for the Xeelee,' said Shira. 'But a single artefact can be enough to galvanize the economy of a race – perhaps give it a significant advantage over its neighbours.' Her face, in the uneven light of the hovering globes, looked still more drawn and tired. 'Michael, we humans are new to this; and the other species are hardly open to questioning. But we believe that wars have been fought – genocides committed – over artifacts the Xeelee must regard as little more than trinkets.'

Shira gave him some examples:

Hyperdrive. Poole's mouth watered.

The construction material: monomolecular sheets, virtually indestructible, which, in the presence of radiant energy, would grow spontaneously from the fist-sized objects known as 'Xeelee flowers'.

Instantaneous communication, based on quantum inseparability –

'No,' Poole protested. 'That's not possible; you can't send information down quantum-inseparability channels.'

Shira smiled. 'Tell the Xeelee.'

Innovation among the junior races was nearly dead, Poole learned. It was a waste of effort, it was universally felt, trying to reinvent something the Xeelee had probably developed a billion years ago. And besides, while you devoted your resources to researching something, your neighbour would probably spend his on a pirated Xeelee version of the same thing and come blazing into your home system . . .

Shira sketched more of the story of mankind.

The light, inefficient yoke of the Squeem was thrown off with (in retrospect) ease, and humans moved out into the Galaxy again, in new ships based on the Xeelee hyperdrive . . . stolen, at second hand, from the Squeem.

Then humans encountered the Qax. And people were made to grow old again.

'And are you here to escape the Qax?'

Shira's mouth closed, softly. Obviously, Poole

thought, he was reaching the boundaries of what Shira was prepared to tell him.

'Well, then,' he said, 'your intention must be to find a way to overthrow them.'

Shira smiled. 'You're an intelligent man, Michael Poole. It must be obvious that I don't wish to answer such questions. I hope you won't force me to be rude –'

Berg snorted and folded her arms. 'Damn it, here's the brick wall I've come up against since this clod of earth came flying up in the path of the *Cauchy*. Shira, what's obvious to me is that you're out to get rid of the Qax. But why the hell won't you let us help you? We might seem primitive to you, but, lady, we can pack a punch.'

'We've discussed this before,' Shira said patiently.

'But she has a point,' Poole said. 'If nothing else, we can offer you AS technology. *You don't have to grow old,* Shira; think about that.'

Shira's expression remained unclouded. 'I doubt if you'll believe me, but that really doesn't matter.'

Harry seemed to shiver. 'This girl gives me the creeps,' he said, blurred.

'I believe you,' Poole said patiently to Shira. 'I understand there are more important things than life itself . . . But still: Miriam has a point. What have you to gain by turning aside the resources of a Solar System?'

'Maybe they just don't trust us to help,' Harry mused. 'Maybe we'd be like chimpanzees working alongside nuclear physicists . . . or, perhaps she's scared of a time paradox.'

Berg shook her head, her sour expression fixed on the girl. 'Maybe. But I've another theory.'

'Which is?' Poole asked.

'That if they let us know what they're really up to, *we'd stop them.*'

Shira's laugh was unconvincingly light. 'This is a pleasant game.'

Poole frowned. 'Well, at least I've learned enough to understand now some of the things that have been puzzling me,' he said.

Shira looked nonplussed.

'Your ship was constructed under the nose of an occupying force,' he said. 'So you were forced to build it in camouflage.'

'Yes.' Shira smiled. 'We are proud of our deception. Until the moment of its launch, when we activated a hyperdrive shell, the earth-craft was indistinguishable from any other patch of Earth, save for the ancient stones which served further to misdirect the Qax.'

'Hence no hull,' Poole said. 'But still, the craft was more than detectable. After all, it has the mass of a small asteroid; there must have been gravitational anomalies, detectable by the Qax from orbit, before its launch.'

Shira shrugged, looking irritatingly amused. 'I cannot speak for the Qax. Perhaps they have grown complacent.'

Poole, sitting cross-legged on the thin cushion, settled back on his haunches. He peered into the girl's calm face. There was something about Shira that troubled him. It was hard to remember that, in the absence of AS treatment, her chronological age was the same as her biological age; and youth, Poole realized with a twinge of sadness, had become a novelty in his world. But for a girl of twenty-five she had an inner deadness that was almost frightening. She had described the bloody history of mankind, the depressing vista of endless, undignified war between the stars, even the Qax Occupation – of which her knowledge was first hand – with flat disinterest.

It was as if, Poole realized uneasily, life held no meaning for this girl.

He leaned forward. 'All right, Shira, let's not play games. I know what you're doing here; what I don't yet know is *why* you're here.'

Shira dropped her eyes to the empty tray, the cooling food. She asked quietly, 'And what is it, in your judgement, that we are intending to do?'

Poole thumped his fist against the Xeelee-material floor. 'Your earth-craft is a honeycomb of singularities. And that, apart from the hyperdrive, is all you seem to have brought back through time. And you've stayed in Jovian orbit. You could have used your hyperdrive to go anywhere in the System, or beyond . . .

'I think you're planning to implode Jupiter; to use your singularities to turn it into a black hole.'

He heard Harry gasp. Berg touched his shoulder. 'My God, Michael; now you know why I wanted you here. Do you think they can do it?'

'I'm sure they can.' Poole kept his eyes locked on Shira's downturned face. 'And it's obvious that the project is something to do with the overthrow, or the removal, of the Qax from their future occupation. But I don't yet know how it will work. Nor have I decided if we should let them do it.'

Shira lifted her head to him now, her weak blue eyes lit by a sudden anger. 'How dare you oppose us? You've no idea what we intend; how can you have the audacity –'

'How can you have the audacity to change history?' Poole asked quietly.

Shira closed her eyes and sat in a lotus-like position for a few seconds, her thin chest swelling with deep, trembling breaths. When she opened her eyes again she seemed calmer. 'Michael Poole, I would prefer you as an ally than as an enemy.'

He smiled at her. 'And I you.'

She stood, her limbs unwinding gracefully. 'I must

consult.' And, without saying any more, she nodded and left.

Poole and Berg picked at the now cold food; Harry watched them through a haze of static.

8

Parz, alone, curled up tightly, floated in Spline entoptic fluid.

'Jasoft Parz. Jasoft. You should wake now.'

Parz uncurled abruptly, the dense liquid and his skin-tight environment suit making the movements of his limbs heavy. He blinked to clear sleep from his eyes. A single light-globe floated with him in the three-yard-wide chamber which contained him; the heavy fluid, disturbed by his movements, cast graceful, waved shadows on the blood-red walls.

For a second he was disoriented, unable to remember where he was, why he was here; he thrashed, helpless as a hooked fish, clumsily swimming towards the nearest wall. Tubes trailed after him like transparent umbilical cords, linking him to a heavy metal box fixed to one wall.

'Parz. Are you awake? It is time.'

The voice of the Qax – of the new Governor of Earth, the bleak, murderous Qax from the future – sounded again, but it had an oddly calming effect on Parz as he clung to thick folds in the fleshy wall of the chamber; his fragmented attention focused on the words, and something of his composure returned.

He whispered, finding his throat closed and dry. 'Yes, I'm awake.'

'I will open the eyelid.'

'No, please.' Jasoft, with a bizarre sense of modesty, felt reluctant to have the curtains of this makeshift sleeping chamber drawn aside before he was fully ready. He pushed away from the wall and operated controls embedded in the right wrist of his suit. 'Give me a minute.'

The Qax did not reply; Parz envisaged its impatience.

Parz's skinsuit, a transparent overlay over thin cotton garments, had been designed for long-duration wear. Now Parz felt the material whisper over his skin; his pores were cleansed, his beard, toe- and fingernails trimmed. A nipple popped out of the inside of his faceplate, which he pressed to his lips, and an ice-cool liquid flavoured like fresh apple juice coursed into his mouth. When he was done he opened his mouth and let ultrasonics work on his teeth.

He emptied his bladder and watched the waste filter back along the pipes to the wall unit for recycling.

His breakfast and toilet over, Parz spent a few minutes bending and stretching, trying to work all of his major muscle groups. He worked particularly hard on his back and shoulders; after eight hours in a foetal position his upper spine – still heavy with age, despite the AS treatments – creaked with a papery stiffness.

When he was done his breathing was a little deeper and he felt the tingle of fresh blood reaching the surface of his flesh. Ruefully, he realized that this was as good as he was going to feel all day. These suits were good at what they did, but living in one was no substitute for a decent cabin: for waking up to a shower with fresh water, and a breakfast of something you could actually bite into, damn it.

Well, that hadn't been an option. Nor had his attendance on this whole damn mission of the Qax's, of course.

'Parz,' the Qax rasped. 'You've had five minutes.'

Parz nodded. 'I'm sorry,' he said. 'I needed time to wake up properly.'

The Qax seemed to think that over. 'Parz, the next few subjective hours could be the most significant in the history of both our species. You are privileged to be the only human of your era to witness these events. And you took time to cleanse yourself after your sleep?'

'I'm human,' Parz snapped. 'Even when the world is coming to an end I have to put my trousers on one leg at a time.'

The Qax considered that. 'And your metaphorical trousers are now on?'

'Open the damn eyelid.'

The walls of the Spline's huge eyeball trembled, sending small shock waves through the heavy entoptic fluid to brush against Jasoft's skin. Muscles hauled at sheets of heavy flesh, and the eyelid lifted like a curtain. Through the rubbery greyness of the Spline's cornea, salmon-pink light swept into the eyeball, dwarfing the yellow glow of Jasoft's light-globe, and causing his slender, suspended form to cast a blurred shadow on the purple-veined retina behind him. Jasoft swam easily to the inside face of the pupil; feeling oddly tender about the Spline's sensations, he laid his suited hands carefully on the warm, pliant substance of the lens.

Outside, the universe was a blurred confusion of pink, gunmetal grey and baby blue; Jasoft kept his eyes steady, giving their image-enhancing software time to work. After a few seconds deconvolution routines cut in with an almost audible click, transforming the blurred patches to objects of clarity, and therefore menace.

There was Jupiter, of course: huge cyclones tracked across its bruised, purple-pink countenance. Another ship glided past – a second Spline, its pores bristling with sensors and weaponry. The eyeball Parz inhabited rotated to follow the second ship, and swirls in the entoptic fluid buffeted Parz, causing him to bounce gently against the lens.

Now Parz's Spline turned, driven by some interior flywheel of flesh, blood and bone; the eye swept away from Jupiter and fixed on the baby-blue patch he'd seen earlier, now resolved into a tetrahedron of exotic matter. Sheets of elusive silver-gold stretched across the triangular faces of the Interface portal, sometimes reflecting fragmented images of Jupiter, and sometimes permitting elusive glimpses of other times, other starfields.

The portal came steadily into Parz's view. The Spline must already be inside the squeezed-vacuum exoticity zone which surrounded the mouth of the wormhole itself, and soon the portal was so close that Jasoft had to press his faceplate against the warm Spline lens to make out its vertices.

'It's almost time,' he whispered.

'Yes, Ambassador,' the Qax growled. 'Almost time.'

The words which sounded in his headpiece were – as ever – bland, synthesized, the product of a translator box somewhere in the Spline. 'Qax, I wish I knew what you were feeling.'

The Qax paused for some seconds. Then, 'Anticipation. Anticipation of satisfaction. My goal is close. Why do you ask this?'

Jasoft shrugged. 'Why not? I'm interested in your reactions. Just as you must be interested in mine. Otherwise, why would you have brought me here?'

'I've explained that. I need a way into human perceptions.'

'Rubbish,' Parz said without anger. 'Why do you bother to justify yourself in that way? Qax, you're travelling back in time to destroy humanity – to eradicate forever the unlimited potential of a species. What do you care about human perception?'

'Jasoft Parz,' the Qax said, its voice almost silky now, the relish audible, 'you are the only human to return through time with this Qax expedition. Fifteen centuries ago humans were still largely confined to the dull star system of their birth. When we have destroyed the home planet – and scoured the neighbouring worlds and spaces – you will be the only human left alive. And, with the termination of your species' line, you will also be the last human. How will that feel?'

Parz felt his lifetime of compromise – of *diplomacy* – weigh down on him, a cargo still heavy despite his AS rejuvenation. He tried, as he'd tried before, to comprehend the significance of the Qax's monstrous act. Surely it was his duty, as the last human, to *feel* the pain of this crime, to suffer on behalf of his race.

But he couldn't. It was beyond him. And, he thought, he had moved beyond hope.

He wondered how he'd feel, though, if he had children of his own.

He nodded, infinitely tired. 'So. You've brought me here so you can watch me, as I watch my race die. I did not understand before; I guess I was hoping for – what? nobility? – from the murderer of my species. But it really is as petty as that. My reaction, the grief of one man, will amplify for you the emotional significance of the event. It will heighten your pleasure. Won't it?'

'Pleasure? I am not psychopathic, Jasoft Parz,' the Qax said. 'But the sweetness of my revenge will be great.'

'Revenge for what?'

'For the destruction of my own world, of the home of the Qax, by the actions of a single human.'

Parz had been told something of the story.

A few centuries after Parz's era, there would be a human: Jim Bolder, an unremarkable man. The Qax would try to employ Bolder, to exploit him for gain. But Bolder would deceive them – somehow trick them into turning starbreakers on their own sun.

The new Governor came from a future in which the comparatively lenient Occupation of Earth had led, inexorably, to the destruction of the Qax home world, to a diaspora in which dozens of the fragile Qax had perished. In this timeline the Qax were marginalized; humans, freed of the Occupation, grew far stronger.

The Qax wanted to change all that.

Ironically, Parz had come to understand, the rebellion of the Friends of Wigner had nothing to do with the ultimate collapse of the Occupation, in this timeline. Whatever the rebels' scheme was it was seen as irrelevant by the Qax – in fact, the sequence of time bridges initiated by the rebellion was actually an *opportunity* for the Qax to move back into time, far beyond Bolder, and to rectify their earlier leniency.

Parz, baffled and disturbed by the philosophy of it all, wondered if a multiplicity of variant worlds would be initiated by this series of trips into the past, of closed timelike curves. In the original variant, the prime timeline, saw no impact on events from either the rebels' activities or the Qax's actions; the timeline would unfold with relentless logic to the Qax dispersal. The Qax, now, hoped to return through time to crush humanity before such events had a chance to occur; this second variant would see the emergence of the Qax as the dominant species in the absence of mankind. The rebels presumably, with their unknown project, hoped to initiate a third variant in which the Occupation would be crushed before the time of Jim Bolder – of whom, of course, the rebels could have no knowledge; to them the Occupation must have looked immense and eternal.

But even that wasn't the end of it, Parz realized; for presumably the actions of the various groups of time travellers would interact to set off a fourth, fifth or sixth variant . . . But most human philosophers seemed to agree, now, that only one of these variants could be considered 'real'; only one could be collapsed into actuality by the observation of conscious minds.

Parz pressed his face against the warm lens material; it yielded like thin rubber. The electric-blue struts of the Interface portal had almost embraced the Spline now; the nearest face, which already blocked out the stars, the moons of Jupiter, was dark and empty, its blackness relieved only by a hint of autumn gold. Parz twisted his head about. He caught a glimpse of the second Spline he'd seen earlier; it hovered above and behind the Qax's ship, following it towards the portal. 'Some armada,' he said. 'Two ships?'

'Two are all that is required. The humans of fifteen centuries ago will have no means of defence against the weaponry of the Spline craft. The second craft will destroy the vessel of these rebels from your present – these Friends of Wigner – while my ship will besiege Earth.'

Parz felt his throat tighten. 'How?'

'Starbreaker beams.'

Parz closed his eyes.

'Maybe your revenge won't be so sweet,' he said, seeking advantage randomly. 'What about causality? Maybe I'll pop out of existence as soon as my ancestors are destroyed. Maybe you will, too. Have you thought about that? And then the destruction of your world by this human hero will never have happened . . . and you'll have no reason, or means, to travel through time to assault the Earth.' But then, he thought further, if the Qax did not travel back through time, surely humanity

111

would survive to destroy the Qax world after all . . .
'We'll be caught in a causality loop, won't we?'

'Jasoft Parz, causality does not operate in such a simplistic fashion. In such a circumstance the different outcomes may all exist simultaneously, like the probabilities expressed by a quantum function. But only one of those possibilities will be collapsed into actuality —'

'Are you sure?' Parz said grimly. 'You're talking about destroying a race . . . about altering history on a cosmic scale, Qax.'

'Yes, we are sure. My intention is to close off all probabilities, all variants of reality in which humanity can survive. After the destruction of your System, you will be the only human left alive.'

'And you and I will disappear into nonexistence,' Parz said grimly.

'No,' the Qax said. 'But the timeline from which we emerged will no longer exist, as a potentiality. We will be stranded, out of time. But my job will be done.'

Yes, Parz thought, what it's saying is possible. It was more than genocide. The Qax was plotting not just the destruction of humankind but the destruction of all variant realities in which humanity might have survived.

The Qax's calculation somehow penetrated Parz's numbed heart more deeply than anything else. How could a sentient being discuss such gruesome events — the destruction of species, of worlds, of *timelines* — in the language of cold logic, of science?

Damn it, Parz protested silently; we're talking about the snuffing out of species — of the potential of countless billions of souls as yet unborn . . .

But, as always, he realized dully, the Qax were doing nothing which humans had not tried to perpetrate on members of their own species in the past.

'Parz, shortly we will be entering the throat of the wormhole. You must be prepared for causality stress.'

'Causality stress?' Parz stared into the blank, gaping mouth of the wormhole portal; the hints of silver-gold were gone now, leaving only a darkness which grew over the stars. 'You know, Qax, you intend to destroy my home world. And yet all I feel now is a personal dread of entering that damn wormhole.'

'You are a limited species, Jasoft Parz.'

'Perhaps we are. Perhaps we're better off that way.'

The Spline trembled; to Jasoft, cushioned as he was by the entoptic matter, the mile-wide animal's shudder was like a mild earth tremor.

'I'm frightened, Qax.'

'Imagine my concern.'

The Spline's shuddering became continuous; Parz felt it as a high-frequency vibration of the entoptic fluid – small waves beating against his flesh like insect wings – and an underlying bass rumble which resounded from the immense skeleton of the Spline itself. The ship was suffering.

'Qax. Talk to me.'

'What about?'

'Anything,' Parz muttered. 'I don't care. Anything to take my mind off this. Tell me the story of how a human destroyed your planet . . . Tell me about Jim Bolder.'

'Will destroy it. Would have destroyed it.'

'Whatever.'

The Qax seemed to consider. 'Perhaps. But, what an odd question for you to ask, Jasoft Parz. I must consider what you have to gain by acquiring such information. Perhaps you have some vain scheme to use the data to rehabilitate yourself in the eyes of your people . . . from the race's greatest traitor, to an unsung hero –'

Parz, surprised, frightened, looked inwards. Traitor? A month ago he would have denied the charge.

But now the Qax had changed the rules. Suddenly

Parz had found himself transformed from a morally dubious collaborating diplomat into a witness to the destruction of his race . . .

The Spline shuddered again, more violently, and through the entoptic medium he seemed to hear a low groan, of pain, or terror.

Could the Qax be right? Was some element of his subconscious still scheming, looking for advantage, even now? Did he, he asked himself with wonder, still entertain hope?

The Qax was silent.

Now the Spline shuddered so hard that Parz was thrown into a soft collision with the wall of the huge eyeball. It felt as if the Spline had jerked through a few hundred yards, as if hauling itself away from some source of pain.

Jasoft closed his eyes and, with a subvocalized command, ordered the software in his eyes to call up an external image of the Spline, transmitted from the companion ship.

His craft was entering the portal face, inching forward as delicately as in any docking, the curves of its flanks almost brushing the powder-blue edges of the tetrahedral framework.

Parz was a hundred hours away from the past.

The Qax spoke abruptly, its decision evidently made. 'The human was – will be – called Jim Bolder. A man of the Occupation era – from not far into your own future, Parz.

'Bolder was one of the last human pilots. Eventually the Qax interdiction on human operation of spacecraft will become complete, Jasoft Parz. Ships will be impounded on landing. The off-Earth human colonies will become self-sufficient. Or they will be closed, their inhabitants returned to Earth. Or they will die.

'Men such as Bolder will lose their vocation, Parz. Their reason to be. This made – will make – it possible to recruit Bolder for a special assignment.'

The clean geometries of the Interface framework looked stark against the flesh of the Spline. At one point the Spline came within a few dozen yards of brushing the frame itself. Flesh toughened against the rigours of hyperspatial travel was *boiling*. As Parz watched, blisters the size of city blocks erupted on that pocked, metal-grey surface; the blisters burst like small volcanoes, emitting sprays of human-looking blood which froze instantly into showers of red ice crystals, sparkling in the blue glow of the framework. Acres of the Spline convulsed, trying to pull the damaged area away from the exotic matter.

'What was Bolder's assignment?' Parz asked.

'Parz, what do you know of galactic drift?'

Galaxies – and clusters and superclusters of galaxies, across half a billion light-years – were moving in great, coherent streams through space. It was as if the galaxies were moths, drawn towards some unseen light . . . Human astronomers had described such drift for centuries, but had never been able satisfactorily to explain it.

'What does this have to do with Bolder?'

'We suspected the drift had some connection with the Xeelee,' the Qax said.

Parz snorted. 'Come on. The Xeelee are powerful, but they're not gods.'

'We sent Bolder to find out,' the Qax said mildly.

Parz frowned. 'How? That's impossible. Even in the fastest of our hyperdrive craft it would take centuries of subjective time –'

'We had access to a Xeelee ship.'

Parz felt his jaw working. 'But that's impossible, too.'

'Such details are unimportant. It is sufficient to know

115

that Bolder survived his journey to the centre of the streaming.'

'To the place where all the galaxies go.'

'Yes,' said the Qax. Although, close enough to the centre, Bolder had found that the structure of all but the most compact ellipticals was shattered; galaxy fragments, stars and worlds tumbled into the immense gravity well at the centre of it all, their blue-shifted light tumbling ahead of them.

'And at the bottom of the well?'

The Qax paused.

To Parz, still studying the Spline from without, it was as if the portal framework were scorching the flesh of the hapless Spline. But it wasn't heat, he knew, but high-frequency radiation and gravity tides raised by the superdense exotic matter which were damaging the Spline so. Parz shuddered in sympathy with the suffering Spline.

The image winked out. Parz, reduced to sudden artificial blindness, realized with a shock that his ship must now be totally inside the wormhole. With a feeling of claustrophobia and panic he snapped out subvocal commands.

His vision cleared.

The eye chamber had been reduced to the darkness within which he had first awoken; his faithful globe light still floated beside him.

So the Spline had shut its eyes. Well, he couldn't entirely blame it.

The ship shuddered, buffeted; entoptic fluid sloshed around the spherical chamber. Parz half-swam to the nearest wall and clung to a ropy nerve channel.

'Gravitational stress,' the Qax murmured in his ear. 'This wormhole is a throat in space and time, Parz: a region of stress, immensely high curvature. The throat is lined with exotic matter throughout; we are traversing a vacuum which runs along the axis, away from the exotic matter. The minimum width of the throat is about a mile. Our velocity is three miles per second –'

'Not fast enough,' Parz gasped.

Vibration travelled through Parz's grasping fingers, up through his arms and to his very core; it felt as if the Spline were being beaten by some immense fist. 'Can the ship endure this?'

'So the simulations tell us,' the Qax said complacently. 'But the creature is scarcely comfortable.'

'Right.' Parz clung to his nerve rope, imagining centuries unravelling around the hurtling Spline. 'Tell me what Bolder found,' he said through chattering teeth. 'At the bottom of the gravity well.'

A Ring, the Qax said. A torus. Composed of some unknown, crystalline substance. A thousand light-years across. Rotating at a respectable fraction of the speed of light.

It was massive. It had caused a well in spacetime so deep that it was drawing in galaxies, including Earth's Milky Way, from across hundreds of millions of light-years.

'I don't believe it,' Parz said, still shaking in sympathy with the Spline.

'It is an artefact,' the Qax said. 'A Xeelee construct. Bolder watched the Xeelee build it.'

Xeelee craft – cup-shaped freighters the size of moons, and fighters with nightdark wings hundreds of miles wide – patrolled the huge construction site. With cherry-red starbreaker beams they smashed the infalling, blue-shifted galactic fragments and plated layers over the growing Ring.

'We believe the Xeelee have already invested billions of years in this project,' the Qax said. 'But its growth is exponential. The more massive it becomes, the deeper the gravity well grows, and the faster matter falls towards the site, feeding the construction crews further.'

'But why? What's the point of it?'

'We speculate that the Xeelee are trying to construct a Kerr-metric region,' the Qax said.

'A what?'

The Kerr metric was a human description of a special solution of Einstein's equations of general relativity. When spacetime was distorted by a sufficiently massive, rotating toroid, it could – open.

'Like a wormhole?' Parz asked.

'Yes. But the Kerr-metric interface would not connect two points in the same spacetime, Parz. It is a throat between spacetimes.'

Parz struggled to understand that. 'You're saying that this – "Kerr-metric region" – is a doorway – a way out of our universe?'

'Crudely, yes. The Xeelee are trying to build an exit from this cosmos.'

'And to do it they're prepared to wreck a region of space hundreds of billions of light-years wide . . .'

Suddenly Parz was blind again. Hurriedly, panicking, he issued commands; but this time his vision would not clear. The darkness in which he was immersed was deeper than that of closed eyes . . . it was, he realized with a terrifying clarity, the darkness of nothingness, of emptiness. 'Qax.' His own voice was muffled; it was as if all his senses were failing together. 'What's happening to me?'

The Qax's voice came to him, distant but clear. 'This is causality stress, Parz. The severance of the causal lines, of the quantum wave functions in which you are embedded. Causality stress is causing sensory dysfunction . . .'

Jasoft felt his body senses softening, drifting away from him; he felt as if he were becoming disembodied,

118

a mote of consciousness without anchor in the external universe.

The Qax continued to speak. Its voice called to Parz like a distant trumpet. 'Jasoft Parz. This is as difficult for me, for any sentient being, as it is for you . . . even for the Spline. But *it will pass*. Do not let it undermine your sanity. Concentrate on what I am saying to you.

'Jim Bolder, in his stolen craft, evaded the Xeelee engineers. He returned to the Qax home system, where his journey had begun. Jasoft, the Qax are a trading nation. Bolder had returned with a treasure valuable beyond price: data on the greatest Xeelee artifact. It will not surprise you that the Qax decided to, ah, retain the data.

'But Bolder tricked us.'

There was a glimmering around Parz now, a ghostly shimmer, a reflection of ripples, like moonlight on a sea.

'The details have never become clear. Bolder should have emerged from hyperspace into a region surrounded by Spline warships, all bearing gravity-wave starbreaker technology . . . He failed to do so. Bolder survived, escaped.

'Starbreakers were used. In the confusion and panic, they brushed the Qax sun. It was enough to cause the sun to become unstable – ultimately, to nova.

'The Qax were forced to flee. Dozens of individuals died in the exodus. Our power was lost, and the Occupation of Earth crumbled . . .'

Jasoft Parz, bewildered and disoriented as he was, could not help but exult at this.

A grey light, without form and structure, spread around him . . . No, not around him, he realized; he was part of this light: it was as if this were the grey light which shone beneath reality, the light against which all phenomena are shadows. His panic subsided, to be replaced by a sense of calm power; he felt as if he were

119

light-years wide and yet no wider than an atom, a million years old and yet fresher than a child's first breath.

'Qax. What the hell is happening?'

'Causality stress, Parz. Perceptual dysfunction. Causality is not a simple phenomenon. When objects are joined once, they become part of a single quantum system . . . and they must remain joined forever, via superlight quantum effects. You should imagine you are walking across a beach, calling into existence a trail of footsteps as you go. The footsteps may fade with time as you pass on, but each of them remains bound to you by the threads of quantum functions.'

'And when I pass out of my own region of spacetime?'

'The threads are cut. Causal bonds are broken and must be reformed . . .'

'Dear God, Qax. Is this pain worth it, just to travel through time?'

'To achieve one's goals: yes,' the Qax said quietly.

'Finish the story,' Jasoft Parz said.

'Finish it?'

'Why are the Xeelee building a way out of the universe? What are they seeking?'

'I suspect if we knew the answer to that,' the Qax said, 'we would know much of the secret truth of our universe. But we do not. The story must remain unfinished, Jasoft Parz.

'But consider this. What if the Xeelee are not seeking something *beyond* their Ring – but are fleeing something in *this* universe?

'What do the Xeelee fear, do you suppose?'

Parz, buffeted, disoriented, could find no reply.

The Spline warship surged through time.

9

The Friend of Wigner, Jaar, was waiting for Michael Poole at the entrance to the *Crab*'s grounded boat.

Poole stood on the boat's exit ramp, bathed in eerie Jovian light. He looked out at the waiting young man, the scatter of Xeelee construction-material buildings in the distance, the glimpse of ancient stones – and over it all the looming, perfect curve of Jupiter.

He felt too old for this.

He'd got through the events of the previous day – the landing, the encounter with Miriam, the bombardment with the unfamiliar – on a kind of psychic momentum. But the momentum had gone now; he'd emerged only reluctantly from a troubled sleep to face the dangers, the pressures of the day, the need to find a way to deal with Miriam's presence here.

Miriam had spent the sleeping period in the boat. Harry had had the decency to abandon his rights-for-AIs rhetoric for a few hours and had gone into stasis to leave them alone. But Miriam and Michael hadn't slept together. What were they, kids? They had talked, and held each other's hands, and had finally stumbled to separate bunks. Somehow, acquiescing to lust didn't seem the right reaction to a century of separation, or the renewal of an antique, and combative, relationship.

He wished he hadn't let Harry talk him into this jaunt. He would have exchanged all he had seen and learned to return to the sanctuary of his station in the Oort Cloud, his slow tinkering at the fringes of exotic-matter physics.

Of course if he got his head cleaned out, as Harry had done, he'd be able to face all this with a fresh eye.

Well, the hell with that.

Poole walked down the ramp and on to the tough English grass. The Friends of Wigner smiled at him; Poole saw a young man, tall and whiplash thin, dressed in the standard-issue pink coverall. Bony wrists and ankles protruded from the coarse material. Under a high, clean-shaven dome of a scalp he shared the pallid, hothouse complexion of Shira, and his eyes were watery-brown. Jaar's stance was a little awkward. Poole guessed that even fifteen centuries hence someone of this height and build would spend his life ducking to avoid looking clumsy, but there was something beyond that, something about the way the Friend's legs looked bowed . . .

Rickets. Was it possible that such a curse had been allowed to return to the Earth? Poole's heart leapt.

'You are Michael Poole. I am honoured to meet you.'

'And you're Jaar – the guide Shira promised?'

'I am a physical sciences specialist. I trust you slept peacefully.'

'Not very.' Poole grinned. 'I have too many questions.'

Jaar nodded with the solemnity of the young. 'You have a fine mind, Mr Poole; it is natural for you to question –'

'And,' Poole went on sharply, 'Shira said she'd send someone who could provide answers.'

Jaar smiled obscurely, and in that expression Poole recognized something of the abstractedness of Shira.

Jaar seemed disengaged, uninterested in this little duel, or indeed in any form of interpersonal contact. It was as if he had much more important things on his mind.

'Shira did say that there was little purpose trying to hide from you anything whose existence you had already deduced.'

'So you've been sent along to humour an old man?'

'No one *sent* me, Mr Poole,' Jaar said. 'I volunteered for the honour.'

'It's me who's honoured, Jaar.'

With a little bow Jaar invited Poole to walk with him. Side by side, they strolled across the pink-stained grass towards the heart of the earth-craft.

Poole said, 'You're only the second Friend I've met . . . and yet you seem very similar, in disposition, to Shira. Forgive my rudeness, Jaar, but are all you Friends so alike?'

'I don't think so, Mr Poole.'

'Call me Michael. But you have an inner calm, a strange certainty – even after running the gauntlet of the Qax navy; even after falling willy-nilly through a hole in spacetime . . .'

'I am sure that what we have come here to do is right.'

Poole nodded. 'Your Project. But you're not allowed to tell me what that is.'

'Like you, I was born with the curse of an inquiring mind. It must be infuriating to have an area of knowledge blocked from you like this . . . I apologize.' Jaar's smile was smooth, bland, unyielding; his bald head seemed oddly egglike to Poole, seamless and devoid of detail. 'But you must not think we are all alike, Michael. The Friends are from very different backgrounds. Granted we were selected for this mission on the grounds of youth and physical fitness, so we share those characteristics; but perhaps we seem similar to you simply because we are from such a removed frame of reference. Perhaps the differences between us are diminished by our distance from you.'

'Perhaps,' Poole said, and he laughed. 'But I'm not naïve, lad.'

'I'm sure that's so,' Jaar said smoothly. 'And yet, lacking AS technology, none of us shares your two hundred years, Mr . . . Michael.' For a precious second he sounded almost mischievous. 'Perhaps you simply aren't used to the company of young people.'

Poole opened his mouth . . . then closed it again, feeling vaguely embarrassed. 'Maybe you're right,' he said.

They walked silently for a while.

An inner calm, a strange certainty . . . Poole wondered if the mysterious purpose of this mission could have some mystical, or religious, content; perhaps it wasn't the scientific or engineering project he had first assumed. He had a sudden, bizarre image of the battered stones of the henge being aligned with a sunrise over the cloudy limb of Jupiter . . .

There were certainly elements of a religious devotion among these strange young people. Their blank demeanour, their lack of *hope for themselves*, he thought. Yes, that was the key to it. Somehow they had no dreams of personal gain, or happiness, in all this. Perhaps the mission plan called for them to sacrifice their lives, Poole wondered; and now he imagined the fragile earth-craft, its mission over, plunging into the forbidding depths of the Jovian atmosphere, ancient menhirs tumbling away like stone chips.

But what religious sect would style itself the Friends of Wigner?

They reached the 'village' which surrounded the ancient henge at the heart of the earth-craft. Jaar led Poole past cones, cylinders and cubes, all a few feet above head-height and composed of the dove-grey

124

Xeelee substance, and scattered over the grass. Save for the signs of habitation it was, thought Poole, like wandering through the play-pen of some child. Knots of young people moved about their tasks calmly and unhurriedly; some of them bore the flat, compact computing devices Berg had called 'slates'.

They reached a hemispherical hut, anonymous among the rest. 'What's this?' Poole asked. 'Home, sweet home? No offence, but I ate enough seaweed with Shira yesterday —'

Jaar laughed, not unpleasantly. 'No, Michael; though I would be honoured if you would be my guest in my quarters later. This building is for access.'

'Access?'

'To the interior of the earth-craft. To the plane of singularities.' Jaar studied him, seeming puzzled. 'That's what you wanted to see, wasn't it?'

Poole smiled. 'What are we waiting for?'

They stepped into the dome, Jaar ducking his head under the razor-sharp lintel. Poole felt light on his feet here, almost buoyant; the surface gravity must be a little less than that outside. Inside the dome a slim cylinder rose from a floor of Xeelee material. A doorway was cut into its wall.

Jaar climbed in, hunching his thin shoulders; Poole followed. Silently the door shut, sealing them in. The chamber was cramped, seamless, filled with a diffuse, pearly light, of which Poole could find no source; it was a little like being inside a neon tube, he thought.

Poole was aware of Jaar studying him with a kind of amused patience. Now Jaar smiled. 'This is an elevator. The terminology hasn't changed since your day. It will take us into the interior.'

Poole nodded, feeling oddly nervous; he wasn't

exactly used to exposing himself to the possibility of physical danger. 'Right. So we're in an elevator shaft, cut through the plane of singularities. Hence the reduced gravity.'

Jaar seemed to respond to his nervousness. 'If you're not ready –'

'You don't have to coddle me along, Jaar.'

'All right.' Jaar touched a section of blank wall. He did not try to hide what he was doing from Poole, even though he must have been aware that Poole would memorize every moment of this trip.

There was no noise. But the floor seemed to fall away. Poole's stomach lurched and, without intending to, he reached behind himself for the stability of the wall.

Jaar murmured, 'It will pass.'

Now, as Poole floated, a band of pressure passed up the length of his body; but it was an inverse, negative pressure, like the pressures of exotic matter, which pulled his stomach and chest outwards rather than compressed them.

Jaar still watched him steadily with his blank brown eyes. Poole kept his face carefully neutral. Damn it, he should have been prepared for this; as Jaar had said he'd deduced the structure of the interior of the craft already. 'The plane of singularities,' he said, his voice reasonably steady. 'We're passing through it. Right?'

Jaar nodded approvingly. 'And the pressure you feel about your chest is the gravitational attraction of the singularities. When you stand on the surface of the earth-craft the plane is below you and draws you down, so simulating the gravitational field of the Earth; but here in the interior of the craft the plane is all around us.'

The gravitational plane had reached Poole's neck now; absurdly he found himself raising his head, as if trying to keep it above water.

126

Jaar said, 'Now, Michael – be ready. You may want to anchor yourself to the walls, as before.'

'This time I've worked it out. We're going to tip over. Right?'

'Be ready.'

Now the plane passed over Poole's head and away from him. For a few seconds there was a disconcerting feeling of sweeping upwards which rapidly changed, as Poole's sensorium went through a hundred-and-eighty degree swivel, to a sense of plummeting head-first downwards. Then came rotation, the sharp pull of Coriolis forces at his belly. The elevator cage was turning about an axis somewhere near his waist. Oddly enough Poole did not feel threatened now; it was like being a small child again, like swinging through the air in the strong, safe arms of Harry. The real Harry.

The turn was completed. The sideways Coriolis died away; with a sigh of relief Poole felt himself settle to a normal-feeling floor. Not quite normal; he felt his ears pop. Jaar smiled kindly at him. 'Don't worry,' he said. 'It took me a while to get used to it.'

Poole frowned, feeling an absurd need to demonstrate his manhood to this young man. 'I've told you you don't need to coddle me. We've passed through the plane; now we've turned upside down, so the holes are beneath our feet again, and everything feels normal. Right?'

Jaar nodded, in unmoved assent. He placed his palm against another section of the wall and the elevator door slid aside.

Jaar stepped out onto a clear, glassy surface. Poole followed, almost stumbling; in the gentle gravity the clear surface was as slippery as hell. When he was steady on his feet, Poole raised his head.

The earth-craft was hollow.

Poole was at the centre of an artificial cave that looked

as if it made up most of the craft's bulk. Above his head there was a dome of Xeelee dove-grey, about twenty yards tall at its highest point, and below him a sheet of glass which met the dome at a seamless horizon. Beneath the glass was a hexagonal array of blue and pink bars, each cell in the array about a yard wide.

Tubes of glass – hollow shafts, each a yard wide – rained from holes in the roof, terminating six feet above the floor. It made the dome look like some huge, absurd chandelier, Poole thought. A blocky control console was fixed to the floor beneath each tube. Through the holes in the roof Poole could see patches of Jovian cloud-pink. The shafts looked like fairyland cannon, pointing at Jupiter.

People – young men and women in pink jumpsuits, Wigner's Friends – moved about the clear surface, talking and carrying the ubiquitous slates, the huge, sparkling pillars dangling unnoticed above their heads. The Friends moved with the mercury-slow grace Poole associated with inhabitants of low-gravity worlds like Luna. Their voices, low and serious, carried clearly to Poole.

The diffuse light seemed to come from the domed ceiling itself, with a little blue-pink toning from the array beneath the floor. It was like being in the imaginary caverns inside the Earth conjured up by one of Poole's favourite authors, the ancient Verne.

Jaar smiled and bowed slightly. 'So,' he said, 'the guided tour. Over your head we have a dome of Xeelee construction material. In fact the construction material passes under the floor we stand on and under the singularity plane, forming a shell within the craft broken only by the access shafts.'

'Why?'

Jaar shrugged. 'The construction material is impervious to all known radiation.'

'So it protects the passengers from riding too close to the black holes.'

'And it prevented the Qax from detecting our activity and becoming overly suspicious. Yes. In addition, our hyperdrive engine has been incorporated into the fabric of the construction-material shell.'

Poole pointed to the floor. 'And under here, the plane of singularities.'

Jaar dropped to one knee; Poole joined him, and they peered through the floor at the enigmatic spokes of blue and pink-violet. Jaar said, 'This surface is not a simple transparent sheet; it is semi-sentient. What you see here is largely a false-colour rendering.

'You have deduced, from your observations of the dimpled gravity field on the surface, that our craft is held together by mini-black hole singularities.' He pointed to a node in the hexagonal array. 'There is one of them. We manufactured and brought about a thousand of the holes with us through time, Michael.'

The holes, the Friend explained, were charged, and were held in place by an electromagnetic lattice. The false colours showed plasma flux lines in the lattice, and high-frequency radiation from infalling matter crushed by the singularities.

Hawking evaporation caused each singularity to glow at a temperature measured in teradegrees. The megawatts generated by the captive, evaporating holes provided the earth-craft's power – power for the hyperdrive, for example.

The evaporation was whittling away at the mass-energy of each hole, inexorably. But it would take a billion years for the holes to evaporate completely.

Poole peered at the gaudy display sombrely; it was difficult to believe that only a few feet beneath him was an object smaller than an electron but with the mass of a city block, a pinpoint flaw in the structure of spacetime itself. And below *that* was a plane of grass from which clung, like flies to a ceiling, the *Crab*'s boat, Berg, Shira and the rest, the toylike buildings of the Friends of Wigner; and – oddest of all – the ancient stones of the henge, dangling there in Jupiter's light like rotting teeth in the upper jaw of an incomplete, furred-over skull.

There must be a layer of air all the way around this craft, he thought. Of course the air must get pretty thin away from the high-gravity regions, close to the centre of the plane of singularities.

Stiffly, he climbed to his feet. 'I'm grateful for what you've shown me,' he said.

Jaar studied him, tall, very bald, disturbingly pale. 'And what do you feel you have learned?'

Poole shrugged, deliberately casual. With a wave of his hand he indicated the cavern. 'Nothing new. All this is impressive, but it's just detail. The singularity array. There is the meat of the mission; that's what you've gone to all this trouble to bring back through time.' He pointed to the shafts which led to the rents in the construction-material dome. 'Those things look like cannon barrels, pointing at Jupiter. I think they *are* cannon – singularity cannons. I think that one by one you're going to release these singularities from their electromagnetic nets and propel them out of those tubes and towards Jupiter.'

Jaar nodded slowly. 'And then what will we do?'

Poole spread his hands. 'Simply wait . . .'

He pictured a singularity – a tiny, all but invisible, fierce little knot of gamma-radiation – swooping in great, slow ellipses around Jupiter, on each orbit blasting a narrow channel through the thin gases at the roof of the atmosphere. There would be a great deal of drag; plasma bow waves would haul at the singularity as it plunged through the air. Eventually, like grasping hands, the atmosphere would claim the singularity.

130

Rapidly spiralling inwards, the hole would scythe through Jupiter's layers of methane and hydrogen, at last plunging into the core of metallic hydrogen. It would come to rest, somewhere close to Jupiter's gravitational centre. And it would start to grow.

'You'll send in more and more,' Poole said. 'Soon there will be a swarm of singularities, orbiting each other like insects inside the solid heart of the planet. And all growing inexorably, absorbing more and more of Jupiter's substance. Eventually some of the holes will collide and merge, I guess, sending out gravitational waves that will disrupt the outer layers of the planet even more.' Maybe, Poole speculated, the Friends could even control the merging of the holes – direct the pulsed gravity waves to sculpt the collapse of the planet.

Until, like a cancer, the holes would have destroyed Jupiter.

As the core was consumed the structure would implode, like a failing balloon; Poole guessed the planet would heat up and there would be pockets of disruption and instability – explosions which would blast away much of the substance of the atmosphere. Tidal effects would scatter the moons, or send them into elliptical orbits; obviously the human inhabitants of the region would have to evacuate. Maybe some of the moons would even be destroyed by tidal stresses and gravitational waves.

'At last,' Poole said, 'there will be a single, massive singularity. There will be a wide accretion disc composed of what's left of the Jovian atmosphere and bits of smashed satellites; and the rest of the moons will loop around the debris like lost birds.'

Jaar's silence was as bland as Xeelee construction material.

Poole frowned. 'Of course, a single singularity would be enough to collapse Jupiter, if that's all you want to

131

do. So why have you brought this great flock of the things?'

'No doubt you've figured that out too,' Jaar said dryly.

'Indeed. I think you're trying to control the size of the final singularity,' Poole said. 'Aren't you? The multiple "seed" singularities will cause a fraction of the mass of the planet to be blown away, detached before the final collapse. I think you've *designed* this implosion to result in a final hole of a certain size and mass.'

'Why should we do that?'

'I'm still working on that,' Poole said grimly. 'But the timescales . . . This could take centuries. I understand a great deal, Jaar, but I don't understand how you can think in those terms, without AS.'

'A man may plan for events beyond his own lifetime,' Jaar said, young and certain.

'Maybe. But what happens when you've shot off the last of your singularities? The earth-craft is going to break up. Even if the inner shell of construction material keeps its integrity, the exterior – the soil, the grass, the very air – is going to drift away, as the source of your gravity field is shot into space.'

He imagined the menhirs like the limbs of giants lifting from the grass, sailing off into Jovian space; it would be a strange end for the ancient henge, far stranger than could have been imagined by those who had carved the stones.

'And what will become of you? You seem determined to refuse any help from us. You must die . . . perhaps within a few months from now. And certainly long before you see your Project come to fruition, with the collapse of Jupiter.'

Jaar's face was calm, smooth, expressionless. 'We will not be the first to sacrifice our lives for a greater good.'

'And the repulse of the Qax is a greater good? Perhaps it is. But –' Poole stared into the Friend's wide brown eyes. 'But I don't think a noble self-sacrifice is all that's happening here. Is it, Jaar? You show no interest in our offers of AS technology. And you could be evacuated before the end. There isn't really any need for your sacrifice, is there? But you don't fear death at all. Death is simply . . . irrelevant.'

Jaar did not reply.

Poole took a step back. 'You people frighten me,' he said frankly. 'And you anger me. You rip Stonehenge out of the ground. Stonehenge, for Christ's sake! Then you have the audacity to come back in time and start the destruction of a planet . . . the gravitational collapse of most of the System's usable mass. Jaar, I'm not afraid to face the consequences of my own actions. After all I was the man who built the time machine that brought you here. But I don't understand how you have the audacity to do this, Jaar – to use up, destroy, so much of humanity's common heritage.'

'Michael, you must not grow agitated over this. I'm sure Shira told you the same thing. In the end, none of this' – he indicated the cavern –'none of us – will matter. *Everything will be made good.* You know we're not prepared to tell you any more than you've figured out already. But you must not be concerned, Michael. What we are doing is for the benefit of all mankind – to come, and in the past . . .'

Poole thrust his face into the young man's. 'How dare you make such claims, lay such plans?' he hissed. 'Damn it, man, you can't be more than twenty-five years old. The Qax are a terrible burden for mankind. I've seen and heard enough to be convinced of that. But I suspect your Project is more, is bigger, is vaster than any threat posed by a simple oppressor like the Qax. Jaar, I think you are trying to change history. But you are no god! I think you may be more dangerous than the Qax.'

Jaar flinched briefly from Poole's anger, but soon the bland assurance returned.

Poole kept the boy in the cavern for some time, arguing, demanding, threatening. But he learned nothing new.

At last he allowed Jaar to return him to the outer surface. On the way up Poole tried to work the elevator controls, as he'd watched the Friend do earlier. Jaar didn't stop him. Of course, the controls did not respond.

When they returned to the grassy plain Poole stalked away to his ship, full of anger and fear.

10

'Michael.' Harry Poole's voice was soft but insistent. 'Michael, wake up. It's started.'

Michael Poole emerged from sleep reluctantly. He pushed back his thin blanket, rolled onto his back and rubbed his eyes. Beside him, he saw, Berg was already awake and sitting up. Poole lifted himself onto his elbows, wincing at a stab in his lower spine: Shira's little hut was quiet enough, and the air of the earth-craft was still and comfortably warm; but – despite Miriam's assurances that the hard surfaces were doing him the world of good – he doubted if he would ever get used to sleeping on nothing more than an inch of coarsely stuffed pallet over a floor of Xeelee construction sheeting.

Miriam Berg was already pulling on her one-piece Friends' jumpsuit. 'What's started, Harry?'

The Virtual construct of his father, coarsened by diffraction, hovered over Poole. 'The high-energy particle flux from the Interface portal has increased. Something's coming, Michael. An invasion from the future – we've got to get out of here.'

Poole, still struggling into jumpsuit and shoes, stumbled to the tepee's open doorway. He squinted in the Jovian light and turned his face to the sky. The

Interface portal hung there, delicate and beautiful, apparently innocent of menace.

'Spline,' Berg breathed. 'They'll send Spline through. The living ships the Friends described, the warships of the Qax, of the Occupation, come to destroy the earth-craft. Just as we've expected.'

There was an edge in Berg's voice Poole had never heard before, a fragility that induced in him an atavistic urge to take her in his arms, shield her from the sky.

Berg said, 'Michael, those things will defeat the best humanity can throw at them – *fifteen centuries from now.* What can *we* do? We haven't got a hope of even scratching their ugly hides.'

'Well, we can have a damn good try,' Poole murmured. 'Come on, Berg. I need you to be strong. Harry, what's happening in the rest of the System?'

The Virtual, sharp and clear here outside the tepee, shrugged nervously. 'I can't send a message out, Michael. The Friends are still blocking me. But the ships in the area have detected the high-energy particle flux.' He met Michael's eyes, mournfully. 'Nobody knows what the hell's going on, Michael. They're still keeping a respectful distance, waiting for us to report back. They don't see any threat – after all, the earth-craft has simply sat here in Jovian orbit for a year, enigmatic but harmless. What can happen now?' He looked vaguely into the sky. 'People are – curious, Michael. Looking forward to this. There are huge public Virtuals, images of the portal and the earth-craft hovering over every city on Earth . . . It's like a carnival.'

'But once the Qax begin their assault –'

'It will be too late.' Berg took Michael's arm; her face was still a mask of fear, he saw, but some of her determination, her cunning, seemed restored. 'Listen to me. The best chance of hitting them is going to be now . . .

in the first few minutes after the Spline emerge from the portal.'

Poole nodded. 'Right. Causality stress.'

'The Spline are living creatures,' Berg said. 'Maybe that's a weakness we can play on; the Qax, and their ships, are surely going to take a while to ramp up to full effectiveness. If we can hit them fast maybe there's a chance.'

Berg was right, of course. There was a kind of inevitability to all of this, Poole thought. *It's going to be up to us*. He closed his eyes, longing for the silence – the lack of decisions – in the Oort Cloud.

Harry laughed, his voice brittle and too bright. 'Hit them fast? Sure. With what, exactly?'

Poole whispered, 'With the singularity cannon.'

Berg looked at Michael sharply, possibilities lancing through her mind. 'But – even if we get the Friends to agree – the cannon wasn't designed as a weapon.'

Michael sighed, looking tired. 'So we adapt.'

Harry said, 'As long as the damn things can be pointed and fired. Tell me how they're supposed to work. You fire black holes into Jupiter . . .'

'Yes,' Michael said. 'A pair of singularities is launched in each cannon shot. Essentially the device is a true cannon; once the singularities are launched, their paths are ballistic. Orbiting each other, a few yards apart, the singularities enter Jupiter's gravity well. The trajectories are designed to merge at a specified point in the body of the planet.'

Berg frowned. 'Ultimately the hole, or holes, will consume Jupiter . . .'

'Yes. The Project's design is to render Jupiter into a single, large black hole of a specified mass –'

'But that could take centuries. I know the holes'

growth would be exponential, but still you're starting from a minuscule base; the holes can only grow as fast as their area allows them.'

'That's true.' He smiled, almost wistfully. 'But the timescale of the Project was longer than centuries; far longer.'

Berg tried to drag thoughts, ideas from her mind, ignoring the lowering sky above her.

How could they use this planetbuster cannon to disable a Spline? If they simply shot off black holes, the tiny singularities would pass through the flesh of the warship. No doubt tidal and other effects would hurt the Spline as the holes passed through, and maybe they'd strike it lucky and disable some key component . . . but probably not; the Spline was a mile wide and the wounds inflicted by the traversing holes would surely be not much worse than laser shots.

A multiple strike, a barrage?

'What if we launched two singularities to come to rest at the centre of mass of the Spline? Could we do that?'

'Of course.' Michael frowned; Berg could almost see trajectory curves rolling through his head. 'We'd simply need to launch the singularities with a low velocity – below the earth-craft's escape velocity, essentially.'

'Yes.' Berg pictured it. Like stones hurled into the air, the singularities would come to rest, hover in the body of the Spline itself . . . But only for a moment, before falling back. What good would that do? It would take days for the holes to consume the Spline's mass – hours, probably, to absorb enough material to inflict any significant damage – not the few seconds they would be present in the volume of the Spline.

Anyway, they wouldn't have hours to spare.

Then what?

'Why would they send the singularities into Jupiter

on such complex trajectories?' Harry asked. 'Why have them merge *before* they reach the centre?'

Michael shook his head. 'You haven't grasped the subtleties of the design,' he said seriously.

'Evidently not,' Harry said dryly.

'Do you understand what happens when two singularities converge, combine?' He mimed, with his two fists, the singularities approaching each other, whirling around each other, finally merging. 'The event horizons merge into a single horizon of greater net area . . . entropy, proportional to the area, increases. The singularities themselves, the flaws in space at the heart of the holes, fall in on each other; blueshifted radiation increases the effective mass until the final merger occurs on Planck timescales – the immense gravitational fields generated effectively deflate time. And the joint event horizon quivers like a soap bubble, generating radiation through quadrupolar effects.'

Berg nodded slowly. 'And what form does this – radiation – take?'

He looked surprised by the question. 'Gravitational, of course. Gravity waves.'

She took a deep breath, felt her blood surge through her veins a little fast. *Gravity waves.*

Michael explained further.

These weren't the dinky little ripples in spacetime, propagating at lightspeed, which had been studied by human astronomers for centuries . . . When two massive singularities merged, the gravity waves were monstrous. Nonlinear distortions of spacetime itself.

'And the radiation is directed,' Michael said. 'It pulses along the axis of the hole pair. By choosing precisely the placement and orientation of the holes at merger inside the carcass of the planet, you can direct gravity-wave pulses as you choose. You can sculpt the implosion of Jupiter by working its substance on a massive scale; it was the Friends' intention, I believe, even to remove some of the mass of the planet before the final collapse. The precise size, angular momentum and charge of the final black hole are evidently important parameters for the success of –'

But Berg was no longer listening. Then the earth-ship wasn't just – *just* – a singularity-cannon platform. It was a gravity-wave gun.

A human-built starbreaker.

They could fight back.

Michael looked up and gasped. The colour of the sky had changed, and cast grey shadows across his face.

Berg looked up. A vast moon of flesh slid complacently towards the zenith, its gunmetal-grey surface pocked with eye sockets and weapon emplacements. Bloody scars a hundred yards wide disfigured the skin-hull. Berg searched for the Interface portal and made out another of the great elephant-ships emerging from the future. One of its limbs brushed the sky-blue wire framework of the portal, and a layer of flesh boiled away as the immense mass of the exotic matter raised *tides* in living tissue.

Spline . . .

It had begun.

Jasoft Parz, suspended in entoptic fluid, clung to the rubbery material of the Spline's cornea and peered out at the past.

Parz's ship was climbing out of Jupiter's gravity well now, on its way to its hyperspace jumpoff point to the inner planets. The wormhole Interface portal was receding; the portal looked like a bluish scar against the swollen cheek of Jupiter. Parz could see that a second Spline ship, the companion of his own, already loomed over the scrap of Earth-green that was the rebels' craft.

Parz sighed. 'The rebel ship is elegant.'

The Qax said, 'It is a scrap of mud hurled into space by hyperactive apes.'

'No. Look at it again, Qax. A camouflaging layer of earth built over a shell of Xeelee construction material . . . They must have stolen a Xeelee flower, constructed this thing in some deep, hollowed-out cavern.' He laughed. 'And all under your watchful gaze.'

'Under my predecessor's gaze,' the Qax said slowly. 'According to the ship's sensors the thing is constructed around a layer of singularities. A thousand of them, the total amounting to an asteroid-scale mass . . .'

Parz whistled. 'That doesn't sound possible. How —'

'Obviously such masses could not be transported from space,' the Qax said. 'The rebels must have evolved some technique of assembling such materials from the substance of the planet.'

Once humans had been able to engineer artefacts of exotic matter. Evidently not all of that technology had been lost, or confiscated by the Qax. Parz imagined wells of magma, shaped and compressed, imploded into a stream of singularities by immense forces . . . He marvelled at the earth-craft. 'It's bold, audacious, ingenious.'

'You sound proud.'

Parz shrugged. 'Why shouldn't I be proud? In impossible circumstances, humans have achieved a remarkable feat. Even to come so far as these rebels have —'

'Keep your sense of perspective,' the Qax snapped. 'This hardly represents a serious threat to the Occupation. For all the ingenuity of its construction we are faced by a single, ramshackle raft, barely capable of maintaining its structural integrity. And it was constructed furtively, like the burrow of a hunted animal. Where is the cause for pride in that?'

141

'Perhaps the rebels see themselves as hunted animals,' Parz said.

The Qax hesitated. 'Your admiration for these criminals is interesting,' it said mildly.

'Oh, you don't need to worry,' Parz said with vague self-disgust. 'I talk a good rebellion. I always have. But when it comes to action, that's a different matter.'

'I know. I understand this feature of your personality. So did my predecessor.'

'Am I as predictable as that?'

'It is a factor which increases your usefulness, in our eyes,' the Qax said.

From behind the curved flank of the Spline, another ship appeared. This, Parz saw through the Spline's lens, was one of the craft indigenous to the period: a squat, ungainly affair, gaudily painted, hovering before the eye of the Spline like some insect. The sensors showed there was a crowd of these barges, clustered around the Interface portal. So far none of them had interfered with the Spline – or attempted to interfere, rather.

Parz said, 'Aren't you concerned about these local craft?'

'They cannot harm us,' the Qax said, sounding uninterested. 'We can afford to take time here, to check through the Spline's systems, before the cross-system hyperspace flight.'

Parz smiled. 'Qax, listening to you I can hear the voice of the commander of a twentieth-century atomic carrier disdaining the painted, dugout canoes of islanders, drifting out to meet him on the curve of some sea. Still, though, the most primitive weapon can kill . . .

'And I wonder why they don't attack anyway.'

He pressed his face to the cornea and glanced around the sky; now that he looked for them he saw how many of the strange local ships there were, and how diverse in design. The political structure in this period was chaotic, he recalled. Fragmented. Perhaps these vessels represented many different authorities. Governments of moons, of the inner planets, of Earth herself; as well as of the central, international agencies . . . Perhaps no war council coalition existed here yet; perhaps there was no one to command an attack on this Spline.

Still, Parz was irritated by the Qax's complacency.

'Aren't you at least worried that these vessels might be raising a System-wide alert? Maybe the inner planets will be able to pack more of a punch against you,' he said grimly. 'And if they're allowed to prepare . . .'

'Jasoft Parz,' the Qax said with a trace of impatience, 'your death-seeking fantasies are beginning to grate. I have monitored none of the dire warnings you seem to yearn for.'

Parz frowned, absently scratching his cheek through the thick, clear plastic of his facemask. 'The situation doesn't make sense, actually, even given the political fragmentation. The Friends have been in this time period for a year. They've had plenty of time to warn the human natives of this era, to co-ordinate, assemble some sort of force to oppose you . . . perhaps even to close the Interface portal.'

'There has been no evidence of such co-ordination,' the Qax said.

'No, there hasn't, has there? Is it possible the Friends haven't warned the natives? – perhaps haven't communicated with them at all, even?' Parz could still make out the Friends' craft against Jupiter, an island of green on a sea of pink. What were the rebels up to? The Friends must have had some project in mind when they made their desperate run to this period . . . but evidently they had not felt the need to enlist the resources of the natives.

Parz tried to imagine how a handful of rebels on a single improvised ship could hope to strike across fifteen centuries at an interstellar power.

'It makes little difference,' the Qax murmured, its disembodied voice like an insect buzzing somewhere behind Parz's eyes. 'The second Occupation craft is minutes away from the rebel craft, now; this absurd episode is nearing its climax.'

'Michael Poole. Miriam.'

Poole dragged his eyes away from the astonishing sky. Shira stood before them; Poole saw that the customary blank composure of her skeletal face was marred by a tightness of the mouth, a pink-white flaring of her small nostrils. Beyond her, the earth-craft was full of motion; Friends bearing slates and other pieces of equipment ran across the wiry grass, converging on the stones at the heart of the craft.

Berg snapped, 'Shira, those are Spline warships up there.'

'We understand what is occurring, Miriam.'

'Then what the hell are you going to do about it?'

Shira ignored this and turned to Poole. 'You must stay inside the tepee,' she said. 'The surface of the earth-craft is not safe now. The Xeelee construction material will shield you from –'

Poole said, 'I'm not going anywhere until you tell me what you're going to do.'

Harry, his image restored to brightness outside the hut, folded his arms and stuck his jaw out. 'Me too,' he said defiantly.

Shira's voice was fragile but steady enough. 'We are not going to respond directly to the incursion of the Qax,' she insisted. 'There is no purpose –'

Berg shouted, 'You mean that after bringing them

144

here you're just going to let them walk in and do what they want?'

Shira flinched at the other woman's fury, but stood her ground. 'You do not understand,' she said, the strain still more evident in her voice. 'The Project is paramount.'

Harry tried to grab Poole's arm; his fingers passed through cloth and flesh in a cloud of pixels. 'Michael. Look at the Spline.'

The first warship had crossed the zenith now and seemed to be receding from the earth-craft. Deep in its crater-like pores Poole saw the glint of blood and metal.

The Spline's partner, the second warship, was clear of the Interface. It was already the size of a large coin, and it grew visibly.

The second ship seemed to be coming straight for them.

'Only two,' Berg muttered.

Poole glanced at her, startled; her face was screwed up tight around peering eyes. 'What?'

'No sign of any more coming through the portal. There's already been time for a third to start appearing.'

Poole shook his head, amazed at her ability to think her way through the looming threat from the sky. 'Do you think something's stopping them, at the other end?'

Berg shook her head with a brief, dismissive jerk. 'No way. Two is all they think they need.'

Shira twisted her hands together anxiously. 'Please,' she said. 'The tepee.'

Poole ignored her. 'What do you think they're doing?'

Berg, her fear gone now, or at least suppressed, tracked the silent motion of the Spline. 'The first one's leaving Jovian space.'

Poole frowned. 'Heading where? The inner Solar System?'

145

'It's logical,' Berg said dryly. 'That's where Earth lies, fat and waiting.'

'And the second?'

'. . . Is coming down our damn throats.'

Shira said, 'You need not fear. When the Project comes to fruition these events will be . . . translated into harmless shadows.'

Poole and Berg, dropping their heads from the ugly movements in the sky, studied the Friend.

'She's crazy,' Berg said.

Shira leaned forward, her blue eyes pale and intense. 'You must understand. The Project will correct all of this. The continuance of the Project is – must be – the top priority for all of us. Including you, our visitors.'

'Even above defending ourselves – defending Earth – against a Spline attack?' Poole asked. 'Shira, this may be the best chance we'll have of defeating the assault. And –'

She didn't seem to be hearing him. 'The Project *must* be seen through,' she said. 'Accelerated, in fact.' The girl looked from one to the other, searching their faces, pleading for understanding; Michael felt as if he could see the practised phrases rolling meaninglessly through her mind. 'You will come with me now.'

'What do you think?' Poole said to Berg. 'Will they force us? Do they have weapons?'

'You know they do,' Berg said calmly. 'You saw what they did to my boat.'

'So we've no way of compelling them to do anything.' He heard the frustration, the despair in his own voice. 'They're not going to oppose the Spline at all; they're putting all their faith in this Project of theirs. The magic Project which will solve everything.'

Berg growled softly.

She lashed out sideways with her bunched fist and caught the Friend squarely on the temple. Shira crumpled and fell to the ground where she lay with her small face fringed by pink-stained grass.

Harry, staring down, said: 'Wow.'

'She won't stay out long,' Miriam said. 'We need to move fast.'

Poole glanced up at the still-growing, rolling form of the Spline warship. 'What do we do?'

'We have to take out both Spline,' Berg muttered.

'Oh, sure,' Harry said. 'Let's take 'em both out. Or, on the other hand, why don't we think big? *I have a cunning plan . . .*'

'Shut up, Harry,' Michael said absently. 'All right, Miriam, we're listening. How?'

'We'll have to split up. Harry, is the *Crab*'s boat ready to lift?'

Harry closed his eyes, as if looking within. 'Yes,' he said.

Shira stirred on the grass, moaning softly.

'Maybe you can get away in the boat,' Miriam said. 'While the Friends are still running about confused, trying to stow everything. Get back to the *Crab* and go after the first Spline, the one that's heading for Earth. Maybe you can catch it before it engages its hyperdrive.'

'And then what?'

Berg grinned tightly. 'How should I know? I'm making this up as I go along. You'll have to think of something.'

'All right. What about you?'

Berg looked up. The second Spline, advancing on the earth-craft, loomed still closer; it was a fleshy moon above them. 'I'll try to do something about that one,' Berg said. 'Maybe I can get to those singularity cannons.'

Shira moaned again and seemed to be trying to lift her face from the grass.

Poole said, 'And her?'

147

Berg shrugged. 'Take her with you. Maybe she'll be able to help you.'

Poole bent, picked up the girl, her protruding eyes open now and trying to focus.

Berg searched Poole's face. 'I need to say goodbye, Michael,' she said.

Harry looked from Poole, to Miriam, and back to Poole; and he winked politely out of existence.

Michael looked beyond the village of Xeelee-material huts, towards the centre of the earth-craft. Three burly Friends were running towards them. No, four. And they were carrying something. Weapons?

He turned back to Berg. 'You'll never make it to the centre of the craft,' he said. 'Come with us.'

Harry's head popped out of space, close to Miriam's ear. 'Sorry, folks,' he said, 'but you haven't a lot of time for this.'

Miriam grinned briefly, ran her hand through her stubble of hair, and took a deep breath. 'But I'm not going to the centre of the craft. Goodbye, Michael.' And she swivelled – and started to run, towards the edge of the world.

Michael Poole stood watching her for one second, mouth open.

Shira wriggled harder in his arms, kicking like a stranded fish.

There was no more time. Michael turned on his heel and ran for his boat, the ungainly burden of Shira flopping in his arms, the disembodied head of his father floating at his side.

The rim of the craft, ahead of her, was a fringe of grass, incongruous against the bruised-purple countenance of Jupiter.

Her mind raced.

From the circular village of the Friends of Wigner, Berg had about a hundred yards to run to the lip of the craft. Well, she could cover that distance in maybe ten seconds, on the flat. But the weakening of gravity as she approached the edge ought to let her speed up – as long as she didn't fall flat on her face – but on the other hand' she'd be climbing out of the earth-craft's gravity well, so she'd feel as if she were running uphill . . .

Yes. Already the ground seemed to be tipping up beneath her.

She tried to work with the weakening gravity, gain whatever advantage she could; she consciously slowed her pace, letting her stride lengthen and carry her further.

She risked a glance backwards. The posse of pursuing Friends had split, she saw; two of them had concentrated on Michael and the girl, and the other two were coming after her. They were fit and covered the grass fast.

They carried laser-guns, of the type which had turned her boat to slag. She imagined coherent photons surging from the weapons and arcing into her back, faster than thought. *You don't dodge a light weapon* . . . She felt her back tense, the muscles locking. Her stride faltered, and she tried to empty her head of everything but the next step.

She seemed to be climbing a one-in-three slope now. She didn't dare look back again, for fear of seeing the earth-craft apparently tip behind her, of tumbling helplessly backwards, her balance lost. And, damn it, her chest hurt. Her lungs were dragging at thinning air; coming this far out of the earth-craft's tiny gravity well was like climbing the mountains of Mars.

She wondered why the Friends didn't just open up. No need to aim; they could just hose the lasers, slice her spine the same way they'd cut open her boat. But they were hesitating. Thinking twice.

They wanted to stop her, not murder her, she realized; they were reluctant to use those weapons.

She didn't have much time for the Friends, but at least they weren't killers. Maybe it would be better if they were.

Her sense of perspective was starting to work on the approaching edge of the world, now. She could see individual blades of grass rushing towards her.

Her lungs hurt like hell. She felt her tongue protrude from her mouth. Her whole chest ached, and the muscles of her back and her upper arms. Her legs, stiffening as she climbed the steepening hill, were shivering, as if they knew what they were approaching.

She ignored it all. Her arms flailing at the thinned air, she drove her feet down into the grass, pushing the earth-craft below her.

The 'plane' continued to steepen; she was flying up a bowl-shaped Alp –

And then there was no more grass beneath her boots.

She tipped forward, stumbling over the edge of the world; her momentum carried her away from the earth-craft and into the pink light of Jovian space, arms and legs spread wide like some unlikely kite. As she spilled slowly forward she saw the posse of Friends sprawl against the grass, weapons abandoned, the thin air drawing their mouths open in cartoon masks of amazement.

She was lost in space, her lungs empty. She hung, seemingly motionless, between the earth-craft and the bulk of Jupiter. Darkness crowded the edge of her vision.

Oh Jesus, Michael, maybe this wasn't such a good plan after all.

*

Michael Poole, running around the edge of the earth-craft village towards his boat, arms aching with the weight of the semi-conscious Shira, was exhausted already.

He saw Berg go flying over the edge of the world. He found time to wonder if she knew what she was doing.

He glanced over his shoulder; the twist of his muscles only added to the breathless ache across his chest. Two of the Friends were still chasing him. They were close enough for him to see the mud spattered over their light pink coveralls, the set grimness of their faces, the glinting plastic of their laser-rifles . . .

Harry hovered beside him, his legs whirling propeller-style in a cartoon running motion. 'I hate to be the bringer of bad news,' he panted, 'but they're gaining on us.'

'Tell me something . . . I don't know.'

Harry glanced easily over his shoulder. 'Actually I don't know why they don't just lase you down where you stand.'

'Save the . . . pep talk . . .' Michael gasped, his shoulders and arms encased in pain, 'and . . . do something!'

'Like what?'

'Use your . . . initiative, damn you,' Michael growled.

Harry frowned, rubbed his chin, and disappeared.

Suddenly there were wails from Poole's pursuers, arcs of laser light above his head, the sizzle of ozone.

Still sprinting, Michael risked another look back.

A ten-foot edition of Harry, a shimmering collage of semi-transparent, fist-sized pixels, had materialized in front of the two Friends. Startled, they'd stumbled to a halt before the apparition and had let rip with the lasers. The pale pink beams lanced harmlessly through the grainy image, dipping slightly as they refracted out of the atmosphere.

But within seconds the Friends had dismissed the

Virtual. Shouting to each other, they shouldered their weapons and set off once more; Harry materialized before them again and again, the basic template of his Virtual body distorted into a variety of gross forms, but the Friends, their strides barely faltering, ran through the ineffectual clouds of pixels.

Poole tucked his head down and ran.

'Michael!'

Poole jerked his head up. The boat from the *Crab* was speeding towards him, a gunmetal-grey bullet shape which hovered a few feet above the plane. The English grass waved and flattened beneath it. An inviting yellow light glowed from the open airlock.

Harry's amplified voice echoed from the distant Xeelee-material buildings. 'Michael, you're going to get approximately one go at this . . . I hope your timing is better than your stamina.'

Michael pounded across the grass, the girl an ungainly bundle in his arms. His breath scraped in his throat. The boat swept towards him at fifty miles per hour, the open hatchway gaping.

A flicker of pink-purple light above his head, a whiff of ozone, and a small hole appeared in the grey-white carapace of the boat. Smoke wisped briefly; the boat seemed to falter, but kept advancing.

It looked as if the Friends were shedding their scruples about using their weapons.

The boat filled his vision.

Poole jumped.

The doorframe caught his right shin, his left foot; pain blazed and he felt the warm welling of blood. He fell hard on the metal floor of the airlock, landing heavily on top of Shira. The girl gasped under his weight, her eyes widening. They slid in a tangle of limbs across the floor, Poole's damaged legs leaving a trail of blood; they were jammed against the back wall of the airlock, and for the second time the air was knocked out of Poole's labouring lungs.

A laser bolt flickered a few inches above Poole's head.

The boat surged away from the ground, the hatch sliding closed slowly; Poole, struggling to rise, was slammed to the floor again, this time away from the girl. His chest heaved. He hadn't been able to draw a single decent breath since his last, desperate few strides across the grass of the earth-craft, and now he felt as if he were in vacuum.

He forced his head up and looked blearily to the closing hatch. He saw a slice of salmon-pink Jupiter, a tranche of stars; already they were out of the toy atmosphere of the earth-world, above its scrap of blue sky, rushing into Jovian space.

Blackness welled up before him. The pain in his legs stabbed through his dimming senses.

The girl moaned, sounding very far away, and he thought he heard Harry's voice. His lungs were empty. He was very cold. He closed his eyes.

Berg turned a half-somersault before the thin air slowed her tumble. Then she was falling, upside down relative to the earth-craft, gravity tugging at her so feebly it seemed as if she were hanging in the sky.

Sucking at the cold air, her arms and legs spread wide, she stared back at the earth-craft. The biggest danger with all of this – the biggest in a whole jungle of dangers, she conceded – was that she might have reached escape velocity. Would she continue to fly out into the Jovian light, her lungs straining to find the last few molecules of oxygen? She tried to taste the air, to sense if it were getting any thinner; but it was impossible to tell.

The earth-craft was laid out like a diagram before her. She was looking up at the flat, quarter-mile-wide dome of dove-grey Xeelee material which formed its base. The dome was breached by circular vents, each about a yard wide, which must be the mouths of the singularity cannon Poole had described. The dome reminded her incongruously of some old sports stadium, ripped from the Earth and hurled into orbit, upside down, around Jupiter; but on the base of this stadium sat a cluster of Xeelee-material buildings and the battered, ancient stones of a henge. Close to the edge of the landscape she could make out her two pursuers; staring after her, they clung to their floor of grass like two pink-clad flies, their weapons pinned to the sward by the inverted gravity.

Beyond the earth-craft the Spline warship climbed across the sky, Jupiter casting long, mottled spotlights onto its elephant hide.

Now there was the faintest breeze whispering past her ears as the earth-craft's weak, complex gravity field stroked her back into the artificial sky. She felt a surge of relief. Well, at least she wasn't going to die of asphyxiation, suspended carelessly over Jupiter.

The earth-craft seemed to be tipping away from her, dipping its domed section and hiding the grass-coated face from her view. Soon, even the Spline ship was hidden by its bulk.

For an odd, brief moment she was alone. She was suspended in a bubble of crisp blue sky; tufts of ragged white cloud laced the air, draping themselves over the edge of the earth-craft. It was utterly silent. It was almost peaceful. She didn't feel any fear, or regrets; she was on a roller-coaster of events now, and there wasn't much she could do except relax, roll with it, and react to whatever happened. She tried to empty her mind, to concentrate just on drawing in each painful breath.

A breeze pushed more steadily at her face now; she felt it riffle her short hair, and her loose jumpsuit billowed gently against her chest and legs.

She watched the dome more carefully, focussing on the nearest of the seemingly randomly placed singularity-cannon vents, about two hundred yards in from the rim of the craft. By measuring it against her thumbnail she saw that the vent was growing. It was like a huge opening mouth.

She found herself sighing with a small, odd regret. So much for her little interlude in the air; it looked as if the world of events was drawing her back in again.

The grey construction-material dome was looming up at her now; she was going to hit about twenty yards up from the earth-lined rim of the craft. Well, she was glad to avoid the vents for the moment; the Xeelee material was monomolecular, and she remembered the razor-sharp edges of the doorway to Shira's hut . . .

The gravity on this part of the dome would be about a quarter of the earth-normal field in the interior of the craft. Enough to cause her to hit hard. She tried to orient herself in the stiffening wind, her arms and legs bent slightly, her hands held before her face.

Michael opened his eyes.

He was breathing normally. Thank God. He took a luxurious draught of thick, warm air.

He was inside the metal box that was the boat's air-lock. The floor felt soft below him . . . too soft. He probed beneath him with his right hand, and found the metal floor a few inches below his spine; inadvertently he shoved himself a little further into the air.

Weightlessness. They'd made it into space.

When he turned his head, his shoulders, chest and neck still ached from their labours in the thin air of the earth-craft. Beside him Shira was curled into a question mark, the diffuse light of the airlock bathing the elegant dome of her head. Her face looked very young in her sleep. Trickles of blood, meandering in the weightless conditions, snaked from her ears.

Poole lifted cautious fingers to his own face. Blood at his nose and ears. And the sudden movement made him rock in the air; his hovering legs dangled and banged together, and the pain from his damaged shins and feet flared anew. He cried out, softly.

Harry's face popped into being just in front of his own. 'You're alive,' Harry said. 'Awake, as a matter of fact.'

Poole found his voice reduced to an ugly scratch. 'Great timing, Harry. Why didn't you run it a bit closer?'

Harry's eyebrows raised a little. 'Piece of cake,' he said.

'Let me sleep.' Michael closed his eyes.

'Sorry. We dock with the *Crab* in one minute. Then we've got to get out of here. We're assaulting a mile-wide sentient warship from the future. Or don't you remember the plan?'

Michael groaned and shut his eyes tighter.

Berg's hands, feet and knees hit the unyielding surface first. The construction material was slick, smoother than ice, a shock of sudden cold against her palms. She let her hands and feet slide away from beneath her. She turned her face away so that her chest and thighs hit the surface comparatively softly.

She lay spreadeagled, flattened against the dome. She lay for a few minutes, the breath hissing through her teeth, her chest flat against the cold Xeelee substance.

She'd had worse landings.

The light changed. She lifted her head. Once more

156

the Spline was rising over the curved horizon of the dome, a malevolent moon of flesh, cratered by eyes and weapon snouts.

11

Harry's voice was strained. 'Michael. The Spline is attacking the earth-craft.'

Michael Poole, the *Crab*'s two gravities heavy on his chest, lay on a couch. The subdued lights of the *Crab*'s lifedome were comfortingly familiar all around him.

Above him, directly ahead of the advancing *Crab*, the Spline they had chosen to chase loomed like a misshapen face, growing perceptibly. Other ships orbited the Spline in a slow, complex gavotte. The whole tableau was almost pleasing to watch; peaceful, silent.

Poole felt tired, his capacity to absorb change exhausted. Lying here was almost like the precious days when he had sailed alone through the Oort Cloud.

The girl Shira, on a couch beside Poole's, her frail frame crushed by the two-gravity thrust, wept softly. Poole turned to her reluctantly. Her face was gaunt. There was moisture under her eyes, her nose, patches of colour in her cheeks; her eyes were like red wounds. Harry's disembodied head floated in shadow some feet above them both, no expression readable.

'Damn it,' said Poole. 'Harry, bring up an image of the earth-craft.'

A section of the dome turned opaque, hiding the Spline and its ineffectual human attendants; the opaque section filled with a salmon-pink wash, an inverted slab of grass-green, a ball of hull-flesh. The little cup-shaped earth-craft, dwarfed, hung beneath the belly of the attacking warship like some absurd pendant; and it hung with its grassy face averted, its construction-material dome turned up to the Spline in submission. Cherry-red fire flickered from the gut of the Spline, dimming Jupiter's light. The earth-craft shuddered visibly.

'Starbreakers,' Shira breathed, eyes wide. 'The Spline is using starbreakers.'

'What did you expect?' Poole said grimly. 'Can the Xeelee material withstand starbreaker beams?'

'I don't know. Perhaps for a while. The earth-craft isn't a warship, Michael.'

Poole frowned. In the magnified and enhanced image on the dome the singularity-cannon portals were obvious breaches in the ship's armour. Presumably the causality stress was still impairing the Spline's power and accuracy. But if the Spline managed to shoot through one of those portals it would be over, no matter how tough this magical Xeelee substance was.

Suddenly there was smoke, flames erupting from one of the cannon mouths. The light was an intense blue, heavily loaded to the ultraviolet. Poole, used to the silent flickering of light and particle weapons, felt weak, awed. Two points of light, intensely bright and whirling around each other, shot out of the cannon and spiralled along the column of smoke and light towards the patient bulk of Jupiter.

Harry said, 'What the hell was that?'

'Singularities,' Poole breathed. 'I can scarcely believe it. They're working their cannon; they've fired off two of their singularities. The Friends are fighting back. Maybe Berg –'

'No.' Shira's face, though damp with weeping, was composed. 'It's the Project. They are proceeding with

159

the Project.' Her eyes were bright, seemingly joyful, as she stared upwards.

Starbreaker light flared. Overloaded, the lifedome turned black, the image imploding, then cleared once more.

Now, above Poole's head, the Spline he was chasing was turning, weapon pits glinting menacingly.

'I think they've spotted us,' Harry said.

The belly of the Spline closed down on the earth-craft like a lid. The nearest cannon-mouth was still yards away.

Berg threw herself flat against the construction-material dome. Hull-flesh rolled above her, silent and awesome, like the palm of some giant hand. Metal artefacts large enough to be artillery pieces stared down at her. Now a huge wounded area swept over her, an inverted pool of blood and disrupted flesh. Something swam in that thick, oil-like blood, she saw: symbiotic organisms – or constructs – patiently tending to the worst of the damage. With acres of charnel-house meat suspended over her head, she found herself gagging; but, of course, there was no smell, no sound; the Spline was still outside the atmosphere of the earth-craft.

Would Xeelee construction material stop the weapons of a Spline warship? Maybe not. But it sure would help . . .

She had to get inside the dome.

Trying to ignore the looming ceiling of flesh, she slithered on her belly towards the hole in the dome.

She was too slow, too damn slow. After a few seconds she stopped, rested her face against the dove-grey cheek of Xeelee material.

This was ridiculous. Crawling wasn't going to make

a difference, one way or the other; it could only slow her down.

Muttering encouragement to herself, keeping her eyes off the nightmare filling the sky, she pushed herself up to a kneeling position, got her legs under her, stood uncertainly.

As if in response cherry-red brightness burst all around her; the dome shuddered like a living thing.

She was thrown to her face.

Then, when the singularity cannon fired, Berg's body actually rattled against the shuddering Xeelee material. She pushed herself away from the dome, leaving smears of blood from her nose, her bruised mouth.

She got to her feet. There was a stink of ozone; a wind pressed at her chest, weak in the thin air. Twin points of light – which must be singularities – climbed a tube of smoke into the pink-stained sky. The points whirled around each other like buzzing fireflies. She gave a hoarse cheer: at last, it seemed, the good guys were fighting back . . .

But then she saw that the smoke tube the singularities were climbing almost grazed the surface of the dome; it passed neatly through the gap between the dome and the lumbering belly of the Spline and arced towards Jupiter.

The Friends weren't trying to attack the Spline, to defend themselves; they were firing their singularities at Jupiter. Even at a time like this, all they cared about was their damn Project.

'Assholes,' Berg said. She started running.

Ignoring the pain of the thinness of the atmosphere in her lungs, the heady stench of scorched air, the buffeting winds, the shuddering dome, she tried to work out what she'd do when she got to the mouth of the cannon. The tubes were about three feet wide, and she'd have about twenty yards to fall to the inner base of the dome; she could probably slide through the first few yards and then use her hands and feet to brake –

Starbreaker light flared hellishly all around her. Abandoning all conscious plans, she wrapped her arms around her face and dived head-first into the cannon tube.

Even though the Spline's weapon-ports must be open now – even though the warship from the future must look like some fleshy wall across the sky, massive and menacing, to the natives of this era – a lone matchstick craft was coming at them out of the flotilla of ships, flaring along a two-gee curve straight for the Spline.

Jasoft Parz could hardly believe it.

The ship was about a mile in length. Its drive-fire plumed from a block of comet-ice; the block was fixed to a long, delicate, open-frame metal stalk, topped by a clear lifedome. The dome was a pool of subdued light; Jasoft could almost imagine he could see humans moving about in it, actual people.

Jasoft recognized the design from the research he'd performed for the dead Governor. This was a GUTship, driven by the phase energy of decoupling superforces. It looked so *fragile*.

Something moved in Jasoft, lost and isolated as he was in the grotesque eyeball of the Spline.

There had to be something he could do to help.

He pushed away from the lens. With short, heavy strokes through the thick entoptic fluid, he cast about the eye chamber, looking for some way to damage his Spline host.

Berg rattled down the translucent singularity-cannon tube.

The barrel seemed to be sheltering her from the blazing red light of the starbreaker assault, but its surface proved to be slick and unyielding; neither her hands nor her feet could gain any kind of purchase on the walls of the tube. So she kicked out at the walls as she collided with them, jamming herself as hard as she could against them: anything to generate a little friction. She knew the lower mouth of the tube was six feet above the crystalline floor of the inner chamber. Berg tried to twist in the tube so she'd land butt-first, protecting her head and arms –

She plummeted out of the cannon.

The plane of singularities, diamond points in a lattice of blue-white light, rushed to meet her, slammed into her back.

For long seconds she lay there spreadeagled, staring up at the Xeelee-material dome. Cherry-red light glimmered in distant cannon mouths.

She gingerly moved her legs, wiggled her fingers. There was a cacophony of pain, but nothing seemed to be broken. Her lungs, back and chest felt like a single mass of bruises, though; and it was hard to expand her lungs, to take a decent breath.

It felt nice to lie here, she thought, just to lie here and to watch the light show . . .

Starbreaker light flared anew beyond the dome – no, she realized with a shock; now it was shining *through* the dome – and as she watched Xeelee construction material blistered, bubbling like melting plastic.

She'd postpone blacking out until later, she decided.

She rolled over and climbed painfully to her feet, ignored the clamouring stiffness, the pain in her legs and chest.

The hollow heart of the earth-craft was a hive of activity. Friends ran everywhere carrying bits of equipment, working control panels, shouting instructions to each other. But there was no chaos, or panic, Berg saw. The Friends knew exactly what they were doing. The scene had something of the air of a great installation – a power plant, perhaps – in the throes of some crisis.

In the commotion no one seemed to have observed her unorthodox entrance. There was damage around her, evidence of the huge Spline assault; close to her there was a burned-out control console, two young, gaunt bodies splayed over it.

A cannon-tube flared, forcing her to shield her eyes; a pair of singularities hurtled out of the plane beneath her feet, dazzled up into a cannon tube and soared beyond the dome like ascending souls. She felt the plane beneath her shudder as the whole craft recoiled from the launch of so much mass.

And now there was a rush of noise above her, like the exhalation of a giant. She glanced up. The damaged area of the dome was beginning to glow white-hot; around a quarter of the dome was sagging, losing its structural integrity under the sustained Spline assault.

There was a smell of burning.

Berg recognized a man – a boy, really – the Friend Jaar, who'd taken Poole on his sightseeing tour of this place. Jaar was working at the centre of a little group of Friends, poring over slates which bore what looked like schematics of singularity trajectories. There was soot, blood smeared over his bare scalp, and his jumpsuit was torn, begrimed; he looked tired, but in control.

In a few strides Berg crossed the chamber. She forced her way through the knot of people and grabbed Jaar's arm, pulling away his slate so he was forced to look at her.

Irritation, hypertension crossed his face. 'Miriam Berg. How did you get in here? I thought –'

'I'll explain later. Jaar, you're under attack. What are you doing about it?'

164

He pulled his arm away from her. 'We are finishing the Project,' he said. 'Please, Miriam —'

She grabbed his shoulders, twisted him round so he was forced to face her. 'Look above your head, damn it! The Spline is using starbreakers. The whole damn roof is going to implode on you, Xeelee material or not. There's not going to be time to finish your precious Project. *You're going to fail*, Jaar, unless you do something about it.'

Wearily he indicated the frantic motion around them. 'We set up a crash schedule for the implementation of the Project, but we're falling behind already. And we've lost lives.' He looked up; he seemed to flinch from the failing dome.

'Why don't you use the hyperdrive?'

'The hyperdrive has already gone,' Jaar said. 'Its components were stored in the structure of the dome; we lost operability soon after the start of the assault —'

'Jesus.' Berg ran stiff fingers through her hair. So there was no way to run; they could only fight. And she wouldn't be fighting merely for the good of humanity, but for her own life . . . 'All right, Jaar; show me how these damn singularity cannons work.'

Jasoft Parz felt rather proud of himself.

He wasn't a scientist, or an engineer, by any stretch of the imagination. But, he was finding, he wasn't completely without resource.

In his life-support box he'd found a spare skinsuit. Using a sharp edge from the box he'd sliced this apart, assembled it into a little tepee-like tent; the substance of the skinsuit, trying to restore its breached integrity, had sealed itself tight along the new seams he'd created.

He'd fixed the little tent over a Spline nerve-trunk and used the facemask of the skinsuit to pump the tent full of breathable air, creating a little bubble of atmosphere in entoptic fluid.

Now he cast through the contents of the life-support box. Maybe he'd have to take the mechanism apart, to start his fire . . .

The Spline warship hung over the lifedome of the *Hermit Crab*, rolling with abrupt, jerky, mechanical motions.

Michael Poole stared at it with something approaching fascination: quite apart from its dominating physical presence there was a vague obscenity about the mixture of gross, swollen life and mechanical deadliness. Michael was reminded of myths of the past, of the undead.

No wonder Earth had been – would be – held in thrall by these things.

Michael glanced at Shira. The Friend, exhausted, dishevelled, crushed by the GUTdrive's continuing two-gravity push, lay flat on the couch next to his. Her eyes were open – staring up – but unseeing. A clean blue glow flickered at the edge of his vision, somewhere close to the perimeter of the lifedome.

Harry's disembodied head drifted like a balloon. 'What was that?'

'Verniers. Attitude jets.'

'I know what verniers are,' Harry grumbled. The head swivelled theatrically to peer up at the Spline. The huge sentient warship was now drifting away from the *Crab*'s zenith. 'You're turning the ship?'

Michael leaned back in his couch and folded his hands together. 'I preset the program,' he said. 'The ship's turning. Right around, through one hundred and eighty degrees.'

'But the GUTdrive is still firing.' The head glanced up

166

at the Spline again, closed one eye as if judging distances. 'We must be slowing. Michael, are you hoping to rendezvous with that thing up there?'

'No.' Michael smiled. 'No, a rendezvous isn't in the plan.'

'Then what is, for Christ's sake?'

'Look, Harry, you know as well as I do that this damn old tub isn't a warship. Apart from a couple of Berry-phase archaeological scanners, I've nothing apart from the ship itself which I can use as a weapon.' He shrugged, lying there. 'Maybe if I'd brought back a few more samples from the Oort Cloud, I could throw rocks —'

'What do you mean,' Harry asked ominously, '"apart from the ship itself"?'

'After all this two-g thrust we've a huge velocity relative to the Spline. When we've turned around there'll be only a couple of minutes before we close with the Spline; even with the GUTdrive firing we'll barely lose any of that . . .

'Do you get it, Harry? We're going to meet the Spline ass-first, with our GUTdrive blazing —'

With slow, hesitant movements, Shira raised her hands and covered her face with long fingers.

'My God,' Harry breathed, and his Virtual head ballooned into a great six-feet-tall caricature. 'We're going to ram a Spline warship. Oh, good plan, Michael.'

'You've got a better suggestion?'

An image flickered into existence on the darkened dome above them: the Spline warship, as seen by the *Crab's* backward-pointing cameras. The gunmetal grey of the Spline's hull was reflected in Harry's huge, pixel-frosted eyes. 'Michael, as soon as that Spline lines itself up and touches us with its damn starbreaker beam, this ship will become a shower of molten slag.'

'Then we'll have died fighting. I say again: have you got a better suggestion?'

'Yes,' said Harry. 'Your first idea. Let's run back out to the cometary halo and find some rocks to throw.'

Beyond Harry's huge, translucent head the Spline's motion seemed to have changed. Michael squinted, trying to make out patterns. Was the rolling of the warship becoming more jerky, more random?

Come to think of it, he'd expected to be dead by now.

Was there something wrong with the Spline?

A quarter of the dome had caved in. Cannon barrels collapsed gracefully. Xeelee construction material shrank back like burning plastic, and through the breaches Miriam could see the harsh glare of the stars, the flicker of cherry-red starbreaker light.

Molten construction material rained over the singularity plane. Friends scurried like insects as shards – red-hot and razor-sharp – sleeted down on them. A wind blasted from the devastated area through the rest of the chamber; Miriam could smell smoke, burning flesh.

'Jesus,' Miriam breathed. She knew she was lucky; the singularity-cannon console she'd been working at with Jaar was well away from the collapsing area. Jaar cried out inarticulately and pushed away from the console. Berg grabbed his arm. 'No!' She pulled him around. 'Don't be stupid, Jaar. There's not a damn thing you can do to help them; the best place for you is here.'

Jaar twisted his head away from her, towards the ruined areas of the earth-craft.

Now a flare of cherry-red light dazzled her. The Spline had found a way through the failed dome and had hit the chamber itself with its starbreaker beam. Raising her hand to shield her eyes from the glow of the dome, she saw that the crystal surface over one section of the singularity plane had become muddied, fractured; cracks were racing across it as if it were melting ice. The area had been scoured of human life. And the singularities themselves, white-hot fireflies embedded in their web of blue light, were stirring. Sliding.

All around the artificial cavern the Friends seemed to have lost their discipline. They stumbled away from their consoles, clung to each other in distracted knots; or they ran, hopelessly, into the devastated area. The singularity-cannon muzzles were silent now; sparks no longer sailed upwards to space.

The Friends were finished, Berg realized.

Berg released Jaar and turned back to the console. She tried to ignore it all – the stench of meat, the wind in her face, the awesome creak of disintegrating Xeelee construction material – and to think through the layout of this cannon control. It was all based on a straightforward touch-screen, and the logic was obvious. Tapping lightly at coloured squares she ran through the direction-finder graphics.

From the corner of her eye she saw schematic diagrams of the earth-ship – huge swaths of the dome-base glaring red – and graphs, lists of figures, data on more subtle damages.

Berg said, 'How bad is it? Are we losing the air?'

Jaar watched her, distracted, his face crumpling in pain. 'No,' he said, his voice a hoarse shout above the chaotic din. 'The breaches in the dome are above the bulk of the atmosphere; the singularity plane's gravity well will keep most of the air in a thick layer close to the surface . . . for the next few minutes anyway. But the air will seep out of that breach. It will absorb all this heat, boil out of the ruined shell . . . and the dome itself may fail further.'

'All right. Tell me about the singularity plane.'

He looked vaguely at the console and lifted a

desultory hand, tapped almost casually at the touch-screen. 'We've lost control of about thirty per cent of the singularities. The integrity of the restraining electro-magnetic net is gone.'

Berg frowned, tried to work it out. 'What does that do to us?'

'We didn't run any simulations of this scenario.' He turned to face her, the sweat on his scalp glistening in the starbreaker light. 'This is a catastrophic failure; we have no options from this point. The loose singularities will attract each other, swarm together. The n-body computations would be interesting . . . The singularity swarms will eventually implode, of course.

'It's over.' His shoulders shook convulsively in their thin covering of begrimed, pink material.

She stared at him. She had the feeling that, just at this moment, Jaar – broken open as he was – would be pre-pared to tell her anything she wanted to know about this damn Project: that all the questions which had plagued her in the months since she'd fallen ass-first into the laps of these Friends of Wigner would at last be settled . . . 'Jesus, I wish I had time for this.' She glared at the console before her, lifted her hands to the touch-screen – but the configuration was different. Blocks of light slid about as she watched; the damn thing was changing before her eyes. 'Jaar, what's happening?'

He glanced down briefly, barely interested. 'Compen-sation for the lost singularities,' he said. 'The mass dis-tribution will continue to change until the disrupted singularities settle down to some form of stable con-figuration.'

'All right.' She stared at the shifting colour blocks, striving to take in the whole board as a kind of gestalt. Slowly she started to see how this new pattern matched the matrix she'd memorized earlier, and she raised her hands hesitantly to the screen –

Then the shifting, the seemingly random configuring, started again.

She dropped her hands. 'Damn it,' she said. 'Serves me right for thinking this was going to be easy.' She grabbed Jaar's arm; he looked down at her with an expressionless face. 'Listen, Jaar, you're going to have to come back out of that shell of yours and help me with this. I can't manage it myself.'

'Help you with what?'

'With firing a singularity.'

He shook his head. It was hard to be sure, but it seemed to Berg that he was almost smiling at her, patient at her ignorance. 'But there's no point. I've already explained that without the thirty per cent we've lost, we can't complete the Project –'

'Damn you,' she shouted over the rising wind, 'I'm not planning to fire these things into Jupiter! Listen to me. I want you to help me fight back against the Spline . . .'

He shook his head, clearly confused and frightened, trying to pull away from her.

'What is it with you people? I know your Project was more important than your own damn life, but the thing has failed now! Why won't you help me keep you alive?'

He stared at her, as if she was speaking a language he no longer understood.

There was a groan, like the cry of some huge animal. She glanced up, cringing; acres of dome were glowing white-hot now, vast sections peeling back to reveal the stars. Xeelee material dangled like scraps of burnt skin.

She might only have seconds left, she realized, before the control systems failed completely – or all the power failed, and she found herself playing billiards with a thousand uncontrolled, city-block-sized black holes – or the damn roof fell in . . .

And she was going to have to waste those seconds holding this guy's hand.

'Jaar,' she shouted, 'your Project is finished. The only way it could succeed, in the future, is for you to start again. To construct new singularities, build a new earth-ship. But the options are limited. We can't run, because the hyperdrive is slag, along with the Xeelee dome. So all we can do is fight. Jaar, you have to help me fight back. We have to destroy the Spline, before it destroys us.'

Still he stared at her emptily, his mouth drooping open.

In frustration she drove her fist into his arm. 'It's for the Project, Jaar. *The Project.* You've got to live, to find a way to start it all again. You see that, don't you? Jaar?'

More of the dome imploded into spinning fragments; starbreaker light flickered.

Jasoft Parz was shaken around his eyeball chamber like a pea in a cup. Bits of his broken-open life-support kit bounced around at the end of his umbilical cord like some ludicrous metal placenta. But the walls of the chamber were fleshy, yielding; and he was cushioned further by entoptic fluid.

It was almost fun.

The life-box was a depressing sight. He'd stripped out so many components in his search for a way to ignite his little bonfire – not to mention bleeding half his air supply away to feed the flames – that he couldn't believe it would sustain him for much longer than a few more minutes.

He doubted it made much difference, now, whatever the outcome of this brief, intense battle; he could see no way he personally was going to be allowed to live through this.

It didn't seem to matter. He hadn't felt as calm in years.

His improvised oxygen-tent was still holding up, despite the buffeting and turbulence of the entoptic fluid; sparking electrical fire sizzled against the raw nerve of the Spline; he must be flooding the nervous system of the disoriented creature with agony. Through the Spline's clouding lens he saw sheets of cherry-red light, lines of fire which seemed to crackle across space. The starbreaker beams were firing at the incoming GUTship, then. But he could see how wild the firing was, how random.

For the first time he allowed himself to suppose that this might actually work.

'Jasoft Parz.' The Qax's synthesized translated voice was, Parz noted with amusement, still as level and empty of meaning as a software-generated travel announcement . . . but it masked a scream of rage. 'You have betrayed me.'

Jasoft laughed. 'Sorry about that. But what did you expect? Who would have thought that a Spline warship would be so easy to disable . . . provided you're in the right place, at the right time. In any event, you're wrong. The truth is that you have betrayed yourself.'

'How?'

'By your insufferable complacency,' Parz said. 'You were so convinced of a simple victory here. Damn it, Qax, I would have emerged from that portal with all guns blazing – hit these men from the past before they understood what was happening! But not you – even despite the fact that you *knew* the Wigner Friends could have prepared resistance to you . . . And, even worse, you carried me – a human, one of the enemy – in your warship's most vulnerable place; and for no other reason than to heighten the exquisiteness of your triumph. Complacency, Qax!'

173

'The Spline is not yet rogue,' the Qax said. 'Its pain-suppression routines are not designed to deal with the damage you have inflicted. But, within seconds, heuristic routines will eliminate the disruption. And, Jasoft Parz, you may anticipate the arrival of antibody drones, to deal with the cause of the damage —'

'I'm weak with terror,' Parz said dryly. Beyond the clouding lens-window of his bathysphere-like cell, comet-ice gleamed, rushing at him; GUTfire blazed like sunlight. 'But I don't think we've got even seconds left, Qax.'

The Spline, engulfed by pain, closed its huge eyelid.

A cannon tube, suspended from the damaged dome, extended downwards; at last its mouth touched the crystalline flooring beneath Berg's feet and merged with it, seamlessly. Two firefly singularities moved imperceptibly closer to the cannon barrel, as if eager to be launched into space. Berg felt the gravity field within which she was embedded alter, subtly; it was like an earth tremor, and it gave her a sensation of falling in the pit of her stomach.

She turned to Jaar. 'Listen to me,' she said rapidly. 'Here's what we're going to do. I want you to reconfigure this damn thing to launch a singularity pair, so that the peak of the trajectory is inside the Spline. But that's not all. *I want the singularities to merge*, just at the second in which they are lodged at the heart of the Spline. Do you understand?'

Jaar looked at her, at first without apparent understanding. Then he got it. His eyes narrowed.

'How quickly can you do it?' she asked.

'Watch me.'

*

174

The collision, when it came, was almost balletic.

GUTdrive fire blistered great swaths of the Spline's writhing flesh; Michael found himself shrinking back from the bloody, carnal acres above his head. But still the Spline seemed to find it impossible to respond; those bizarre cherry-red beams, lightspeed rents in spacetime, continued to lance out – but it fired at random, consistently missing the *Crab*.

'There's something wrong,' Harry breathed. 'It should have sliced us open by now. Why hasn't it?'

And now the *Crab* entered the Spline itself, its burning GUTdrive breaching the elephant-flesh hull. Creation light boiled away blood, flesh in a vast, obscene, soundless explosion; the Spline's huge body seemed to recoil. At last the comet-ice tail of the *Crab* disappeared, still glowing, into the carcass of the Spline.

There was a cloud of motion around the huge wound; Michael squinted to see.

'Little robots,' Harry said, amazed.

'Antibody drones,' said Shira lifelessly; she stared at the scene with dull fascination.

Harry said, 'The robots are damaging our hull. We're under attack. For the first time.'

'Maybe,' said Poole. 'But I don't think it really matters now.'

The star-core glow of the GUTdrive was extinguished at last, killed by the toiling antibody drones. But still the mass of comet-ice, the long, crumpling body of the *Crab*, slid steadily into Spline flesh.

It was almost sexual, Michael thought.

The singularity shot, with its reduced launch velocity, seemed to crawl up the translucent cannon shaft. Berg had absurd visions of the singularities rolling out of the mouth of the barrel, falling back to the crystal floor with an anticlimactic plop –

The singularities reached the mouth of the cannon shaft and soared out of sight, eclipsed by the Xeelee-material dome of the chamber.

Berg's energy seeped out of her, now that it was done – for better or worse. She clasped the console, feeling her legs sagging under her.

Purple-red light flared silently through the cracks in the shattered dome. The Spline's deadly starbreaker beams flickered, died.

All over the devastated earth-craft Friends turned their faces up to the uncertain glow, oddly like flowers to the Sun.

Half the dome was gone now. Beyond it, the Spline blocked out the stars.

Its starbreaker beams stilled, the huge warship rolled across the impassive sky. An immense, bloody crater – covering fully an eighth of the Spline's surface area – deformed its hull, Berg saw; and she couldn't help but wince in sympathy. And, as the Spline rolled, she realized that the crater was matched by a second – if anything, even deeper – at the ship's opposite pole. Weapon-navels pooled with blood. The Spline's roll across the stars was erratic, as if some internal balance system was failing.

'Implosion wounds from the directional gravity waves,' said Jaar, his voice calm, evaluating. He nodded thoughtfully. 'It worked.'

Berg closed her eyes. She sought feelings of triumph. Even of relief. But she was still stranded on a damn eggshell that would probably fall apart spontaneously, without any more help from the Spline. And, lest she forget, there was a merged mini-black hole, its devastating work on the Spline complete, falling out of the sky towards her . . .

She said, 'Come on, Jaar, you beautiful bastard. If we're going to live through this we've still got work to do –'

The Spline imploded.

The GUTdrive module drove into its heart like a stiletto. Muscles convulsed in compression waves which tore through the body of the Spline like seismic events. All over the surface of the ship vessels exploded, spewing fast-freezing fluids into space.

The Qax was silent.

Jasoft Parz clung to nerve cables; the eye chamber rolled absurdly as the Spline sought escape from its agony. Parz closed his eyes and tried to *feel* the suffering of the Spline – every spasm, every bursting vessel.

He had been brought here to witness the destruction of Earth. Now he was determined to witness the death of a Qax, embedded in the consciousness of the Spline; he tried to sense its fear at the encroaching darkness, its frustration at its own mistakes, its dawning realization that the future – of Jim Bolder, the Qax diaspora – would, after all, come to pass.

Failure, and death.

Jasoft Parz smiled.

The *Crab* had come to rest at last, its tail section buried in the ravaged heart of the Spline. The lifedome, perched on the crumpled shaft of the ship, overlooked the Spline's carcass like, Michael thought, a viewing platform over some ghastly resort of blood and ripped flesh.

He lay on his couch, the tension draining out of him. Shira, beside him, even seemed to be asleep.

'I need a shower,' he said.

'Michael.' Harry's Virtual head hovered at the edge of the dome, peering out. 'There's something out here.'

Michael laughed. 'What, something other than a wrecked sentient warship from the future? Surprise me, Harry.'

'I think it's an eyeball. Really; a huge, ugly eyeball, yards wide. It's come out of its socket; it's drifting at the end of a kind of cable . . . an optic nerve extension, maybe.'

'So?'

'So I think there's somebody inside.' Harry grinned. 'I think he's seen me. He's waving at me . . .'

12

Michael Poole followed Jasoft Parz, the strange bureaucrat from the future, through the entrails of the dead Spline.

They worked their way through gravity-free darkness broken only by the shifting, limited glow of the light-globe Parz had rescued from his bizarre eyeball-capsule; the semi-sentient device trailed Parz, doglike. The corridor they followed was circular in cross-section and little more than head-high. Poole's hands sank into walls of a greyish, oily substance, and he found himself worming his way past dark, floating ovals a foot or more wide. The ovals were harmless as long as he avoided them, but if he broke the crusty meniscus of any of them a thick, grainy blood-analogue flowed eagerly over his suit.

'Jesus,' he muttered. 'This is disgusting.'

Parz was a few yards ahead of him. He laughed, and spoke in his light, time-accented English. 'No,' he said. 'This is life aboard the finest interstellar craft likely to be available to humans for generations to come – even after my time.' Parz was a thin, dapper man of medium height; his receding hair was snow white and his face was gloomy, downturned, his chin weak. He looked, Michael thought, like a caricature of an aging bureaucrat

– a caricature saved only by his striking green eyes. Parz, in his clear, skin-tight environment suit, moved more easily through the claustrophobic, sticky conditions than did Poole in his bulky space-hardened gear; but Poole, watching Parz slide like a fish through the cloacal darkness, found himself relishing the cool dryness inside his own suit.

A fleshy flap a yard square opened in the floor of this tunnel-tube. Poole jumped back with a cry; ahead of him Parz halted and turned. Fist-sized globes of blood-analogue came quivering out of the flap, splashing stickily against Poole's legs, and then out shot an antibody drone – one of the little robots which seemed to infest the carcass of this damn ship. This one was a flattened sphere about a foot across; it shot from wall to wall, rebounding. Then, for a moment, the drone hovered before Poole; tiny red laser-spots played over Poole's shins and knees, and he tensed, expecting a lance of pain. But the laser-spots snapped away from him and played over the walls and blood-globules like tiny searchlights.

The drone, jets sparkling, hurtled off down the passageway and out of sight.

Poole found himself trembling.

Parz laughed, irritatingly. 'You shouldn't worry about the drones. That one was just a simple maintenance unit –'

'With lasers.'

'It was only using them for ranging information, Mr Poole.'

'And they couldn't be used for any more offensive purposes, I suppose.'

'Against us? The drones of this Spline are thoroughly used to humans, Mr Poole. It probably thinks we're part of a maintenance crew ourselves. They wouldn't dream of attacking humans. Unless specifically ordered to, of course.'

'That cheers me up,' Poole said. 'Anyway, what was it doing here? I thought you said the damn Spline was dead.'

'Of course it is dead,' Parz said with a trace of genteel impatience. 'Ah, then, but what is death, to a being on this scale? The irruption of your GUTdrive craft into the heart of the Spline was enough to sever most of its command channels, disrupt most of its higher functions. Like snapping the spinal cord of a human. But – is it dead?' Parz hesitated. 'Mr Poole, imagine putting a bullet in the brain of a tyrannosaurus. It's effectively dead; its brain is destroyed. But how long will the processes of its body continue undirected, feedback loops striving blindly to restore some semblance of homeostasis? And the antibody drones are virtually autonomous – semi-sentient, some of them. With the extinguishing of the Spline's consciousness they will be acting without central direction. Most of them will simply have ceased functioning. But the more advanced among them – like our little visitor just now – don't have to wait to be told what to do; they actively prowl the body of the Spline, seeking out functions to perform, repairs to initiate. It's all a bit anarchic, I suppose, but it's also highly effective. Flexible, responsive, mobile, heuristic, with intelligence distributed to the lowest level . . . A bit like an ideal human society, I suppose; free individuals seeking out ways to advance the common good.' Parz's laugh was delicate, almost effete, thought Poole. 'Perhaps we should hope, as one sentient species considering another, that the drones find tasks sufficient to give their lives meaning while they remain aware.'

Poole frowned, studying Parz's round, serious face. He found Jasoft Parz oddly repellent, like an insect; his humour was too dry for Poole's taste, and his view of the world somehow over-sophisticated, ironic, detached from the direct, ordinary concerns of human perception.

Here was a man, Poole thought, who has distanced himself from his own emotions. He has become as alien as the Qax. The world is a game to him, an abstract puzzle to be solved – no, not even that: to be admired dustily, as one might marvel at the recorded moves of some ancient chess game.

No doubt it had been an effective survival strategy for someone in Parz's line of work. Poole found pity in his heart for the man of the future.

Parz, proceeding ahead of Poole along the tunnel, continued to speak. 'I've never been aboard a dead Spline before, Mr Poole; I suspect it could be days before the normal functions close down completely. So you'll continue to see signs of life for some time.' He sniffed. 'Eventually, of course, it will be unviable. The vacuum will penetrate its deepest recesses; we will witness a race between corruption and freezing ice . . .' He hesitated. 'There are other ships in the area who could take us off? Human ships of this era, I mean.'

Poole laughed. 'A whole flotilla of them, flying every flag in the System. A damn lot of use they've been.' The navies had been arriving in strength. But the key battles had been over in minutes, long before most of the inner System worlds were even aware of the invasion from the future. But, Poole had learned, the space battles had made spectacular viewing, projected live in huge Virtuals in the skies of the planets . . . 'We've asked them to hold off for a few more hours, until we finish this investigation; we wanted to make sure this thing was safe – dead – deactivated – before letting anyone else aboard.'

'Oh, I think it's safe,' Parz said dryly. 'If the Spline could still strike at you, be assured you'd be dead by now. Ah,' he said. 'Here we are.'

Abruptly the vein-like tunnel opened out around Jasoft. He drifted into empty space, his light-globe following patiently. The white light of the globe shone feebly over the walls of a cavern which Poole, peering carefully from the tunnel, estimated to be about a quarter-mile across. The walls were pink and shot through with crimson veins as thick as Poole's arms; blood-analogue still pulsed along the wider tubes, he noticed, and quivering globes of the blood substance, some of them yards across, drifted like stately galleons through the darkness.

But there was damage. In the dim light cast by the globe-lamp, Poole could make out a spear of metal yards wide which lanced across the chamber, from one ripped wall to another: the spine of the embedded *Crab*. The lining of the chamber had done its best to seal itself around the entrance and exit wounds, so that a tide of flesh lapped around the *Crab*'s spine at each extremity. And even now Poole could see the fleeting shadows of drones – dozens of them – drifting around the spine, sparking with reaction jets and laser-light as they toiled, too late, to drive out this monstrous splinter. Poole stared up at the immense intrusion, the huge wounds, with a kind of wonder; even the spine's straight lines seemed a violation, hard and painfully unnatural, in this soft place of curved walls and flesh.

He unwrapped a line from his waist and fixed one end to the pulsing wall of the chamber. As the jaws of the clip bit, Poole found himself wincing, but he forced himself to tug at the clip, feeling its strong teeth tear a little into the Spline's flesh, before trusting himself to push away from the wall after Parz.

Parz, propelled by a compact reaction-pack built onto the spine of his skinsuit, swam with a stiff grace around the chamber. His suit was slick with gobbets of blood-analogue, Poole noticed, giving Parz the odd and obscene appearance of something newborn. 'This is the stomach-chamber,' Parz said. 'The Spline's main – ah, hold, if you will. Where the Qax customarily reside. At least, the Occupation-era Qax I have described; the turbulent-fluid beings.'

Poole glanced around the dim recesses of the space; it was like some ugly, fleshy cathedral. 'I guess they needed the elbow room.'

Parz glanced across at Poole. His green eyes glimmered, startling. 'You shouldn't be surprised to feel uncomfortable, moving through this Spline, Mr Poole. It's not a human environment. No attempt has been made to adapt it to human needs, or human sensibilities.' His face seemed to soften, then, and Poole tried to read his expression in the uncertain light. 'You know, I'd give a lot to see the Spline of a few centuries from now. From my time,' he corrected himself absently. 'After the overthrow of the Qax, when human engineers adapt the Splines for our own purposes. Tiled vein-corridors; metal-walled stomach-chambers . . .'

'The overthrow of the Qax?' Poole asked sharply. 'Parz, what do you know?'

Parz smiled dreamily. 'Only what I was told by the Governor of occupied Earth . . . The second Governor, that is. Only what it told me of the future, when it was convinced I would die before seeing another human.'

Poole felt the blood pulse in the veins of his neck. 'Jasoft, for the first time I'm glad I rescued you from that ridiculous eyeball.'

Parz turned away. Half-swimming, he made his way towards one section of the stomach-chamber wall, some way from the areas violated by the irruption of the *Crab*. He came to rest beside a metal canister, a coffin-sized box which was fixed to the fleshy wall by a web of metal strands.

'What is it?' Poole asked. 'Have you found something?' He made his way clumsily across the deserted space of the chamber towards Parz.

The two of them huddled over the box, the light-globe hovering close; the small tent of light cast over them was strangely intimate. Parz ran quick, practised hands over the box, fingering touch-screens which, Poole noticed, refused to light up. His face was quite clear to Poole, but his expression was neutral. Unreadable.

Parz said, '"Look on my works, ye mighty, and despair."'

'What?'

'This is Qax.' He slapped the box with one gloved palm. 'The Governor of Earth. Dead, harmless . . .'

'How?'

'The Qax preferred to run their Spline craft by direct conscious control, with their own awareness alongside the continuing sentience of the Spline.'

Poole frowned. 'Can't have been comfortable for the Spline.'

'The Spline didn't have much choice,' said Parz. 'It's an efficient method. But not without its risks.

'When the collision with your ship terminated the Spline's higher functions, perhaps the Qax could have disengaged. But it didn't. Driven by its hatred – and, perhaps, by hubris, right to the end – it stayed locked inside the Spline's sensorium. And when the ship died, the Qax died with it.'

Poole fingered the metal webbing, thoughtfully. 'I wonder if the Spline could be salvaged, somehow. After all, the hyperdrive alone is worth centuries of research. Maybe we could link up the *Crab*'s AI to what's left of the Spline's functions.'

Parz frowned. 'But if the Qax's method is any guide, you need a sophisticated conscious entity as a front end, something which can feel its way into what's left of the Spline's – identity. Sympathetically. Do you understand?'

Poole nodded, smiling. 'I think so. And I know just the conscious entity to try it.'

Parz was silent for a moment. His gloved fingers stroked the surface of the metal canister almost tenderly, and he seemed to be rocking back and forth in the thick intestinal air. Poole leaned closer, trying to read Parz's expression; but the half-shadowed face, with its mask of age tightened by AS, was as empty as it had ever been. 'Jasoft? What are you thinking?'

Parz looked up at him. 'Why,' he said with a note of surprise, 'I think I'm mourning.'

'Mourning a Qax?' A creature, thought Poole, whose fellows had turned Earth's cities to glass – who would have, given a little more fortune, scraped humanity out of the Solar System before most people had even learned the name of their destroyers – and who had turned Parz himself into a quisling, a man unable even to face his true self . . . 'Jasoft, are you crazy?'

Parz shook his head slowly; folds of the clear skinsuit creased at his neck. 'Poole, one day humans are going to bring about the destruction of the Qax's home world. We'll almost wipe them out.

'. . . But they're *unique*. There are only – have only ever been – a few hundred of them. Yet each one has the seed of immortality – the potential to live long enough to witness star-corpses shine by proton decay.

'Poole, this is the second Qax I've seen die.' Parz bent his head to the metal case, apparently looking inward. 'Yes,' he said. 'Yes, I'm mourning.'

Poole stayed with him in the silence of the dead Spline.

*

Miriam Berg, Jaar at her side, walked into the devastated heart of Stonehenge.

The ground had been ripped open, wadded into thick furrows; grass clung to the broken turf like hair to flesh. And the ancient stones had been scattered, shivered to rubble by the casual brush of a gravity-wave starbreaker beam.

Jaar touched her shoulder and pointed into the sky, towards the bulk of Jupiter. 'Look up there,' he said.

Miriam stared hard along the line of his long arm, squinting with the effort. There was a shadow: a rough rectangle silhouetted against the gaudy pink of Jupiter, turning slowly as it sailed away from the earth-craft. 'The last of the henge,' she said.

'Well, at least one of the old stones has survived. It will sail around Jupiter for a hundred thousand years, perhaps.'

Berg shook her head. 'Damn it. I should feel happier, I guess. We've saved the human race! . . . But what a cost.'

Jaar inclined his head towards her with awkward tenderness. 'Miriam, I think the first builders of this old henge – had they been able to imagine it – would have been happy with such a monument as that orbiting menhir.'

'Maybe.' Miriam looked around at what was left of the earth-craft. The Xeelee-material huts of the Friends had been flattened like canvas tents in a gale; she could see Friends picking sadly through the debris. Although the earth-craft's essential life-support equipment had survived inside the singularity-plane chamber, she knew that most of the Friends' personal possessions had been abandoned up here during the assault: their records of families and places lost fifteen centuries in the future – much that made life worth living from day

187

to day, when there was time for less weighty concerns than the fate of the universe.

Berg found herself shivering; her chest and lungs – which had not healed properly following her leap out to the edge of the atmosphere during the attack – ached dully, a constant, brooding presence. And the air of the craft was noticeably thinner, now. The weakening of the earth-craft's gravity field, as generated by the devastated plane of singularities, was marked; in some places the craft had been rendered virtually uninhabitable. The Friends' latest estimate was that fully forty per cent of their stock of singularities had been fired or lost while the Spline starbreakers had riffled through the craft's defences like fingers through paper. Many of the singularities launched before Berg had made it into the dome had hit their primary target. Jupiter, it seemed, had probably been seeded with enough singularities to cause its ultimate implosion, and – one day, centuries away – there would be a single, spinning singularity on the site now occupied by the greatest planet. But the singularity wouldn't be of the right size, or the right spin, or whatever the hell were the mysterious criteria of success the Friends had laid down for themselves. And now there weren't enough singularities left for them to finish the job.

'So,' she said to Jaar. 'What next, for the Friends of Wigner?'

He smiled a little wistfully, his large, fragile-looking head swivelling as he surveyed the battered earth-craft. 'The craft has suffered too much damage to remain habitable for long –'

'Atmosphere leakage?'

He looked at her. 'Yes, but more significantly the loss of the hyperdrive when the construction-material dome was crushed –' He closed his long fingers into a fist. 'And without the hyperdrive we have no effective radiation shielding. This skimpy blanket of atmosphere will scarcely suffice to protect us in Jovian space, and I doubt if we could survive even one close encounter with the Io flux-tube.'

'Right.' Berg looked up at the sky nervously; suddenly her situation – the fact that she was standing on a lump of rock, lost in orbit around Jupiter, *with nothing over her head but a few wisps of gas* – seemed harshly real; the sky seemed very close, very threatening.

'We'll have to evacuate, of course,' Jaar said stiffly. 'We will accept assistance from your contemporaries, Miriam. If we may.'

'You needn't fear,' she said as kindly as she could. 'I'll speak to Michael, if you'll let me; he can intercede with the authorities. There are plenty of ships in the area.'

'Thank you.'

'And then what, Jaar?'

'Then we go on.' His brown eyes were pale and intense and filled once more with unshakable faith; she found herself returning his gaze uncomfortably. 'We find a way to resume the Project.'

'But, Jaar –' She shook her head. 'Your Project has nearly brought disaster down on us all already. Hasn't it? You mustn't lose sight of this simple fact, my friend – *we were lucky to defeat the Qax invasion from the future*. If they hadn't been so slow to react, so complacent, so sure we posed no threat to them – then they could have destroyed the race. Is your Project worth such a risk again?'

Jaar replied with intensity, 'Berg, your words in the singularity chamber, at the height of the struggle with the Spline – that I must survive, in order to fight another day, to continue with the Project – changed me, convinced me. Yes, the Project is worth all of that. It's worth any risk – believe me, *any price*.'

189

'Look, I said all that when the roof was caving in. Literally. It was a ploy, Jaar. I was trying to manipulate you, to get you to fight, to make you do what I wanted you to do.'

'I know that.' He smiled. 'Of course I know that. But the motives behind your words don't reduce their truth. Don't you see that?'

She studied his long, certain face, and wrapped her arms closely around her, troubled.

Harry Poole, downloaded into the nervous system of the Spline, was in agony.

Jesus Christ . . .

The Spline's body and sensorium encased him like the inside of his own (corporeal) head. He felt its vast, intimidating bulk all around him; the toughened outer flesh-hull felt as if it were third-degree burnt; the pits for weapons and sensors felt like open wounds.

The Spline must be in constant, continual pain, he realized; yes, they had been adapted for survival in space and hyperspace, but clumsily, he saw now. He felt like an amputee, nerve ends crudely welded to steamhammers and jacks.

Was this a price worth paying, even for special longevity? . . . And the Qax must have endured this horror, too. Then again, he thought, perhaps pain had a different meaning for one as alien as a Qax.

The shock of Poole's crude attack had been enough to kill the Spline. The pain Harry suffered now was like the agony of a new birth into a universe of darkness and terror.

. . . And yet, as he became accustomed to the size and scale of the Spline, to the constant howl of pain, Harry became aware of – compensating factors.

Some of his sensors – even some of the Spline's

ancient, original eyes, like the one ravaged by Jasoft Parz – still worked. He saw the stars through the eyes of a sentient starship; they were remote yet accessible, like youthful ideals. He could still turn; the Spline could roll. Vast, hidden flywheels of bone moved somewhere inside him, and he felt the centrifugal wrench of rotation as if the stars themselves were rolling around him, tugging.

And, burning like a fire in his gut, he felt the power of the hyperdrive. Cautiously he flexed those strange, indirect muscles; and he thrilled at the power he could direct – the power to unravel the dimensions of space-time itself.

Yes, there was grandeur in being a Spline.

He opened pixel-eyes inside the lifedome of the wrecked *Crab*. His son was staring up at him. 'I can fly,' Harry said.

Jasoft Parz had shed his skinsuit, snakelike; now he floated in the air, one of Michael's roomier dressing gowns billowing around him. 'From what your companion Berg reports, these Friends of Wigner sound determined to revive their Project.'

Michael Poole lay back in his couch in the *Crab*'s lifedome and steepled his fingers behind his head. 'But the Friends are going to need access to singularity-manufacturing technology on an industrial scale, if they are to rebuild their earth-craft. And that surely means keeping the Interface access to the future open. We simply don't have the infrastructure for such an endeavour, in this time period.'

Harry, his huge Virtual head floating in the air above Poole's couch, nodded wisely. 'But then we're leaving the door unlocked against whatever else the Qax choose to throw down their wormhole pipe at us. Not to mention any companions of Miss Splendid Isolation over there.' He nodded towards Shira; the girl sat at a data console scrolling idly through some of Michael's research results, studiously ignoring the conversation.

Parz said, 'The Qax were utterly complacent in their invasion of this timeframe. And so – perhaps – no message, no report of the disaster, was sent back through the Interface to the future. But the Qax Occupation authorities will surely send through more probes, to investigate the outcome. We have bought time with our victory, but nothing more, as long as the Interface remains open.'

Shira looked up. 'Are you so sure you can close the portal?' she asked quietly. 'You designed it, Michael Poole; you must know that spacetime wormholes are not hinged hatches one can open and close at will.'

'We'll find a way, if we have to,' Michael said seriously.

'And if the Qax, or the Friends of the future, choose not to allow it?'

'Believe me. We'll find a way.'

Parz nodded, his green eyes narrowing. 'Yes. But perhaps we should begin considering now how to do such a thing. We may need the option rapidly, should we decide to use it – or should it become necessary to do so.'

Harry opened a pixel-blurred mouth and laughed. 'In case of emergency, break laws of physics.'

'Start working on it, Harry,' Michael said wearily. 'Shira, it's not impossible. Wormholes are inherently unstable. Active feedback has to be built into the design, to enable a hole to endure . . .'

But Shira had turned away again and was bent over her data. In the semi-darkness of the lifedome, with her face lit from beneath by the pink-blue glow of Poole's old data, her eyes were huge and liquid.

She was shutting them out once more.

'If only the Friends would let us in on their secret,' Michael said, half to himself. 'Then perhaps we could assess the risks, analyse the potential benefits against the costs of allowing them to go ahead.'

'But they won't,' Harry said. 'All they'll tell us is how the Project will make it all right in the end.'

'Yes,' Parz said. 'One senses from their words that it is as if the Project will not merely justify any means, any sacrifice – but will somehow *nullify the sacrifice itself*, in its development.' He looked at Michael. 'Is that possible?'

Michael sighed, feeling very tired, very old; the weight of centuries pressed down on him, evidently unnoticed by the Virtual of his father, by this faded bureaucrat, by the baffling, enigmatic girl from fifteen centuries away. 'If they won't tell us what they're up to, maybe we can try to work it out. We know that the core of the Project is the implosion, the induced gravitational collapse of Jupiter, by the implanting of seed singularities.'

'Yes,' Parz said. 'But there is a subtle design. We know already that the precise form of that collapse – the parameters of the resulting singularity – is vital to the success of the Project. And that's what they hoped to engineer with their singularity bullets.'

Harry frowned hugely. 'What's the point? One singularity is much like another. Isn't it? I mean, a black hole is black.'

Michael shook his head. 'Harry, a lot of information gets lost, destroyed, when a black hole forms from a collapsing object. A black hole forming is like an irruption of disorder into the universe. But there are still three distinguishing quantities associated with any hole: its mass, its electrical charge and its spin.'

A non-rotating, electrically neutral hole, Michael said,

would have a spherical event horizon – the Schwarzs-child solution to Einstein's ancient, durable equations of general relativity. But a rotating, charged object left behind a Kerr-Newman hole: a more general solution to the equations, a non-spherical horizon.

Parz was performing gentle, weightless somersaults; he looked like a small, sleek animal. 'Kerr-Newman predicts that if one may choose mass, charge and spin, one may sculpt event horizons.'

Harry smiled slowly. 'So you can customize a hole. But my question still stands: so what?'

'One could go further,' Parz said, still languidly somersaulting. 'One could construct a naked singularity.'

'A *naked* singularity?'

Michael sighed. 'All right, Harry. Think of the formation of a hole again: the implosion of a massive object, the formation of an event horizon.

'But, *within* the event horizon, the story isn't over yet. The matter of the dead star keeps imploding; nothing – not pressure from the heat of the core, not even the Pauli exclusion principle – can keep it from collapsing all the way.'

Harry frowned. 'All the way to what?'

'A singularity. A flaw in spacetime; a place where spacetime quantities – mass/energy density, space curvature – all go off the scale, to infinity. Inside a well-behaved black hole, the singularity is effectively cloaked from the rest of the universe by the event horizon. The horizon renders us safe from the damage the singularity can do. But there are ways for singularities to form *without* a cloaking event horizon – to be 'naked'. If a star is spinning rapidly enough before its collapse, for instance . . . Or if the mass distribution is not compact enough in the first place – if it is elongated, or spiky.

'The singularity in such a solution wouldn't be a point,

as would form at the centre of a spherically symmetric, non-rotating star. Instead, the material of the star would collapse to a thin disc – like a pancake – and the singularity would form within the pancake, and along a spike through the axis of the pancake – a spindle of flawed spacetime.

'The naked singularity would be unstable, probably – it would rapidly collapse within an event horizon – but it would last long enough to do a lot of damage –'

Harry frowned. 'I don't like the sound of that. What damage?'

Poole locked his hands behind his head. 'How can I explain this? Harry, it's all to do with *boundary conditions* . . .'

Spacetime could only evolve in an orderly and predictable way if its boundaries, in space and time, were themselves orderly. The boundaries had to satisfy what were called 'Cauchy conditions'; causality itself could only flow from stable Cauchy boundaries.

There were three types of boundary: in the beginning there was the initial singularity – the Big Bang, from which the universe expanded. That was one boundary: the start of time.

Then there were boundaries at infinity: *spacelike infinity* contained all the places infinitely remote from the observer . . . and then, far ahead, at *timelike infinity*. At the end of all worldlines.

The initial singularity, and the boundaries at spacelike and timelike infinity, were all Cauchy boundaries . . .

But there was another class of boundary.

Naked singularities.

*

'It sounds fantastic,' Harry said.

'Maybe it is. But nobody can think of any reason why such objects shouldn't form. There are some quite easy ways for this to happen, if you wait long enough. You know that black holes aren't really "black", that they have a temperature –'

'Yes. Hawking evaporation. Just like the holes in the earth-craft.'

'Small holes like those in the earth-craft's singularity plane will simply implode when they have evaporated completely. But in the far future, when the singularities at the heart of galaxy-mass holes begin to emerge from within their evaporating horizons . . .

'Harry, naked singularities are *non-Cauchy boundaries* to spacetime. There is no order, no pattern to the space-time which might evolve from a naked singularity; we can't make any causal predictions about events. Some theorists hold that if a naked singularity were to form then spacetime – the universe – would simply be destroyed.'

'Jesus. Then maybe they can't form after all?'

'You should have been a philosopher, Harry.'

'I should?'

'That's the principle of Cosmic Censorship – that there's something out there, something like the Pauli principle maybe, which will stop the formation of naked flaws. That's one theory.'

'Yeah. But who is this Cosmic Censor? And can we trust him?'

'The trouble is that we can think of too many ways for naked singularities to be formed. And nobody can think of a particularly intelligent way for Cosmic Censorship to come about . . .'

Parz, hovering, had listened to all this with eyes closed. 'Indeed. And perhaps that is the goal of the Friends.'

Michael felt the pieces of the puzzle sliding around in his head. 'My God,' he said softly. 'They've hinted at a power over history. Do you think they could be so stupid?' He looked up at the Virtual. 'Harry, maybe the Friends are trying to change history using a naked singularity . . .'

'But they could never control it,' Parz said, eyes still closed. 'It would be utterly random. At best, like lobbing a grenade into a political discussion. It will change the agenda, yes, but in an utterly discontinuous fashion. And at worst —'

'At worst they could wreck spacetime,' Michael said.

Harry looked down at him, serious and calm. 'What do we do, Michael? Do we help them?'

'Like hell,' Michael said quietly. 'We have to stop them.'

Shira looked up from her data screens, her long neck seeming to uncoil. 'You don't understand,' she said calmly. 'You're wrong.'

'Then you'll have to explain it to me,' Michael said tiredly. 'Harry, do you have that option I asked for?'

Harry's smile was strained. 'We can close the Interface, the AIs say. But I don't understand how. And I don't think you're going to like the solution.'

Michael felt an enormous weight, oppressive, seeming to strive to crush his chest. 'I don't like any of this. But we're going to do it anyway. Harry, start when you can.'

He closed his eyes and lay back on the couch, hoping for sleep to claim him. After a few seconds the surge of the Spline's insystem drive pressed him deeper into the cushions.

13

At the zenith, the Interface portal was a tiny, growing flower of electric blue. The Spline ship was already within the thousand-mile region of exotic space, the squeezed vacuum which surrounded the wormhole mouth.

Jasoft Parz settled, birdlike, onto the deck in the new artificial gravity of the Spline drive; he took a seat and watched Michael closely, his green eyes sharp, fascinated.

Shira got out of her chair and walked unsteadily across the deck. Her eyes were huge, bruised, the shape of her skull showing through her thin flesh. 'You must not do this,' she said.

Michael began, 'My dear –'

Harry cut in, 'Michael, we're in the middle of a storm of messages. I'm surprised the hull of the dome hasn't burned off under comm-laser fire . . . I think you'll have to deal with this. All the ships within a thousand miles are aware we're moving, and a dozen different authorities want to know what the hell we're doing.'

'Can any of them stop us before we reach the Interface?'

Harry considered. 'Probably not. The Spline, even disabled as it is, is so damn big it would have to be blown out of the sky to be stopped. And there's no armour heavy enough to do that, in range.'

'Okay. Ignore them.'

'And we're getting messages from the earth-craft,' Harry reported. 'Also inquiring politely as to what we think we're doing.'

Shira's hands twisted together. 'You must listen to them, Michael.'

'Answer me honestly, Shira. Can the Friends do anything to stop us?'

Her mouth worked and her eyes seemed heavy, as if she could barely restrain hysterical tears; and Michael felt an absurd, irrational urge to comfort her. 'No,' she said at last, quietly. 'Not physically, no. But –'

'Then ignore them too.' Michael thought it over. 'In fact, Harry, I want you to disable the whole damn comms panel . . . Any equipment the Spline is carrying too. Permanently; I want you to trash it. Can you do that?'

Again a short hesitation. 'Sure, Michael,' Harry said uncertainly. 'But – are you sure that's such a good idea?'

'Where we're going we're not going to need it,' Michael said. 'It's just a damn distraction. In,' he studied the zenith, 'what, forty minutes? –'

'Thirty-eight,' Harry said gloomily.

'– we're going to enter the Interface. And we're going to close it. And there's nothing more anybody can say that will make a bit of difference to that.'

'I'm not going to argue,' Harry urged, 'but – Michael – *what about Miriam?*'

'Miriam's a distraction,' Michael said firmly. 'Come on, Harry, do it. I need your support.'

There was a silence of a few seconds. Then: 'Done,' Harry said. 'We're all alone, Michael.'

'You are a fool,' Shira told Michael coldly.

Michael sighed and tried to regain a comfortable

posture on his couch. 'It's not the first time I've been called that.'

'Might be the last, though,' Parz said dryly.

'You think you are solving the problem, with one bold, audacious stroke,' Shira said, her water-blue eyes fixed on Michael's face. 'You think you are fearless, in the face of unknown dangers – an encounter with the future, even with death. But you are not fearless. You are afraid. You fear even *words*. You fear the words of your contemporaries – how many lectures have I endured on how important it was that we should allow you into our confidence . . . that we should share the immense problems with which we grappled? And now you – as arrogant as you are foolish – turn your back even on your own kind. You fear the words of the Friends themselves – even of me – you fear the logic, the *truth* in our convictions.'

Michael massaged the bridge of his nose, wishing he didn't feel so damned tired. 'Quite a speech,' he said.

She drew herself upright. 'And you fear yourself. For fear of your own weakness of resolve, you dare not even consider the possibility of consulting the one closest to you, Miriam, who is less than a light-second away. You would rather, as you put it, "trash" your comms equipment than –'

'Enough,' Michael snapped.

She drew back a little at the sharpness of his tone, but she held her ground; pale eyes glittered from her bony face.

Michael said, 'To hell with any of that. It's academic, Shira. The rules have changed; the outside universe might as well not exist as far as what happens to this ship from now on is concerned; we've established that. There's only the four of us now – you, me, Parz and Harry –'

'– and several hundred drones,' Harry put in uncertainly, 'who I'm having a certain amount of difficulty controlling –'

Michael ignored him. 'Just the four of us, Shira, in this bubble of air and warmth. And the only way this ship is going to get turned aside is if you – *you* – convince me, and the others, that your Project is worth the incalculable risk it entails.' He studied her, trying to gauge her reaction. 'Well? You have thirty-eight minutes.'

'Thirty-six,' Harry said.

Shira closed her eyes and drew in a deep, shuddering breath. 'All right,' she said. She crossed the deck to her chair, her gait stiff and ungainly, and sat down.

Michael, watching her, felt himself come alive with anticipation, rejuvenated by the prospect of having his questions answered at last.

Shira talked to them of Eugene Wigner, and of the von Neumann catastrophe.

Like the alive-dead condition of Schrödinger's cat, events remained in a state of unreality until observed by a conscious observer. But each act of observation merely added another layer of potentiality to the core events, themselves unrealized until observed in turn.

The chains of quantum functions, in Wigner's view, extended to infinity in an unending chain, an infinite regress.

'Thus, the paradox of Wigner's friend,' Shira said.

Michael shook his head impatiently. 'But this is pure philosophical debate,' he said. 'Wigner himself believed that the regress was not infinite . . . that the chain of wave-functions terminates as soon as a conscious mind makes an observation.'

'That is one view,' Shira said quietly. 'But there are others . . .'

Shira described the theory of the 'participatory universe'.

Life – intelligent life – was, under this hypothesis, essential for the very existence of the universe. 'Imagine a myriad of box-cat-friend chains of quantum functions, all extending through time, without end. Constantly,' Shira said, 'life – consciousness – is calling the universe into existence by the very act of observing it.'

Consciousness was like an immense, self-directed eye, a recursive design developed by the universe to invoke its own being.

And if this were true, the goal of consciousness, of life, said Shira, must be to gather and organize data – all data, everywhere – to observe and actualize all events. For without actualization there could be no reality.

Arising from a million chance beginnings, like the stirring of the chemical soup of Earth's ancient seas, life had spread – was continuing to spread – and to observe, to gather and record data using every resource available.

'We live in an era somewhere near the start of the contact between species, on an interstellar scale,' Shira said. 'There is war, death, destruction, genocide. But one can, from a Godlike perspective, regard it all as interfacing – as a sharing, a pooling, of information.

'Ultimately, surely, the squabbling species of our day will resolve their childish differences – differences of special prejudice, of narrow interests, of inadequate perception – and move together, perhaps under the leadership of the Xeelee, towards the ultimate goal of life: the gathering and recording of all data, the observation and invocation of the universe itself.'

More and more resources would be devoted to this goal – not just in extent, as life spread from its myriad points of origin, but in depth and scope. At last all the energy sources available for exploitation, from the gravitational potential of galactic superclusters down to the zero-point energy inherent in space itself, would be suborned to the great project of consciousness.

Shira described the future of the universe.

In a few billion years – a blink of cosmic time – Earth's sun would leave the Main Sequence of stars, its outer layers ballooning, swallowing the remains of the planets. Humanity would move on, of course, abandoning the old in favour of the new. More stars would form, to replace those which had failed and died . . . but the formation rate of new stars was already declining exponentially, with a half-life of a few billion years.

After about a thousand billion years, no more stars would form. The darkened galaxies would continue to turn, but chance collisions and close encounters would take their cumulative toll. Planets would 'evaporate' from their parent suns, and stars would evaporate from their galaxies. Those stars remaining in the time-ravaged star systems would lose energy, steadily, by gravitational radiation, and coalesce at last into immense, galactic-scale black holes.

And those holes themselves would coalesce, into holes on the scale of galactic clusters and superclusters; from all across the universe the timelines would converge, merging at last into the great singularities.

But life would prevail, said Shira, continuing to exploit with ever-increasing efficiency the universe's residual sources of energy. Such as the dim shining of the star-corpses, kept at a few degrees above absolute zero by the slow decay of protons.

And there would still be work to be done.

Black hole evaporation would continue, with the eventual shrinking and disappearance of event horizons even on the scale of galaxies and clusters of galaxies; and naked singularities would emerge into the spreading sweep of spacetime.

Perhaps the universe could not exist beyond the formation of a naked singularity. Perhaps the formation of such a flaw would cause the cessation of time and space, the ending of being.

'And perhaps,' Shira said, 'life's purpose, in the later stages of the evolution of the universe, is to manipulate event horizons in order to prevent the formation of naked singularities.'

'Ah.' Parz smiled. 'Another elegant idea. So our descendants might be retrained to work as Cosmic Censors.'

'Or as Cosmic Saviours,' Michael said dryly.

Harry asked, sounding awed, 'How do you manipulate event horizons?'

'No doubt there are lots of ways,' Michael said. 'But even now we can imagine some fairly crude methods. Such as forcing black holes to merge before they get a chance to evaporate.'

'The Wigner paradox is inescapable,' Shira said. The chains of unresolved quantum states would build on and on, growing like flowers, extending into the future, until the observations of the cosmos-spanning minds to come would rest on aeon-thick layers of history, studded with the fossils of ancient events. 'At last,' Shira said, her voice steady and oddly flat, 'life will cover the universe, still observing, still building the regressing chains of quantum functions. Life will manipulate the dynamic evolution of the cosmos as a whole. One can anticipate the pooled resources of life exploiting even the last energy resource, the sheer energy of the expansion of spacetime itself . . .

'Consciousness must exist as long as the cosmos itself – for without observation there can be no actualization, no existence – and, further, consciousness must become coextensive with the cosmos, in order that *all* events may be observed.'

Parz laughed softly, wondering. 'What a vision. Girl, how old are you? You sound a thousand years old.'

But, Shira went on, the chains of quantum functions would finally merge, culminate in a final state: at the last boundary to the universe, at timelike infinity.

'And at timelike infinity resides the Ultimate Observer,' Shira said quietly. 'And the last Observation will be made —'

'Yes,' Parz said, 'and so collapsing all the chains of quantum functions, right back through time – through the wreckage of the galaxies, down to the present and on into history, past Wigner, his friend, the cat and its box – what a charming notion this is —'

'Retrospectively, the history of the universe will be actualized,' Shira said. '*But not until the final Observation.*' For the first time since resuming her seat she turned to Michael. 'Do you understand the implications of this, Michael Poole?'

He frowned. 'These ideas are staggering, of course. But you've gone one step further, haven't you, Shira? There's still another hypothesis you've made.'

'I . . . Yes.' She bowed her head in an odd, almost prayerful attitude of respect. 'It is impossible for us to believe that the Ultimate Observer will simply be a passive eye. A camera, for all of history.'

'No,' Michael said. 'I think you believe that the Ultimate Observer will be able to *influence* the actualization. Don't you? You believe that the Observer will have the power to study all the nearly-infinite potential histories of the universe, stored in the regressing chains of quantum functions. And that the Observer will select, actualize a history which is – what?'

'Which is simply the most aesthetically pleasing, perhaps,' Parz said in his dry, aged way.

'Which maximizes the potential of being,' Shira said. 'Or so we believe. Which makes the cosmos through all of time into a shining place, a garden free of waste, pain and death.' She lifted her head abruptly. Michael was moved by the contrast between the skeletal gauntness of the girl's intense face and the beauty – the power, the wistfulness – of her concepts.

Harry said, his voice heavy with wonder, 'A god at the end of time. Is it possible?'

Michael found he wanted to reach the girl, and he tried to put tenderness into his voice. 'I understand you now, I think,' he said. 'You believe that none of this – our situation here, the Qax occupation of Earth, the Qax time-invasion – is real. It's all transitory, in a sense; we are simply forced to endure the motion of our conscious-ness along one of the chains of quantum functions which you believe will be collapsed, discarded, by your Ultimate Observer, in favour of –'

'Heaven,' Harry said.

'No, nothing so crude,' Michael said. He tried to imagine it, to look beyond the words. 'Harry, if she's right, the ultimate state – the final mode of being of the cosmos – will consist of global and local optimization; of the maximizing of potential, everywhere and at every moment, from the beginning of time.' Shining, Shira had said. Yes, shining would surely be a good word for such an existence . . . Michael closed his eyes and tried to evoke such a mode; he imagined this shoddy reality burning away to reveal the grey light of the underlying optimal state.

Tears prickled gently at his closed eyes. If one were vouchsafed a glimpse of such a state, he thought, then surely one would, on being dragged back to the mire of this unrealized chain of being, go insane.

If this was the basis of the faith of the Friends, then no wonder the Friends were so remote, so intense – so careless of their everyday lives, of the pain and death of others. History as it existed was nothing more than

206

a shabby prototype of the global optimization to come, when the Ultimate Observer discarded all inferior worldlines.

And no wonder then, he thought, the Friends were so leached of humanity. Their mystical vision had removed all significance from their own lives – the only lives they could experience, whatever the truth of their philosophy – and it had rendered them deeply flawed, less than human. He opened his eyes and studied Shira. He saw again the patient intensity which resided inside this fragile girl – and he saw now how damaged she was by her philosophy.

She was not fully alive, and perhaps never could be; he pitied her, he realized.

'All right, Shira,' he said tenderly. 'Thank you for telling me so much.'

Parz sighed, almost wistfully; his small, closed face showed a refined distress. 'But she hasn't yet told us all of it. Have you, girl?' With an edge in his voice, he went on, 'I mean, if you truly believe such a wondrous vision – that the history we have lived through, the present and future we must endure – are merely prototypes for some vast, perfect version which will one day be imposed on us from the end of time – then what is the Project all about? Why do you need to do anything to change your condition in the here-and-now? Why not simply endure this pain, let it end, and wait for it all to be put right at the end of things?'

She shook her head. 'In my time, humans are help-lessly subjugated to the Qax. We were able to assemble the resources for our rebellion, but it was only the fortu-itous arrival of your ship from the past which gave us the opportunity to do so.

'Such a rebellion could never happen again.

'Michael Poole, we believe the Qax Occupation will result, at last, in the decline of man. The Qax –

inadvertently, perhaps – will destroy humanity. And thereby they will terminate all possible timelines in which humanity survives the Occupation Era, joins the greater, maturing community of species which is to come, and adds to the wisdom of those mighty races at the end of time. The Qax will stop the transmission of any data about what humans were and might have been into the future. This is a crime on the largest of scales – and would be worth opposing even if we were not of the species affected . . .

'But we are. And we believe we have to thwart the Qax, to safeguard the future role of humanity.'

Poole pulled his lip. 'Jasoft, what do you make of this diagnosis?'

Parz spread his hands. 'She may be right. The Qax of my era weren't planning for our destruction before this disastrous sequence of events, ironically initiated by the Friends themselves – we've been too useful, economically. But perhaps in the end, we could not have survived an extended subjugation . . .

'And, looking ahead, we know that Shira's prediction must come true, but in ways she could not anticipate. The human Jim Bolder will cause the destruction of the Qax home world, drive them to diaspora. After this, it seems, the elimination of humanity will become a racial goal for the Qax.'

Poole nodded; he'd studied Shira's reactions throughout this discourse, but her face was blank, unreacting, blandly pretty. *She's not listening*, he realized. *Perhaps she can't.*

'Very well. Then, Shira, tell us how turning Jupiter into a black hole will help you achieve your aims. Is the singularity to be some form of super-weapon?'

'No,' Shira said calmly. 'Such is not our intention. Not directly.'

'No,' said Michael, staring at the girl. 'You're not

208

weapons-manufacturers, or warriors. Are you? I think you see yourself as part of the great upwards streaming of life, towards this marvellous, cosmic future you've described. I think you want to preserve something. Information of some kind. And send it beyond the current perilous era into this distant, glorious future, when those wise Observers of the universe will pick up your message and understand its true meaning.'

Parz was staring at him, baffled.

Michael said, 'Jasoft, I think they are turning Jupiter into a vast time capsule. They're constructing a black hole; a black hole which will evaporate in – what? Ten to power forty, fifty years from now? Jupiter will be like a vast tomb, timed to open. A naked singularity will be exposed. These cosmic engineers, these tinkerers with the dynamic evolution of the universe, will come to investigate; to extinguish the peril exposed to the universe and its future/past.'

'Ah.' Jasoft smiled. 'And when they do come, they will find a message. A message left for them by the Friends.'

Harry laughed. 'This conversation gets more and more bizarre. What will this message say? How do you strike up a conversation with god-like cosmic designers ten to power forty years in the future? "Hello. We were here, and had a hell of a lot of trouble. What about you?"'

Michael smiled. 'Oh, you might be a bit more imaginative than that. What if you stored the human genome in there, for instance? The future consciousness could reconstruct the best of the race from that. And with a bit of tinkering you could store the "message" in the consciousness of the reconstructed humans. Imagine that, Harry; imagine emerging from some fake womb, with your head full of memories of this brief, glorious youth of the universe – and into a cosmos in which the formation, life and death of even the last, shrivelled star is a memory, logarithmically distant . . .'

Shira smiled now. 'There is no limit, given the technology,' she said. 'One could imagine converting an Earth-mass to data, lodging it within the event horizon. One would have available ten to power sixty-four bits – equivalent to the transcription of ten to power thirty-eight human personalities. Michael, one might imagine storing every human who ever lived, beyond the reach of the Qax and other predators.'

'But how would you store the data? We know already that a black hole is a vast source of entropy; if an object of whatever complexity implodes into a hole, all bits of data about it are lost to the outside universe save its charge, mass and spin –'

'Singularities themselves are complex objects,' Shira said. 'Unimaginably so. Our understanding of them has advanced enormously since your time. It may be possible to store data in the structure of the spacetime flaw itself –'

'But,' Parz said, his round, weak face broken by a sly smile, 'with respect, my dear, you still haven't told us precisely what your message to these superbeings of the future would be. Even if you succeeded in transmitting it.'

Michael settled back on his couch. 'Why, that much is obvious,' he said.

Shira watched him, utterly erect and tense. 'Is it?'

'You're trying to get a message to the Ultimate Observer.' He heard Parz call out wordlessly, but he pressed on. 'You want to influence the way the Observer selects the optimal lifeline of the cosmos; you want to ensure that data about humanity reaches the post-Qax future, and that the Observer selects worldlines in favour of humanity.' Michael smiled. 'I'm right, aren't I? I have to admire your capacity for thinking big, Shira.'

Shira nodded, stiffly. 'Our goal is a valid one, from a racial point of view.'

He inclined his head in return. 'Oh, certainly. None more valid. And once the final Observation takes place, the events we have endured will not have taken place, and the means you have employed are justified . . . because if the end is met, *the means won't even have occurred.*'

'It's utterly outrageous,' Parz said, green eyes sparkling. 'But wonderful! I love it.'

Shira sat silently, her eyes still locked disconcertingly on Michael's.

'Well, at least we know what's going on now,' Harry said brightly. 'But now comes the difficult bit. Do we help them . . . or try to stop them?'

The dot of blue light at the zenith had grown to the size of a fist.

Shira shrugged, almost casually. 'I have no more influence to exert on you. I can only rely on your wisdom.'

'Right.' Michael pursed his lips. 'But you weren't so keen on trusting to that wisdom earlier, were you?'

'We did not believe you would understand,' she said simply. 'We calculated it was more likely to yield success if we proceeded alone.'

'Yes,' said Parz coldly. 'Perhaps you were wise to attempt such a course, my dear. I have learned that these people, from fifteen centuries before our shared era, are behind us in knowledge and some experiences, but are our peers – more than our peers – in wisdom. I suspect you knew what the reaction of these people would be to your schemes; you knew they would oppose you.'

Shira looked at Michael uncertainly.

He said, somewhat reluctantly, unwilling to be cruel

211

to this young, earnest girl, 'He's talking about hubris, Shira. Arrogance.'

'We are attempting to avert the extinction of the species,' Shira said, her voice fragile.

'Maybe. Shira, to my dying day I will honour the courage, the ingenuity of the Friends. To have constructed the earth-craft under the very eyes of the Qax; to have hurled yourselves unhesitatingly into an unknown past . . . Yes, you have courage and vision. But – *what right do you have to tinker with the history of the universe?* What gives *you* the wisdom to do that, Shira – regardless of the validity of your motives? Listen, you scared us all to death when we thought you were just trying to create a naked singularity. That would have set off an unpredictable explosion of acausality. But in fact you're trying to disrupt causality deliberately – and on the largest scale.'

'You dare not oppose us,' Shira said. Her face was a mask of anger, of almost childish resentment.

Michael closed his eyes. 'I don't think I dare allow you to go ahead. Look, Shira, maybe the whole logic of your argument is flawed. For a start, the philosophical basis for the whole thing – that particular resolution of the Wigner paradox – is speculative, just one among many.'

Parz nodded. 'And where is the evidence of this advance of life that you've based your hopes on? The most advanced species we know are the Xeelee. But the Xeelee don't fit the description, give no evidence of sharing the goals you've advanced. They show no signs of having the gathering and recording of data as their key racial motive. Indeed their goal seems to be very different – the construction of their Kerr-metric gateway to another universe – and they seem prepared to destroy data, in the form of structures on an intergalactic scale, to do it. So how will this cosmic eye, this Ultimate

Observer of yours, ever come about, if even the Xeelee don't want to lead us towards its formation?'

Her nostrils flared. 'You're not going to help us. You're going to try to stop us. Michael Poole, you are —'

Poole held his hands up. 'Look, don't bother insulting me again. I'm sure I'm a fool, but I'm a fool who doesn't trust himself where a final solution to the history of the universe is concerned. I'd do anything to avert the imposition of such a solution, I think.'

'Perhaps the Project won't, or can't, succeed,' Shira said. 'But it remains humanity's best and only hope of removing the Qax yoke.'

'No,' he said. He smiled, an immense sadness sweeping over him; he felt irrationally ashamed at his systematic demolition of this young person's ideals. 'That's the clinching argument, I'm afraid, Shira. The fact is, we don't need your Project.' He nodded to Parz. 'Jasoft has told us. Humans will get out from under the oppression of the Qax. It will take a long time, and will mean the near destruction of the Qax — but it will be done, we know that now, and it will come from the simple, surprising, actions of a single man. From the unpredictability of humanity.' He studied her empty face, the surface of an incomplete personality, he realized now. 'Ordinary humanity will beat the Qax in the end, Shira. But that's beyond your imagining, isn't it? We won't need your grandiose schemes to win freedom by sabotaging history.'

'But —'

'And the only way that outcome can be subverted, as far as I can see,' Michael pressed on, 'is if we leave that portal open; if we allow the Qax themselves more chances to change history — in their favour. I'm sorry I had anything to do with building the damn thing, unleashing all this trouble in the first place. Now, all I want to do is to put that right . . .'

213

'You'll be killed,' Shira said, clutching at straws.

He laughed. 'Funnily enough, that doesn't seem to matter so much any more . . . But I don't want to take you all with me, if I don't have to. Harry, give me an option to get them off before we hit.'

'Working,' Harry said calmly. 'Thirteen minutes to the portal, now.'

Parz seemed to squirm, uncomfortable, in his chair. 'I'm not certain I deserve such a reprieve,' he said.

'Then think of it as an assignment,' Michael said briskly. 'I need you to get this girl off the ship. Do you think she's going to go voluntarily?'

Parz studied Shira briefly, as she continued to stand before Michael, clenching and unclenching her small fists. 'Perhaps not,' he said sadly.

'Twelve minutes,' Harry said.

14

From a scarred, bruised socket in the elephant-grey hide of the Spline, a three-yard-wide eyeball popped into space, trailing a length of thick optic nerve. Antibody drones, squabbling and scrambling over each other, swarmed over the translucent surface of the eyeball and along the length of the nerve trunk. Red laser light sparked from the mouths of a dozen of the drones, sawing at the trunk; at last the trunk parted, with fully a yard of its length disintegrating into laser-sliced fragments. The warship surged up towards the blue mouth of the Interface portal; drones, scrabbling to hang on, slid away from the abandoned eyeball and from the severed trunk, still spitting at each other with tiny, fierce bolts of laser light.

As the Spline receded to a knot of bruised flesh, Jasoft Parz turned and surveyed the interior of the eye chamber. His only companion, the Wigner Friend girl Shira, floated somewhere near the eyeball's geometric centre, her thin body curled into a loose foetal position, her eyes half-closed. Studying her, Parz felt suddenly vulnerable in this chamber, dressed as he was only in this ill-fitting, rather worn gown of Michael Poole's. The entoptic fluid had been drained, the eyeball hurriedly pumped full of air to accommodate the two of them;

and he had forgone his skinsuit, in order to share the dangers Shira would have to face.

He shivered with a sudden chill of fear, feeling naked. He sought something to say.

'You must not fear the future, my dear. Michael Poole has done his best to preserve us from the fate he has decreed for himself. We have air in this chamber sufficient for many hours, and Poole has given us heating elements, a packet of water and food. We should survive long enough to be picked up by the craft of this era. And I've every reason to believe you'll soon be reunited with your own people, on the earth-craft.'

Now she swivelled her head to face him; her watery-blue eyes seemed bruised, as if from weeping. 'Cold comfort coming from a servant of the Qax, Jasoft Parz.'

He tried not to flinch. 'I can't blame you for that,' he said patiently. 'But such labels are behind us now, Shira. We are here, you and I, in this ancient time frame; and here, after the destruction of the Interface, we will spend the rest of our lives. You must begin to accept that, and think forward —'

'I accept I am trapped,' she said. 'I accept little else.'

'Trapped in the past? You shouldn't think of it like that. We have been brought to a new era – in many ways a better era, a golden age in man's history. Think of it, Shira; the humans of this era are looking outwards, only beginning to explore the potentialities of the universe in which they are embedded, and the resources of their own being. They have banished many of the ills, social as well as physiological – hunger, disease, untimely death, which, thanks to the Qax, our lost contemporaries endure. There are many projects here for you to —'

'You don't understand,' she snapped. 'I do not mean trapped merely in the past. I mean trapped in the *future*. Thanks to the destruction of the Project by the insane arrogance of Michael Poole, I am trapped in this single, doomed timeline.'

'Ah. Your vision of globally optimized event chains –'

'Don't speak to me of visions, collaborator.' Her words were delivered in an even, matter-of-fact tone, and were the more stinging for that. 'What visions have sustained you?'

He felt the muscles of his cheeks twitch. 'Look, Shira, I'm trying to help you. If you want to insult me, then that's fine. But sooner or later you're going to have to accept the fact that, like me, you're trapped here. In the past.'

She turned her head away again, quite gracefully, and bowed it towards her knees; her body rocked a little in the air. 'No,' she said.

He began to feel irritated. 'What do you mean, "no"? Once the damn Interface is closed down you'll have no way back to the future.'

Now, unexpectedly, she smiled. 'No short cut. No, I accept that. But there is another way back. The longer way.'

He frowned.

She went on, 'I mean to accept AntiSenescence treatment here. If I'm offered it, or can buy it. And then –'

'– And then it's a simple matter of living through fifteen centuries – *fifty generations* – waiting for the re-emergence of singularity technology. So you can start all over again. Is that what you mean?'

Her smile lingered.

'How can you think in such terms?' he demanded. 'You got to know Michael Poole; after two centuries of life his head was so full of detritus, of layers of experience, that at times he could barely function. You saw that, didn't you? Why do you think he spent decades, literally, alone in that GUTship in the cometary halo?

And you're talking, almost casually, about lasting more than seven times as long. How can any purpose endure through such an immense timescale? It's – beyond the human . . .'

The girl did not reply, but her smile lingered on, inwardly directed; and Parz, despite his superiority in years to this girl, felt as if he had become something weak and transient, a mayfly, beside the immense, burning purpose of Shira.

Harry crystallized onto the empty couch beside Michael. The image was weak and wavering, the pixels crowding and of uneven size – evidently Harry didn't have available the processing power he'd used earlier – but there was at least an illusion of solidity, of another presence in the lifedome, and Michael felt grateful enough for that.

Michael lay back on his couch, trying to achieve a state of inner, and outer, relaxation, but he was betrayed by knots of tension in his forehead, his neck, his upper back. He watched the Interface portal blossom open above his head. It spanned most of the dome now. The Spline warship, with the *Crab* embedded within, was moving along a trajectory which passed the cheek of Jupiter tangentially and from Michael's position, the portal now hung against a backdrop of velvet space, of distant, inhabited stars. The portal's clean blue-violet geometry – and the burnished-gold effect of the glimmering faces of the tetrahedron, the shadowy reflections of other times and places – were really quite beautiful.

Harry said, his voice scratchy, 'I suppose you do know what you're doing?'

Michael couldn't help but laugh. 'It's a bit late to ask that now.'

Harry cleared his throat. 'I mean, this whole caper has been improvised. I just wondered if you had any clearer ideas about your precise intentions when, say, you were ramming a lump of comet-ice down the throat of a Spline warship from the future.'

'Well, it worked, didn't it?'

'Yeah, through sheer luck. Only because the Spline was bemused by causality stress, and poor old Jasoft started setting fire to the Spline's nervous system.'

Michael smiled. 'It wasn't luck. Not really. What beat the Qax in the end was their own damned complacency. Jasoft was a loophole, a weakness, which they brought back through time with them. If it hadn't been for Jasoft Parz they would have left some other hole, another Achilles' heel for us to exploit. They were so certain they could scrape us out of the Solar System without any trouble, so certain there was nothing we could do to resist them –'

'All right, all right.' Harry threw up his ghostly hands. 'Come on, Michael. How are we going to destroy the wormhole?'

'I don't know for sure.'

'Oh, terrific.' Harry's face turned fuzzy for a moment and Michael imagined that more processing power was being diverted from the image. Now it downgraded further, until the illusion of a solid presence in the chair beside Michael was almost lost.

'Harry, is there some problem? I thought we were on routine running until we hit the Interface.'

Harry's voice came to him through a sea of phasing and static. 'It's these drones,' he said. 'They're just too damn smart.'

'I thought you had them under control. You organized them to cast off the eye chamber with Shira and Parz, to cut the nerve trunk –'

'Yeah, but I'm not experienced at handling them.

219

Remember, they're not simple remotes; they have a lot of processing power of their own. It's like – I don't know – like trying to get work done by a few thousand strong-willed ten-year-olds. Michael, one bunch of them has gone ape. They've formed into a raiding party; they're working through the carcass in search of the high-density power sources. They're being resisted by others because the damage they're doing is going to be detrimental to the functioning of the Spline in the long run. But the resistance isn't organized yet . . . and any drone which opposes them is chewed up by those damn little laser jaws of theirs.'

Michael laughed. 'What's going to be the outcome?'

'I don't know . . . The raiders are heading for the heart of the Spline, now. And I mean the heart, literally; a city-block of power-cells and muscle stumps centred around the hyperdrive unit. The area of greatest energy density. If the raiders get through there'll be hell to pay; the rest of the ship's systems will be too drained of power to be able to do anything about it, and ultimately they'll decommission the hyperdrive . . . But it might not get that far. Other drones are forming up to oppose them. It looks as if there's going to be a pitched battle, soon, somewhere in the region of the heart. But at the moment my money is on the rogue, rebel drones; the defenders just haven't got the leadership –'

Michael cut in, 'Oh, for God's sake, Harry, will you shut up about the drones? Who cares about the damn drones, at a time like this?'

Harry frowned, blurredly. 'Look, Michael, this isn't a joke. These rebels could disable the hyperdrive, out from under us. And you want to use the hyperdrive in your scheme to wreck the Interface, don't you?'

'What's the timescale for all this?'

Harry turned away, flickering. 'Twenty minutes for the battle to resolve itself. Another ten for the rebels, assuming they win, to cut their way into the heart and get to the hyperdrive and other power sources. Let's say thirty, total, at the outside, before we lose hyperdrive functionality.'

Michael pointed up at the Interface. 'And how long before we're in the guts of that thing?'

Harry thought for a few seconds. 'Six minutes, tops.'

'Okay, then. That's why you should forget about the damn drones. By the time they've done their worst it will all be over, one way or the other.'

Harry pulled a face. 'All right, point taken. But it doesn't get you out of explaining to me how you're going to blow up the Interface portal.' Harry turned his head up to the blue-glowing portal, and – with an evident surge of processing concentration – he produced blue-violet highlights on his Virtual cheekbones. 'I mean, if we simply ram that portal, the corpse of this damn ship is going to be cut up like ripe cheese, isn't it?'

'Right. I doubt if you could do much harm to a structure of exotic matter by smashing it with a lump of conventional material; the density difference would make it as absurd as trying to knock down a building by blowing it a kiss . . . We're going to enter the Interface as best we can in this tub –'

'And then what?'

'Harry, do you understand how the hyperdrive works?'

Harry grinned. 'Yes and no.'

'What's that supposed to mean?'

'It means that I've now merged with the residuum of the Spline's consciousness. And the operation of the hyperdrive is buried in there somewhere . . . But it's like working the muscles that let you stand up and walk about. Do you understand me?' He looked at Michael, almost wistfully, his face more boyish than ever. 'The

Spline core of me knows all about the hyperdrive. But the human shell of Harry, what's left of it, knows damn-all. And – I find I'm scared, Michael.'

Michael found himself frowning, disturbed by Harry's tone. 'You sound pathetic, Harry.'

'Well, I'm sorry you don't approve,' Harry said defiantly. 'But it's honest. I'm still human, son.'

Michael shook his head, impatient with the sudden jumble of emotions he found stirring inside him. 'The hyperdrive,' he said sternly. 'All right, Harry. How many dimensions does spacetime have?'

Harry opened his mouth, closed it again. 'Four. Three space, one time. Doesn't it? All wrapped up into some kind of four-dimensional sphere . . .'

'Wrong. Sorry, Harry. There are actually *eleven*. And the extra seven is what allows the hyperdrive to work . . .'

The grand unified theories of physics – the frameworks which merged gravitation and quantum mechanics – predicted that spacetime ought to assume a full eleven dimensions. The logic, the symmetry of the ideas would allow little else.

And eleven dimensions there turned out to be.

But human senses could perceive only four of those dimensions, directly. The others existed, but on a tiny scale. The seven compactified dimensions were rolled into the topological equivalent of tight tubes, with diameters well within the Planck length, the quantum limit to measurement of size.

'Well, so what? Can we observe these compactifed tubes?'

'Not directly. But, Harry, looked at another way, the tubes determine the values of the fundamental physical constants of the universe. The gravitational constant, the charge on the electron, Planck's constant, the uncertainty scale . . .'

Harry nodded. 'And if one of these tubes of compact-ification were opened up a little –'

'– the constants would change. Or,' said Michael sig-nificantly, 'vice versa.'

'You're getting to how the hyperdrive works.'

'Yes . . . As far as I can make out, the hyperdrive suppresses, locally, one of the constants of physics. Or, more likely, a dimensionless combination of them.'

'And by suppressing those constants –'

'– you can relax the compactification of the extra dimensions, locally, at least. And by allowing the ship to move a short distance in a fifth spacetime-dimension, you can allow it to traverse great distances in the con-ventional dimensions.'

Harry held up his hands. 'Enough. I understand how the hyperdrive works. Now tell me what it all means.'

Michael turned to him and grinned. 'Okay, here's the plan. We enter the Interface, travel into the wormhole –'

Harry winced. 'Let me guess. And then we start up the hyperdrive.'

Michael nodded.

The Interface portal was immense over them, now. One glimmering pool of a facet filled Michael's vision, so close that he could no longer make out the electric blue struts of exotic matter which bounded it.

'Three minutes away,' Harry said quietly.

'Okay.' As an afterthought Michael added: 'Thanks, Harry.'

'Michael – I know this won't, and mustn't, make a damn bit of difference – but I don't think there's any way I can survive this. I can't function independently of the Spline any more; I've interwoven the AI func-tionalities of Spline and *Crab* so much that if one fails, so must the other . . .'

Michael found himself reaching out to the Virtual of his father; embarrassed, he drew his hand back. 'No.

223

I know. I'm sorry, I guess. If it's any consolation I'm not going to live through it either.'

Harry's young face broke up into a swarm of pixels. 'That's no consolation at all, damn you,' he whispered distantly.

The Interface was very close now; Michael caught reflections of the Spline in that great, glimmering face, as if the facet were some immense pool into which the warship was about to plunge.

Harry crumbled into pixel dust, reformed again, edgily. 'Damn those drones,' he grumbled. 'Look, Michael, while there's enough time there's something I have to tell you . . .'

The intrasystem freighter settled over the battered, gouged-out Spline eyeball. Cargo-bay doors hung open like welcoming lips, revealing a brightly lit hold.

The eye bumped against the hold's flat ceiling, rebounding softly; a few yards of chewed-up optic nerve followed it like a grizzled remnant of umbilical cord, wrapping itself slowly around the turning eye. Then the hold doors slid shut, and the eye was swallowed.

In an airlock outside the hold, Miriam Berg pressed her face to a thick inspection window. She cradled a heavy-duty industrial-strength hand-laser, and her fingers rattled against the laser's casing as the hold's pressure equalized.

She cast her eyes around the scuffed walls of the hold with some distaste. This was the *Narlikar* out of Ganymede, an inter-moon freighter run by a tinpot two-man shipping line. She knew she shouldn't expect too much of a ship like this. The D'Arcy brothers performed a dirty, dangerous job. Normally this hold would contain water ice from Ganymede or Europa, or exotic sulphur compounds excavated with extreme peril from the stinking surface of Io. So that would explain some of the stains. But sulphur compounds didn't scratch tasteless graffiti onto the hold walls, she thought. Nor did they leave sticky patches and half-eaten meals all over – it seemed – every work surface. Still, she was lucky there had been even one ship in the area capable of coming to pick up this damn eyeball so quickly. Most of the ships in the vicinity of the Interface portal were clean-lined government or military boats – but it had been the D'Arcy brothers, in their battered old tub, who had come shouldering through the crowd to pick her up from the earth-craft in answer to the frantic, all-channel request she'd put out when she'd realized what Poole was up to.

She watched the Spline eyeball bounce around in the hold's thickening air. It was like some absurd beachball, she thought sourly, plastered with dried blood and the stumps of severed muscles. But there was a clear area – the lens? – through which human figures, tantalizingly obscure, could be seen.

Michael . . .

Now a synthesized bell chimed softly, and the door separating her from the hold fell open. Towing the laser, Berg threw herself into the eyeball-filled hold.

The air in the hold was fresh, if damn cold through the flimsy, begrimed Wignerian one-piece coverall she'd been wearing since before the Qax attack. She took a draught of atmosphere into her lungs, checking the pressure and tasting the air –

'Jesus.'

– and she almost gagged at the mélange of odours which filled her head. Maybe she should have anticipated this. The gouged-out Spline eyeball *stank* like three-week-old meat – there was a smell of burning, of scorched flesh, and subtler stenches, perhaps arising from the half-frozen, viscous purple gunk which seemed to be seeping from the severed nerve trunk. And underlying it all, of course, thanks to her hosts the D'Arcys, was the nose-burning tang of sulphur.

Every time the eyeball hit the walls of the hold, it squelched softly.

She shook her head, feeling her throat spasm at the stench. Spline ships; what a way to travel.

After one or two more bounces, air resistance slowed the motion of the sphere. The eyeball settled, quivering gently, in the air at the centre of the hold.

Beyond the Spline's clouded lens she could see movement; it was like looking into a murky fishtank. There was somebody in there, peering out at her.

It was time.

Her mind seemed to race; her mouth dried. She tried to put it all out of her head and concentrate on the task in hand. She raised her laser.

The D'Arcys, after picking her up from the earth-craft, had loaned her this hand-laser, a huge, inertia-laden thing designed for slicing ton masses of ore from Valhalla Crater, Callisto. It took both hands and the strength of all her muscles to set the thing swinging through the air to point its snout-like muzzle at the Spline eyeball, and all her strength again to slow its rotation, to steady it and aim. She wanted to set the thing hanging in the air so that – with any luck – she'd slice tangentially at the eyeball, cutting away the lens area without the beam lancing too far into the inhabited interior of the eyeball. Once the laser was aimed, she swam over and, pressing her face as close to the clouding lens as she could bear, she peered into the interior. There were two people in there, reduced to little more than stick-figures by the opacity of the dead lens material. With her open palm she slapped at the surface of the lens – and her hand broke through a crust-like

226

surface and sank into a thick, mouldering mess; she yanked her hand away, shaking it to clear it of clinging scraps of meat. 'Get away from the lens!' She shouted and mouthed the words with exaggerated movements of her lips, and she waved her hands in brushing motions.

The two unidentifiable passengers got the message; they moved further away from the lens, back into the revolting shadows.

Taking care not to touch the fleshy parts again, Berg moved away and back to her laser. She palmed the controls, setting the dispersion range for five yards. A blue-purple line of light, geometrically perfect, leapt into existence, almost grazing the cloudy lens; Berg checked that the coherence was sufficiently low that the beam did no more than cast a thumb-sized spot of light on the hold's far bulkhead.

Shoving gently at the laser, she sliced the beam down. As the opaque lens material burned and shrivelled away from laser fire, brownish air puffed out of the eyeball, dispersing rapidly into the hold's atmosphere; and still another aroma was added to the mélange in Berg's head – this one, oddly, not too unpleasant, a little like fresh leather.

A disc of lens material fell away, as neat as a hatchway. Droplets of some fluid leaked into the air from the rim of the removed lens, connecting the detached disc by sticky, weblike threads.

She still couldn't see into the meaty sphere; and there was silence from the chamber she had opened up.

Berg thumbed the laser to stillness. Absently she reached for the detached lens-stuff and pulled it from the improvised hatchway; the loops of entoptic material stretched and broke, and she sent the disc spinning away.

Then, unable to think of anything else to do, and

quite unable to go into the opening she'd made, she hovered in the air, staring at the surgically clean, leaking lip of the aperture.

Thin hands emerged, grasped the lip uncertainly. The small, sleek head of Jasoft Parz emerged into the air of the *Narlikar*. He saw Berg, nodded with an odd, stiff courtesy, and – with an ungainly grace – swept his legs, bent at the knees, out of the aperture. He shivered slightly in the fresh air outside the eyeball; he was barefoot, and dressed in a battered, begrimed dressing gown – one of Michael's, Berg realized. Parz seemed to be trying to smile at her. He hovered in the air, clinging to the aperture of the eye with one hand like an ungainly spider. He said, 'This is the second time I've been extracted from a Spline eyeball, after expecting only death. Thank you, Miriam; it's nice to meet you in the flesh.'

Berg was quite unable to reply.

Now a second figure emerged slowly from the eye. This was the Wigner girl Shira, dressed – like Berg – in the grubby remnants of a Wigner coverall. The girl perched on the lip of the aperture, her legs tucked under her, and briefly scanned the interior of the freighter's hold, her face blank. She faced Berg. 'Miriam. I didn't expect to see you again.'

'No.' Berg forced the words out. 'I . . .'

There was something like compassion in Shira's eyes – the closest approximation to human warmth Miriam had ever seen in that cold, skull-like visage – and Berg hated her for it. The Friend said, 'There's nobody else, Miriam. There's only the two of us. I'm sorry.'

Berg wanted to deny what she said, to shove past these battered, stained strangers and hurl herself headfirst into the eyeball, search it for herself. Instead she kept her face still and dug her nails into her palm; soon she felt a trickle of blood on her wrist.

Parz smiled at her, his green eyes soft. 'Miriam. They – Michael and Harry – have contrived a scheme. They are going to use the wreckage of the Spline to close the wormhole Interface, to remove the risk of any more incursions from the Qax occupation future. Or any other future, for that matter.'

'And they've stayed aboard. Both of them.'

Parz's face was almost comically solemn. 'Yes. Michael is very brave, Miriam. I think you should take comfort from –'

'Bollix to that, you pompous old fart.' Berg turned to Shira. 'Why the hell didn't he at least speak to me? He turned his comms to slag, didn't he? Why? Do you know?'

Shira shrugged, a trace of residual, human concern still evident over her basic indifference. 'Because of his fear.'

'Parz calls him brave. You call him a coward. What's he afraid of?'

Shira's mouth twitched. 'Perhaps you, a little. But mostly himself.'

Parz nodded his head. 'I think she's right, Miriam. I don't think Michael was certain he could maintain his resolve if he spoke to you.'

Berg felt anger, frustration, surge through her. Of course she'd known people die before; and her lingering memories of those times had always been filled with an immense frustration at unfinished business – personal or otherwise. There was always so much left to say that could now never be said. In a way this was worse, she realized; the bastard wasn't even dead yet but he was already as inaccessible as if he were in the grave. 'That's damn cold comfort.'

'But,' Jasoft Parz said gently, 'it's all we can offer.'

'Yeah.' She shook her head, trying to restore some sense of purpose. 'Well, we may as well go and watch the fireworks. Come on. Then let's see if these tinpot freighters run to shower cubicles . . .'

The freighter's bridge was cramped, stuffy, every flat surface coated with notes scrawled on adhesive bits of paper. Only the regal light of Jupiter, flooding into the squalid space through a clear-view port, gave the place any semblance of dignity. The D'Arcy brothers, fat, moon-faced and disconcertingly alike, watched from their control couches as Berg led her bizarre party onto their bridge. Berg said gruffly, 'Jasoft. Shira. Meet your great-grandparents.'

Then, leaving the four of them staring cautiously at each other, Miriam turned her face to the clear-view port, lifted her face to the zenith. Against the cheek of Jupiter the frame of the Interface portal was a tetrahedral stencil; and the Spline warship, the lodged wreckage of the *Crab* clearly visible even at this distance, was like a bunched fist against the portal's geometric elegance.

As she watched, the warship entered the Interface; blood-coloured sparks ringing the Spline where the battered carcass brushed the exotic-matter frame of the portal.

Berg considered raising a hand in farewell.

The sparks flared until the Spline was lost to view.

Miriam closed her eyes.

15

The lifedome of the *Crab* was swallowed by the encroaching darkness of the Interface portal. Michael, staring up through the dome, found himself cowering.

Blue-violet fire flared from the lip of the lifedome; it was like multiple dawns arising from all around Michael's limited horizon. Harry, from the couch beside Michael's, looked across fearfully. Michael said, 'That's the hull of the Spline hitting the exotic-matter framework. I'd guess it's doing a lot of damage. Harry, are you –'

The holographic Virtual of Harry Poole opened its mouth wide – impossibly wide – and screamed; the sound was an inhuman chirp that slid upwards through the frequency scales and folded out of Michael's sensorium.

The Virtual smashed into a hail of pixels and crumbled, sparkling.

The Spline shuddered as it entered the spacetime wormhole itself; Michael, helplessly gripping the straps which bound him to his couch, found it impossible to forget that the vessel which was carrying him into the future was no product of technology, but had once been a fragile, sentient, living thing.

Harry's head popped back into existence just above

Michael's face. Harry looked freshly scrubbed, his hair neatly combed. 'Sorry about that,' he said sheepishly. 'I should have anticipated the shock as we hit the exotic matter. I think I'll be okay now; I've shut down a lot of the nerve/sensor trunks connecting the central processor to the rest of the ship. Of course I've lost a lot of functionality.'

A vast sense of loss, of alienation, swept over Michael; Harry's face was an incongruously cheerful blob of animation in a vision field otherwise filled with the emptiness of a spacetime flaw. He forced himself to reply. 'I – hardly think it matters any more. As long as we can power up the hyperdrive.'

'Sure. And I've my battalions of loyal antibody drones protecting the remaining key areas of the ship; they ought to be able to hold out until it doesn't matter one way or the other.' The Virtual head plummeted disconcertingly towards Michael until it hovered a mere foot above his nose; it peered down at him with exaggerated concern. 'Are you okay, Michael?'

Michael tried to grin, to come back with a sharp reply, but the feeling of desolation was like a black, widening pool inside his head. 'No,' he said. 'No, I'm not damn well okay.'

Harry nodded, looking sage, and receded into the air. 'You have to understand what's happening to you, Michael. We're passing from one time frame to another. Remember how Jasoft Parz described this experience? The quantum functions linking you to your world – the nonlocal connections between you and everything and everybody you touched, heard, saw – are being stretched thin, broken . . . You're being left as isolated as if you'd only just been born.'

'Yes.' Michael gritted his teeth, trying to suppress a sensation of huge, psychic pain. 'Yes, I understand all of that. But it doesn't help. And it doesn't help, either, that I've just left behind Miriam, everyone and every-thing I know, without so much as a farewell. And it doesn't help that I face nothing but death; and that only the level of pain remains to be determined . . . I'm scared, Harry.'

Harry opened his mouth to speak, closed it again; convincing-looking tears brimmed in his eyes.

An unreasonable anger flared in Michael. 'Don't you get sentimental on me again, you damn – facsimile.'

Harry's grin was slight. 'Should we activate the hyperdrive?' he asked softly. 'Get this affair over and done with?'

Michael closed his eyes and shook his head, his neck muscles stiff and tight, almost rigid. 'Not yet. Wait until we're well inside the throat of the wormhole.'

Harry hesitated. 'Michael, what exactly will the hyperdrive operation do to the wormhole?'

'I don't know for sure,' Michael said. 'How can I know for sure? No one's tried such a damn fool experi-ment before. Look, a wormhole is a flaw in spacetime, kept open by threads of exotic matter. And it's an unstable flaw.

'When the hyperdrive operates, the dimensionality of spacetime is changed, locally. And if we do that inside the wormhole itself – deep inside, near the midpoint, where the stress on the flawed spacetime will be highest – I don't see how the wormhole feedback control systems can maintain stability.'

'And then what?'

Michael shrugged. 'I've no idea. But I'm damn sure the Interface will no longer be passable. And I'm hoping that the collapse we initiate will go further, Harry. Remember that more wormhole links have been set up, to the future beyond Jim Bolder and his heroics. I don't want to leave the opportunity for more Qax of that era to come back and try wrecking history again.'

'Can we close the other wormholes?'

Poole shrugged. 'Maybe. Wormholes put spacetime under a lot of stress, Harry . . .'

'. . . And us?' Harry asked gently.

Michael met the Virtual's gaze. 'What do you think? Look, I'm sorry, Harry.' He frowned. 'Well, what were you going to tell me?'

'When?'

'Your big secret. Just before we hit the exotic matter.'

Harry's head shrank a little in an odd, shy gesture. 'Ah. I was vaguely hoping you'd forgotten that.'

Michael clicked his tongue, exasperated. 'My God, Harry, we've just minutes to live and you're still a pain in the arse.'

'I'm dead.'

'. . . What?'

'I'm dead. The real Harry Poole, that is. The original.' Harry's eyes held Michael's and his tone was level, matter-of-fact. 'I've been dead thirty years, now, Michael. More, in fact.'

Michael, lost in quantum isolation, tried to make sense of this ghostly news. 'How did you – he –'

'I reacted adversely to a stage of the AS treatment. Couldn't accept it; my body couldn't take any more. One in a thousand react like that, they tell me. I lived a few more years. I aged rapidly. I, ah – I stored this Virtual as soon as I understood what was going to happen. I didn't have any specific purpose in mind for it. I didn't plan to transmit it to you. I just thought, maybe, it might be of use to you one day. A comfort, even.'

Michael frowned. 'I don't know what to say. I'm sorry. I . . . know how much your youth, your –'

'My good looks, health and potency.' Harry grinned. 'Don't be afraid to say it, Michael; I'm kind of beyond modesty. All the things I wanted to keep, which irritated you so much.'

'I know how much life meant to you.'

Harry nodded. 'Thank you. I'm thanking you for him. He – Harry – died before I, the Virtual, was animated. I share his memories up to the point where he took the Virtual copy; then there's a gap. Before the end of his life he left me a message, though.'

Michael shook his head. 'He left one of his own Virtuals a message. Well, that's my father.'

'Michael, he said he didn't fear death.' Harry looked thoughtful. 'He'd changed, Michael. Changed from the person I was, or am. I think he wanted me to tell you that, in case you ever encountered me. Perhaps he thought it would be a comfort.'

The Spline shuddered again, more violently now, and Michael, staring beyond the dome, seemed to see detail in what had previously been formlessness. Blue-white light, sparking from tortured hull-flesh, continued to flare at the edge of his vision. Fragments of light swam from a vanishing point directly above his head down the spacetime walls and, fading, shot down over his horizon. They were flashes, sheets of colourless light; it was like watching lightning behind clouds. This was radiation generated, he knew, by the unravelling of stressed spacetime, here deep in the throat of the flaw. He gripped the couch. For the first time he had a genuine sensation of speed, of limitless, uncontrollable velocity. The lifedome was a fragile, vulnerable thing above him, no more protection than a canvas tent as he plummeted through this spacetime flaw; and he tried not to cower, to hide his head from the sky which stretched over him.

'Why didn't he tell me?'

Harry's expression hardened. 'He didn't know how to tell you. He was genuinely concerned about causing you pain – I hope you believe that. But the basic reason was that the two of you haven't shared a moment of closeness, of – of *intimacy* – since you were ten years old. That's why.' He glared down at Michael. 'What did you expect? He turned to his friends, Michael.'

'I'm sorry.'

'So am I,' said Harry earnestly. 'So was he. But that was the way it was.'

'That's the trouble with living so damned long,' Michael said. 'Soured relationships last for ever.' He shook his head. 'But still . . . I'd never even have heard about it if you hadn't been transmitted to persuade me to come in from the Oort Cloud.'

'They – the multi-government committee set up to handle this incident – thought I'd have a better chance of persuading you if you didn't know; if I didn't tell you about the death.'

Michael almost smiled. 'Why the hell did they think that?'

'What do multi-government committees know about the relationship between father and son?'

The walls of the wormhole seemed to be constricting like a throat. Still the lightning-like splashes of light shone through the walls. 'I think it's time,' Michael said. 'You'll handle the hyperdrive?'

'Sure. I guess you don't need a countdown . . . Michael. You have a message.'

'What are you talking about? Who the hell can be contacting me now?'

Harry, his face straight, said, 'It's a representative of the rebel antibody drones. They're not unintelligent, Michael; somehow they've patched in to a translator circuit. They want me to let them talk to you.'

'What do they want?'

'They've ringed the hyperdrive. The drones consider it – ah, a hostage.'

'And?'

'They're willing to sue for peace. In the spirit of

interspecies harmony. They have a long list of conditions, though.' Harry frowned down at Michael. 'Do you want to hear what they are? First –'

'No. Just tell me this. Do you still control the hyperdrive?'

'Yes.'

Michael felt the tension drain out of his neck muscles, it seemed for the first time in days; a sensation of peace swept over him. He laughed. 'Tell them where they can stick their list.'

Harry's head ballooned. He smiled, young and confident. 'I think it's time. Goodbye, Michael.'

The hyperdrive engaged. The Spline warship convulsed.

Ribbons of blue-white light poured through the cracking walls of spacetime; Michael could almost feel the photons as they sleeted through the absurd fragility of the lifedome.

A lost corner of Michael's consciousness continued to analyse, even to wonder. He was seeing unbearable shear stresses in twisted spacetime resolving themselves into radiant energy as the wormhole failed. At any moment now the residual shielding of the lifedome would surely collapse; already the flesh of the Spline corpse must be boiling away. Knowing what was happening didn't really help, of course – something which, Michael thought, it was a bit late to discover.

Harry's Virtual imploded, finally, under the pressure of the godlike glare beyond the dome.

Bits of the wormhole seemed literally to fall away before the *Crab*. Cracks in spacetime opened up like branching tunnels, stretching to infinity.

Michael wasn't sure if that should be happening. Maybe this wouldn't go quite according to plan . . .

Spacetime was shattering. Michael screamed and pressed his fists to his eyes.

*

On the earth-craft, the image of the Interface portal glittered on every data slate.

Miriam Berg sat on scorched grass, close enough to the centre of the earth-craft to see, beyond the ruined construction-material homes of the Friends of Wigner, the brownish sandstone shards that marked the site of the ancient henge.

Jasoft Parz, clothed in a fresh but ill-fitting Wignerian coverall, sat close to her, his short legs stretched out on the grass. The *Narlikar*'s only boat stood on blackened earth close by her. The D'Arcys had brought her back here, after her retrieval of Shira and Jasoft Parz.

She was aware that Parz's green eyes were fixed on her. That he was almost radiating sympathy.

Well, damn him. Damn them all.

Her legs tucked under her, Miriam stared at the slate on her lap, at the delicate image of the portal it contained, as if willing herself to travel into the slate, shrinking down until she, too, could follow Michael Poole through the spacetime wormhole. If she concentrated really hard, she could shut out all the rest of it: this strange, rather chilling man from the future beside her, the distant activities of the Friends, even the damned thin air and irregular gravity of the devastated earth-craft.

The moment stretched. The portal glimmered like a diamond on her slate.

Then, with shocking suddenness, blue-white light flared silently inside the portal, gushing from every one of the tetrahedral frame's facets. It was as if a tiny sun had gone nova inside the frame. The light of the wormhole's collapse glared from the slates carried by Parz, the Friends, as far as she could see; it was as if everyone held a candle before them, and the light generated by that failing spacetime flaw illuminated all their young, smooth faces.

238

The light died. When she looked again at her slate the portal was gone; broken fragments of the exotic-matter frame, sparking, tumbled away from a patch of space which had become ordinary, finite once more.

She threw the slate face down on the grass.

Jasoft Parz laid his slate more gently on the ground. 'It is over,' he said. 'Michael Poole has succeeded in sealing the wormhole; there can be no doubt.'

Berg shoved her fingers, hard, into the battered earth, welcoming the pain of bent-back nails. 'Those damn struts of exotic matter will have to be cleared. Hazard to navigation.'

He said, 'It is over, you know. You'll have to find ways of letting it go.'

'Letting what go?'

'The past.' He sighed. 'And, in my case, the future.'

She lifted her head, studied the huge, brooding bulk of Jupiter. 'The future is still yours . . . your own future. There is plenty for you to explore here. And the Friends, of course.'

He smiled. 'Such as?'

'AS treatment for a start. And, for the first time in your lives, some modern – sorry, ancient – health checks.'

Jasoft smiled, quietly sad. 'But we are aliens on our native planet. Stranded so far from our own time . . .'

She shrugged. 'There are plenty of you, including the Friends. And they're young, basically fit. You could found a colony; there's plenty of room. Or head for the stars.' She smiled, remembering the strange voyage of the *Cauchy*. 'Of course we don't yet have the hyperdrive to offer you. Strictly sublight only . . . But the wonder of the journey is no less for that, I can assure you.'

'Yes. Well, Miriam, such projects might attract these young people, if not me . . .'

She looked at him now. 'What do you mean? What about you, Jasoft?'

He smiled and spread his long, age-withered fingers. 'Oh, I think my story is over now. I've seen, done, learned more than I ever dreamed. Or deserved to.'

Her eyes narrowed. 'You're going to refuse further AS treatment? Look, if you feel some guilt about the function you performed in the Qax Occupation Era, nobody in this age is going to –'

'It's not that,' he said gently. 'I'm not talking about some complicated form of suicide, my dear. And I don't suffer greatly from guilt, despite the moral ambivalence of what I've done with my life. I certainly believe I left my era for the last time aboard that damn Spline warship having done more good than harm . . . It's just that I think I've seen enough. I know all I could wish to know, you see. I know that, although the Project of these rebels – the Friends of Wigner – has failed, Earth will ultimately be liberated from the grip of the Qax. I don't need to learn anything more. I certainly don't feel I need to see any more of it laboriously unfold. Do you understand that?'

Berg smiled. 'I think so. Though I must chide you for thinking small. The Friends of Wigner have projects which extend to the end of time.'

'Yes. And, as for their future, I suspect they are already engaged on designs of their own.'

She nodded. 'You've told me what Shira said. Take the long way home, by surviving through the centuries until the era of your birth returns . . . and then what? Start the whole damn business over again?'

'Perhaps. Though I hear they've done a little more thinking since I spoke to Shira. You mention a sublight star trip. I think that would appeal to the Friends, if only because it would let them exploit relativistic time-dilation effects –'

'– and get home that bit quicker; in a century instead of fifteen.' She smiled. 'Well, it's one way to waste your life, I suppose.'

'And you, Miriam? You've been a century away yourself; this must be almost as great a dislocation for you as it is for me. What will you do?'

She shrugged, ruffling her hair. 'Maybe I'll go with the Friends,' she murmured. 'Maybe I'll take them to the stars and back, journey through fifteen centuries once more –'

'– and see if Michael Poole emerges into the Qax occupation future, dashing valiantly from the imploding wormhole?' He smiled.

She looked up to the Jupiter-roofed zenith, trying to make out the pieces of the shattered portal. 'It might make me feel better,' she said. 'But, Jasoft, I know I've lost Michael. Wherever he is now I can never reach him.'

They sat for a moment, watching images of shattered, tumbling exotic matter through the discarded slates. At length he said, 'Come. It is cold here, and the air is thin. Let us return to the *Narlikar* boat. I would like some more warmth. And food.'

She dropped her head from the sky. 'Yeah. That's a good idea, Jasoft.'

She stood, her legs stiff after so long curled beneath her. Almost tenderly Jasoft took her arm, and they walked together to the waiting boat.

Spacetime is friable.

The fabric of spacetime is riddled with wormholes of all scales. At the Planck length and below, wormholes arising from quantum uncertainty effects blur the clean Einsteinian lines of spacetime. And some of the wormholes expand to the human scale, and beyond –

sometimes spontaneously, and sometimes at the instigation of intelligence.

Spacetime is like a sheet of ice, permeated by flaws, by hairline cracks.

When Michael Poole's hyperdrive was activated inside the human-built wormhole Interface, it was as if someone had smashed at that ice floe with a mallet. Cracks exploded from the point of impact, widened; they joined each other in a complex, spreading network, a tributary pattern which continually formed and reformed as spacetime healed and shattered anew.

The battered, scorched corpse of the Spline warship bearing the lifedome of the *Crab*, Michael Poole, and a cloud of rebellious antibody drones emerged from the collapsing wormhole into the Qax Occupation Era at close to the speed of light. Shear energy from the tortured spacetime of the wormhole transformed into high-frequency radiation, into showers of short-lived, exotic particles which showered around the tumbling Spline.

It was like a small sun exploding amid the moons of Jupiter. Vast storms were evoked in the bulk of the gas giant's atmosphere. A moon was destroyed. Humans were killed, blinded.

Cracks in shattering spacetime propagated at the speed of light.

There was already another macroscopic spacetime wormhole in the Jovian system: the channel set up to a future beyond the destruction of the Qax star, the channel through which Qax had travelled towards the past, intent on destroying humanity.

Under the impact of Poole's hammer-blow arrival – as Poole had expected – this second spacetime flaw could not retain its stability.

The wormhole mouth itself expanded, exoticity ballooning across thousands of miles and engulfing the mass-energy of Michael Poole's unlikely vessel. The icosahedral exotic-matter frame which threaded the wormhole mouth exploded, a mirror image of the destruction witnessed by Miriam Berg fifteen centuries earlier. Then the portal imploded at lightspeed; gravitational shockwaves pulsed from the vanishing mouth like Xeelee starbreaker beams, scattering ships and moons.

Through a transient network of wormholes which imploded after him in a storm of gravity waves and high-energy particles, Michael Poole hurtled helplessly into the future.

16

Chains of events threaded the future.

A human called Jim Bolder flew a Xeelee nightfighter into the heart of the Qax home system, causing them to turn their starbreaker weapons on their own sun.

The Qax occupation of Earth collapsed. Humans would never again be defeated, on a significant scale, by any of the junior species.

Humans spread across stars, their spheres of influence expanding at many times lightspeed. A period known as the Assimilation followed during which the wisdom and power of other species were absorbed, on an industrial scale.

Soon, only the Xeelee stood between humans and dominance.

The conflict that followed lasted a million years.

When it was resolved only a handful of humans, and human-derived beings, remained anywhere in the universe.

The Projects of the Xeelee, the inexorable workings of natural processes, continued to change the universe.

Stars died. More stars formed, to replace those which had already failed . . . but as the primal mix of hydrogen and helium became polluted with stellar waste products, the formation rate of new stars declined exponentially.

And darker forces were at work. The stars aged . . . too rapidly.

The Xeelee completed their great Projects, and fled the decaying cosmos.

Five million years after the first conflict between human and Qax, the wreckage of a Spline warship emerged, tumbling, from the mouth of a wormhole which blazed with gravitational radiation. The wormhole closed, sparkling.

The wreck – dark, almost bereft of energy – turned slowly in the stillness. It was empty of life.

Almost.

Quantum functions flooded over Michael Poole like blue-violet rain, restoring him to time. He gasped at the pain of rebirth.

Humans would call it the antiXeelee.

It was . . . large. Its lofty emotions could be described in human terms only by analogy.

Nevertheless – the antiXeelee looked on its completed works and was satisfied.

Its awareness spread across light-years. Shining matter littered the universe; the Xeelee had come, built fine castles of that shining froth, and had now departed. Soon the stuff itself would begin to decay, and already the antiXeelee could detect the flexing muscles of the denizens of that dark ocean which lay below.

The function of the antiXeelee had been to guide the huge Projects of the Xeelee, the Projects whose purpose had been to build a way out of this deadly cosmos. In order to achieve their goals, the Xeelee had even moved back through time to modify their own evolution, turning their history into a closed timelike curve, a vacuum diagram. The antiXeelee was the consciousness driving this process, travelling – like an antiparticle – back in time from the moment of its dissolution to the moment of its creation.

Now the job was done. The antiXeelee felt something like contentment at the thought that its charges had escaped, were now beyond the reach of those . . . others, who the Xeelee had in the end been unable to oppose.

The antiXeelee could let go.

It spread wide and thin; soon, with a brief, non-localized burst of selectrons and neutralinos its awareness would multiply, fragment, shatter, sink into the vacuum . . .

But not yet. There was something new.

It didn't take Michael long to check out the status of his fragile craft.

There was some power still available to the lifedome from its internal cells. That might last – what, a few hours? As far as he could tell, there was no functional link between the dome and the rest of the *Hermit Crab*, nor had the links set up by Harry to the Spline ship survived . . . save for one, glowing tell-tale on the comms desks which Michael studiously ignored; the damn rebel drones could chew the ship up as far as he was concerned, now.

So he had no motive power. Not so much as an in-system boat; no way of adjusting his situation.

He didn't grouse about this, nor did he fear his future, such as it was. It was a miracle he'd even survived his passage through the wormhole network . . . This was all a bizarre bonus.

Harry was gone, of course.

The universe beyond the lifedome looked aged, dead, darkened. The lifedome was a little bubble of light and life, isolated.

Michael was alone, here at the end of time. He could feel it.

He gathered a meal together; the mundane chore, performed in a bright island of light around the lifedome's small galley, was oddly cheering. He carried the food to his couch, lay back with the plate balancing on one hand, and dimmed the dome lights.

God alone knew where he was . . . if 'where' could have a meaning, after such a dislocation in spacetime. The stars were distant, dark, red. Could so long have passed? – or, he wondered, could something, some unknown force, have acted to speed the stars' aging in the aeons beyond the flashbulb slice of time occupied by humans?

There was no large-scale sign of human life, or activity; nor, indeed, of any intelligent life.

Intelligence would have had time to work, Michael reflected. After millions of years, with a faster-than-light hyperdrive and singularity technology in the hands of hundreds of species, the universe should have been transformed . . .

The reconstruction of the universe should have been as obvious as a neon sign a thousand light-years tall.

. . . But the universe had merely aged.

He knew from the subjective length of his passage through the wormholes that he couldn't have travelled through more than a few million years – a fraction of the great journey to timelike infinity – and yet already the tide of life had receded. Were there any humans left, anywhere?

He smiled wistfully. So much for Shira's grand dreams of life covering the universe, of manipulating the dynamic evolution of spacetime itself . . .

There would be no 'Ultimate Observer', then. The Project of the Friends of Wigner could not, after all, have succeeded: there would have been nobody to hear the elaborately constructed message. But, Michael thought as he gazed out at the decayed universe, by God it had been a grand conception. To think of finite humans, already long since dust, even daring to challenge these deserts of time . . .

He finished his food, set the plate carefully on the floor. He drank a glass of clean water, went to the free-fall shower, washed in a spray of hot water. He tried to open up his senses, to relish every particle of sensation. There was a last time for everything, for even the most mundane experiences.

He considered finding some music to play, a book to read. Somehow that might have seemed fitting.

The lights failed. Even the comms telltale from the drones winked out.

Well, so much for reading a book.

By the dimmed starlight, half by touch, he made his way back to his couch.

It grew colder; he imagined the heat of the lifedome leaking out into the immense heat sink of the blackened, ancient sky. What would get him first? – the cold, or the failing air?

He wasn't afraid. Oddly, he felt renewed: young, for the first time in a subjective century, the pressure of time no longer seeming to weigh on him.

Perhaps he was finding that peace of death, the readiness to abandon the cares of a too-long life, which his father had discovered before him. And he found, at last, a contentment that he had lived long enough to see all he had.

He crossed his hands on his chest. He was beginning to shiver, the air sharp in his nostrils. He closed his eyes.

*

Something like curiosity, a spark of its awareness, stirred the antiXeelee.

Here was an artefact.

How had this cooling wreckage got here, to this place and time?

There was something inside it. A single, flickering candle of consciousness . . .

The antiXeelee reached out.

There was a ship, another ship, hanging over the lifedome.

Michael, dying, stared in wonder.

It was something like a sycamore seed wrought in jet black. No lights showed in the small, pod-like hull. Nightdark wings which must have spanned hundreds of miles loomed over the wreck of the *Crab*, softly rippling.

The Friends of Wigner had told Michael of ships like this. This was a nightfighter, the wings sheet-discontinuities in the fabric of spacetime.

Xeelee.

The cold sank claws into his chest; the muscles of his throat abruptly spasmed, and dark clouds ringed his vision.

Not now, he found himself pleading silently, his failing vision locked onto the Xeelee ship, all his elegiac acceptance gone in a flash. *Just a little longer. I have to know what this means. Please . . .*

The antiXeelee plucked the guttering flame from the candle.

The last heat fled from the wrecked craft; the air in the translucent dome began to frost over the comms panels, the couches, the galley, the abandoned body.

The antiXeelee cupped the flame, almost amused by its tiny fear, its wonder, its helpless longing to survive.

The flame was spun out into a web of quantum functions, acausal and nonlocal.

Michael was – discorporeal; it was as if the jewel of consciousness which had lain behind his eyes had been plucked out of his body and flung into space.

He did not even have heartbeats to count.

But there was something here with him, he sensed: some – entity. It was like a great ceiling under which he hovered and buzzed, insect-like. He sensed a vast, satisfied weariness in its mood, the contentment of the traveller at the end of a long and difficult road. For a long time he stayed within the glow of its protection.

Then it began to dissolve.

Michael wanted to cry out, like a child seeking its huge parent. He was buffeted, battered. It was as if a glacier of memories and emotions was calving into a hundred icebergs around him; and now those icebergs in turn burst into shards which melted into the surface of a waiting sea . . .

And he was left alone.

It was impossible to measure time, other than by the slow evolution of his own emotions.

He endured despair. Why had he been brought to this point in spacetime, preserved in such a fashion, and then so casually abandoned?

The despair turned to anger, and lasted a long time.

But the anger faded.

He became curious and began to experiment with his

awareness. Physically he seemed to be composed of a tight knot of quantum wave functions; now, cautiously, he began to unravel that knot, to allow the focus of his consciousness to slide over spacetime. Soon it was as if he was flying over the arch of the cosmos, unbound by limits of space or time.

Throughout the galaxy he found the works of man. He lingered over places and artefacts abandoned by history, dwelling as long over a drifting child's toy as over some huge spacebound fortress.

Everywhere he found relics of war. Ruined stars and worlds, squandered energy. But he found no people – no sentience – anywhere.

At first Michael labelled the places he visited, the relics he found, in human terms; but as time passed and his confidence grew he removed this barrier of conscious thought. He allowed his consciousness to soften further, to dilute the narrow human perception to which he had clung.

All about him were quantum wave functions. They spread from stars and planets, sheets of probability that linked matter and time. They were like spiders' webs scattered over the aging galaxies; they mingled, reinforced and cancelled each other, all bound by the implacable logic of the governing wave equations.

The functions filled spacetime and they pierced his soul. Exhilarated, he rode their gaudy brilliance through the hearts of aging stars.

He relaxed his sense of scale, so that there seemed no real difference between the width of an electron and the depth of a star's gravity well. His sense of time telescoped, so that he could watch the insect-like, fluttering decay of free neutrons – or step back and watch the grand, slow decomposition of protons themselves . . .

Soon there was little of the human left in him.

Then, at last, he was ready for the final step.

Human consciousness was an artificial thing. Once humans had believed that gods animated their souls, fighting their battles in the guise of humans. Later they had evolved the idea of the self-aware, self-directed consciousness. Now Michael saw that it had all been no more than an idea, a model, an illusion behind which to hide.

He, the last man, need no longer cling to such outmoded comforts.

There was no cognition, he realized. There was only perception.

With the equivalent of a smile he relaxed. His awareness sparkled and subsided.

He was beyond time and space. The great quantum functions which encompassed the universe slid past him like a vast, turbulent river, and his eyes were filled with the grey light which shone beneath reality, the light against which all phenomena are shadows.

Time wore away, unmarked.

And then . . .

There was a box, drifting in space, tetrahedral, clear-walled.

From around an impossible corner a human walked into the box. A rope of woven bark trailed behind him. The human was dressed in treated animal skins. He was gaunt, encrusted in filth, his skin ravaged by frost.

He stared out at the stars, astonished.

*

Michael's extended awareness stirred. Something had changed . . .

History resumed.